Special Agent

NOEL B. GERSON

Special Agent

E. P. DUTTON & CO., INC. | NEW YORK

FIRST EDITION
10 9 8 7 6 5 4 3 2 1

Library of Congress Cataloging in Publication Data

Gerson, Noel Bertram, 1914–
Special agent.

I. Title.
PZ3.G323So [PS3513.E8679] 813'.5'2 76–14776

ISBN: 0–8415–0451–2

Published simultaneously in Canada
by Clarke, Irwin & Company Limited, Toronto and Vancouver

For Marilyn

Introduction

"What do you know about the FBI?" my editor asked me at lunch as we were discussing subjects for a new novel.

Well, I had worked with the Federal Bureau of Investigation on a number of cases during World War II, when I had been a Military Intelligence officer, but that had been a long time ago.

Other than that, like millions of other Americans, I had been fascinated by the recent and continuing revelations, allegations and rumors, some admitted and some denied, about FBI misconduct over a period of years. Congressional investigations uncovered some shockers, and alert reporters did the rest. As these lines are being written, in the spring of 1976, the FBI is still in the news.

The list is not pretty. Abuses of civil rights. The harassment of citizens, including members of radical and fringe political groups, by means of unauthorized electronic surveillance, illegal burglaries, the sending of anonymous letters and other "dirty tricks." An alleged payoff, something unique in FBI history, a case whose outcome has not yet been determined. Even the charge that a bank gave interest-free loans to FBI agents.

I was intrigued. Was the FBI an organization of heroes, villains or just plain people with clay feet? Was its late Director, J. Edgar Hoover, a truly great American or something else? Was the FBI's standing as the world's foremost investigative body deserved?

I had two choices.

The first was that of digging into the FBI's past and determining whether the various charges were true, and if so, of assessing the degree of malfeasance. That approach would require a book of nonfiction. I concluded it was not for me, largely because a number of highly competent investigative reporters for newspapers and news magazines were already at work in this field.

My second alternative was that of writing a novel about the FBI of today. I had no way of knowing whether the "new," post-Hoover FBI was still winking at the law or trying to perform its functions within its limitations. I decided to make this FBI my subject.

Discarding all preconceived notions, I made up my mind to write a book that, to the best of my ability, would be an accurate portrait of the FBI as it exists today. In order to achieve this goal it was necessary for me to become well acquainted with the men and women who make up the FBI, and to understand what motivates them, how they behave and why. Above all, I had to gain an understanding of the spirit of today's FBI.

This book is the result of that research, conducted over the period of one year.

Thanks to the good offices of United States Attorney General Edward H. Levi, I was given an introduction to the Bureau. Director Clarence M. Kelley cooperated willingly and opened the FBI doors to me. I was on my way.

I couldn't ask for more help than I was given by Assistant Director Don Moore, the head of the External Affairs Division, who issued instructions that I was to be given every assistance, and that nothing was to be withheld from me. Since that time I have come to know a great many Special Agents, from high-ranking executives to recent graduates of the FBI Academy at Quantico, Virginia. I've sat with them in their offices and observed the flow of papers across their desks. I've accompanied them on their field assignments and have become familiar with the problems of "street agents." I've learned the headaches and the rewards of Special Agents in charge of Field Offices. I've gained an understanding of the troubles faced by top-level Inspectors and hard-working squad supervisors.

I've spent countless off-duty hours with FBI Special Agents, too, eating meals with them, drinking with them, socializing with them and their wives. I've made it my business to become acquainted with employees on the lower levels, clerks and secretaries and stenographers.

Some FBI men have spoken with painful candor about the past. Others have been defensive, and a few have slammed the door on yesterday. But my interest in the past sins of the Bureau served me only for purposes of background. I concentrated on the people who make up the FBI in the late 1970's, how they perform their duties; above all, I tried to find out whether they are true to their public trust.

I am grateful to Bill Gunn of the External Affairs Division for his help, beyond the call of duty, and for the generous assistance of Martin McNerney, who is in charge of New Agent Training at the FBI Academy.

This book could not have been written without the cooperation of Special Agent Broni Maceys, an FBI veteran of almost three decades, who shared his expertise with me. I am also grateful for the technical assistance of Special Agent David Miller.

Above all, I want to thank Tom Dugan, Special Agent in Charge of the New Haven, Connecticut Field Office, whose help, candor and hospitality were responsible for much of the information and so many of the insights I needed.

If there are FBI "types," they appear in these pages. But it goes almost without saying that individual characters are strictly the products of my own imagination, and that any resemblance they may bear to real, living persons is coincidental.

—N.B.G.

Special Agent

1

"FBI Special Agents are not supercops. In fact, we aren't cops at all, so you can forget the glamorous exploits you've seen on television. We're not Nazi storm troopers. And we're not a sly gang playing tricks on individuals or invading the privacy of American citizens with electronic gadgets. Okay?" David Daniels, Special Agent in Charge of the Winthrop Field Office, leaned back in his swivel chair, ran a hand through his graying hair, and looked in turn at each of the reporters gathered in his large, impressive office overlooking the Winthrop Common.

This was the first Field Office of his own since his promotion, and he was proud of his assignment, proud of his office with its oak paneling and United States and FBI flags on standards in two corners. The whole state of Connecticut was under his jurisdiction, and he had a staff of 214 to assist him in the fulfillment of his obligations, 93 of them Special Agents, the rest clerks and stenographers. On his first day on the new job, he was eager to organize and get rolling, but public relations had intervened, forcing him to call a press conference even before he met his new staff. With the Bureau on the firing line these days, the image problem took priority.

A reporter from the Hartford *Courant* sipped coffee from a steaming paper cup. "You've told us what you aren't, Mr. Daniels. What are you?"

"A special investigative branch of the Department of Justice, charged with specific areas of responsibility under laws passed by the Congress. But that isn't what you want to know. The Bureau has eight thousand, six hundred Special Agents. G-men, as we were once called. Hard-working, decent guys who obey the law ourselves, and try to carry out our assigned functions inside it, not outside it. I might add that we're the most incorruptible law-enforcement body in the world, and I can't stress that point too strongly."

The representative of the New Haven *Register* smiled.

"I'm not kidding," Dave said. "You people deal with police. I needn't tell you that police forces—not only in the United States, but in every country on earth—are riddled with graft and corruption. It's a major problem everywhere. But not in the FBI. Sure, we've had a few guys who have been caught, but damn few. I'm told Scotland Yard is pretty much on the up-and-up, but we're still better. Not only do we know it, but our enemies know it. Ask the KGB in Moscow how many of our agents they've subverted lately. See if the organized crime hoodlums can name even one agent they've persuaded to accept a payoff."

A woman reporter from the New London *Day* raised her hand. "How do you justify harassments like anonymous letters that were sent out ten to fifteen years ago under COINTELPRO, your so-called counterintelligence program?"

Dave felt older than his fifty-three years. "I'm not justifying anything. We obeyed orders. I merely ask you to keep in mind the spirit of those times, those of you who are old enough to remember the hysteria that gripped the country."

"What about J. Edgar Hoover's private files on the personal weaknesses and idiosyncrasies of Congressmen, Senators, and even Presidents?" she demanded.

"First of all, I don't know—and neither do you—that such files ever existed. I was a Resident Agent in a small Illinois town in those days, and Mr. Hoover didn't take me into his confidence." Dave paused, waiting for the laugh to subside. "I'm going to level with you, and what I'm going to say isn't news anymore. First. Director Hoover made the Bureau into the number one law-enforcement agency, devoting his whole life to the job, so let's give him credit for it. Two. Director Hoover stayed on the job far too long. He should have retired years before he died, but he was a national institution and didn't even know he should have quit. Now, before somebody asks me whether he was senile in his last years, I honestly don't know. On the few occasions I was called into his office I never said much except, 'Yes, sir.' "

The assistant city editor of the Winthrop *Herald,* who was covering the conference himself instead of assigning a reporter, cleared his throat. "One more question about J. Edgar—"

"Sorry," Dave said, cutting in. "I don't care to speculate or gossip about the past. I have a job to do, and it's going to occupy my full time. Okay? Anytime you want to know what's happening at the FBI, call me or drop in. When I can, I'll tell you what you want to know. When I must, I'll put you off. But you can always depend on one thing. I'll be honest with you. Any more questions this morning, ladies and gentlemen?"

Supervisor Raymond Merrill shifted the holster containing his .38 revolver to a more comfortable position on his belt, initialed another of the endless raw interview 302 forms piled on his desk, and glanced out of the large plate-glass window at one side of his private cubicle. The bullpen, where the street agents and stenographers worked, was filled. In the old days eighty percent of the agents were expected to be working outside the office at any given time, and even though that rule had been relaxed somewhat by Director Kelley, Ray Merrill still felt a trifle uncomfortable when he saw so many desks occupied. Just as it made him uneasy to be wearing a yellow and green striped shirt to work. Times had changed, to be sure, but he still entertained the suspicion that Mr. Hoover was whirling in his grave.

This was no ordinary day; every Special Agent wanted to be on hand. The new SAC (Special Agent in Charge) had come in for the first time this morning, and the hired hands wanted to greet him in person. Ray and the other supervisors had met him the previous month during a private two-day visit, when he had learned for the first time that Assistant Special Agent in Charge Joe Butler wouldn't be moved into the top job.

Ray hadn't yet figured out the new SAC, but that would come in time. No two SACs were alike, and in these days of increased local autonomy, when it was necessary to follow only the general guidelines from Bureau headquarters, an agent's career depended on the attitudes and principles, likes and dislikes of the SAC under whom he served.

Of far greater importance was the undeniable, unpalatable fact that Joe Butler would stay on at the Winthrop Field Office as ASAC. Not that Ray disliked or resented Butler. On the contrary, he was an amiable person, fair in his dealings with his immediate subordinates and better able than most to remain vertical after consuming a pitcher of Manhattans.

What bothered Ray was that he stood first in line, at least in his own opinion, to take over as ASAC when Joe was moved. Instead, at the age of forty, his career—like his personal life—had come to a dead halt. Two years had passed since Helga had divorced him because she couldn't stand his schedule and never knew when he was coming or going.

But forty was the age when life began or ended, and Ray was in a cul-de-sac. He was no longer a street agent, but—big deal—he had his own squad. Bank robberies and ITSMV (Interstate Traffic in Stolen Motor Vehicles). Nine agents. He could spend the rest of his Bureau career at this same desk. He could hang on, hoping against hope for promotion, until he was fifty-five, the new retirement limit that would go into effect in another twenty-four months.

Ray was tired of waiting for the breaks that would call him to the favorable attention of an SAC or an Inspector from the Bureau. Tired of the torrents of paper that had been pouring across his desk since his promotion a year and a half ago, yet unwilling to admit, except in rare moments, that he missed the freedom and variety of life on the street. Tired, too, of proving himself weekend after weekend with a young woman.

Ray forced himself to concentrate on a batch of 302 forms. An interview with a teller of a bank in Torrington that had been robbed. Interviews with the bank cashier and two witnesses. An interview with a Groton garage owner suspected of dismantling and reconstructing stolen cars. That one needed more careful study, and he put it aside. An interview with a state trooper who had apprehended a minor member of a stolen car ring; trooper's arrest report was attached.

Ray looked up again, and something in the bullpen caught his eye. He dropped his ballpoint pen, walked to the door of his office, and beckoned.

Special Agent John Philip Hedley jumped to his feet and almost sprinted into the cubicle. At twenty-four he was the youngest member of the Office, and as a new agent, graduated from the Academy only a month previous, he never lost sight of the fact that this was a first-office assignment. "You want to see me, sir?"

Ray looked him up and down and actually envied the kid his youth, his clean-cut virility, and his verve. Most of them looked like that when they were fresh out of Quantico, eager and ambitious, ready to tear the Mafia apart, all set to invade a nest of Red spies singlehanded. Give him a decade—five years here, another in a two-man Resident Agency in some small city—and he'd be thoroughly housebroken by the time he moved into a semi-permanent spot, conducting investigations and dictating raw 302 reports in his sleep.

"Hedley," he said, "you're entitled to wear your hair long, until it almost touches your collar. Your prerogative, under the new rules." The rules weren't all that new, even if they seemed to be, but no matter. It was the principle that was important. "I was just wondering how well you know the new S-A-C." The initials were always pronounced individually.

John Philip Hedley was bewildered. "I've never even met him, Mr. Merrill."

Ray leaned back in his chair. He knew he was being a bastard, that he could make his point without nastiness, but new agents needed discipline, and it did them no favor to coddle them. "I just wonder how you know he thinks it's okay for us to wander around the office in shirtsleeves."

"I don't, sir. I mean, I'll put on my jacket right away!" Johnny Hedley was rattled.

"Hold on. That isn't what I said. Maybe he doesn't mind shirtsleeves, and maybe he's a stickler for jackets. Maybe he doesn't notice feet on the desk, or maybe he's a spit-and-polish fiend. What I'm trying to get across to you is that an S-A-C is God Almighty in his own bailiwick. There are fifty-nine of them in the Bureau, Hedley, fifty-nine of the Lord's anointed, and no two are the same. Cross one and you'll go to a little one-man

Resident Agency somewhere. You'll stay there until you rot, helping county sheriffs track down military deserters, conducting applicant interviews, and interrogating itinerant whores for stray information. Maybe you'd like that kind of job. Some do."

"I don't dig you, Mr. Merrill."

Ray softened. "Play it safe, kid. Wear your jacket today. Watch the Ay-Sack. When Mr. Butler starts wandering around in shirt-sleeves, then the supervisors will do it. After that, you're safe. Got it?"

Johnny Hedley was relieved. Yes, sir, and thanks very—"

The ringing of a telephone interrupted him. "Merrill," Ray said, and in an instant his lethargy vanished. "Full details, Burroughs." The call was brief, but he wrote rapidly, and as soon as he slammed the instrument into its cradle he reached for a microphone that would carry his voice to the state's Resident Agencies as well as to the bullpen.

"Your attention, please," he said, his voice calm in spite of his tension. "The Third National Bank, Milford, located on the Boston Post Road, was robbed at oh-nine-forty-three hours this morning." A glance at the electric clock on his wall told him it was now 9:46. "Two men made the holdup and a third waited in their car. All in their twenties. White, clean-shaven, no distinguishing marks. Getaway made heading east on the Post Road in a Ford Pinto sedan, black, Nineteen Seventy-five, two-door. Preliminary estimate is that more than fifteen thousand dollars was taken, most in specie, some in coins. Over."

The Winthrop Field Office moved into high gear. Street agents not occupied on special assignments dropped whatever they were doing and ran out to their waiting Bureau cars. Teletypes in the adjoining communications center clattered, confirming the information to Resident Agencies and notifying the Connecticut State Police as well as local police departments and sheriffs' offices within a four-hundred-mile radius.

Within moments only squad supervisors remained in their offices, and only a handful of agents in the bullpen were still at their desks. The stenographers continued to type as though nothing out of the ordinary had happened.

Ray flipped a lever that connected him with the ASAC.

"I heard," Joe Butler said. "Sounds like the same trio that hit Two State Savings in Stonington day before yesterday. Any license report?"

"Not yet, sir, but Burroughs hopes to have it very soon. I'm taking charge of this case myself, Mr. Butler, so I'll notify you by radio whenever he reports."

"All right," the ASAC said. "I'll save you time and feed NCIC." The FBI's National Crime Information Center was one of the most potent, efficient law-enforcement tools on earth. A huge, complex computer, it stored vast quantities of information, and when fed even fragments about individuals, automobiles, and other data, it responded, both by radio and teletype, in as little as thirty seconds, revealing everything ever accumulated and filed on the subject. "I'll also ask Commissioner Red Martin of the State Police to block all highway exits. Have you notified the S-A-C?"

Ray's professional composure was jarred. "He's brand-new, sir, and he's just holding his first press conference!"

ASAC Butler was nettled. "You know the rules, Merrill, but never mind. I'll tell him." It was the right of the Special Agent in Charge to lead a bank robbery manhunt in person if he so elected. "You get going."

Ray saw that Hedley was still standing in a corner. New agents spent their first year after graduation in on-the-job training, always in the company of someone more experienced, so Hedley was obliged to remain at the office until assigned. "You're coming with me, kid."

"Yes, sir!" Johnny sprinted down the corridor beside the older man, in his eagerness outdistancing him. But he had the presence of mind to hold one of the building's three elevators for the supervisor.

Ray had his car keys in his hand as they ran to the parking lot across the street. In what seemed like a single motion he turned on his ignition and two-way radio, plugged his flashing light into the cigar-lighter socket, and snapped on his siren. "This is Merrill, agent-in-charge, Third National Bank robbery, Milford."

As the car roared out of the lot and headed toward the Connecticut Turnpike they listened to a National Crime Information Center report. "Interesting," Ray said. "Certain characteristics—

the number of men, their description, and the relatively small amount stolen—correspond with the Stonington robbery and another last week in Westerly, Rhode Island. All in the same area, you'll note." He broke off to receive a report from Agent Burroughs in Milford, giving him a New York license number for the getaway car.

"Now NCIC has something it can sink its teeth into!" Johnny Hedley said.

Ray made no reply as he continued to converse with various agents, a State Police sergeant, and a desk man at the New Haven police headquarters. Then a State Police cruiser fell in behind him, its siren adding to the din his own was making, and he waved cheerfully.

Johnny was astonished by his calm. "It begins to look like we'll close in on those guys, doesn't it?"

Ray nodded. "Four to one we'll nail them. Within an hour." Only seven minutes had passed since the robbery had taken place.

Johnny's hand slid to his .38.

Ray noticed the gesture and grinned. "Saw an exciting cops and robbers film last night, huh?"

In his embarrassment the new agent didn't know what to reply.

"Always be ready to use a weapon," Ray said, "and remember what they taught you at the Academy. When you shoot, shoot to kill. But there's something else to keep in mind that they probably didn't stress there. No matter what kind of case you're on, you may not fire your gun for months at a time, even years. If it weren't for obligatory target practice sessions every other month, my gun would be rusty."

"How come, sir?"

"I'll let you in on one of the world's worst-kept secrets, Hedley. The Bureau's best protection is its reputation. The enemy, regardless of whether they're in organized crime, foreign spies or saboteurs, or just punks out for a thrill, all know that every man who carries our badge, from Mr. Kelley down to new agents like you, is a crack shot. With any kind of pistol, rifle, riot gun, or whatever. Desk officer or field agent, it doesn't matter. Standing, sitting, or on the move. Our record is extraordinary. When we shoot, we get our man."

Ray interrupted himself to turn up the two-way radio as the Field Office came on the line. "NCIC," the voice of ASAC Butler said, "reports that the trio in the Ford Pinto with New York plates are armed and dangerous. Two have prison records, and at least one has been involved in several shooting scrapes. So watch your step."

It was difficult to determine whether Johnny's sigh was caused by anticipatory pleasure or anxiety.

"Maybe you'll get your wish, kid," Ray said. "But don't shoot until the agent-in-charge—that's me—gives the word. This is real life, not Hogan's Alley."

Hogan's Alley was a mock street at the Academy firing range, and students were subjected to a variety of surprise assaults and attacks there to test the speed of their reflexes and their ability to distinguish friends from foes. He had earned high scores at Hogan's Alley, but as Mr. Merrill said, that was just training.

Two state troopers who had left their cars were diverting Turnpike traffic to an exit, and masses of flashing lights directly ahead caused Ray to slow down. "Dandy," he said, "the roadblock is all set."

He parked on the shoulder, then sauntered forward, seemingly unconcerned.

Johnny saw that an old trailer truck had been parked broadside, blocking all three lanes, and behind it were stationed a number of men, some in civilian clothes and some in the uniforms of troopers. He recognized several older colleagues from the Winthrop Field Office who were armed with rifles, and others, whom he didn't know, apparently were Resident Agents from Bridgeport, New Haven, and other cities in the area. There were a number of blue-uniformed policemen from various communities on hand, too, and at least a dozen cruisers and other vehicles were parked on the shoulder.

Creating order out of the chaos was a hatless man with fading, reddish hair, who wore a trench coat, and Johnny observed that men moved in a hurry when he addressed them.

"Good to see you, Commissioner," Ray said as he shook hands.

"The same to you, Mr. Merrill. I was on my way down from Hartford to welcome your boss, so I thought I'd join the party. Do you want to make it your show?"

"Since you're here, Commissioner, just tell us what you want us to do," Ray said.

Johnny knew now what his instructors at the Academy had meant when they had stressed that the Bureau maintained a low profile. For more than forty years the FBI had taken command whenever possible, and had claimed a lion's share of credit. But Director Kelley had changed all that, and his policy was paying handsome dividends. Now state and local law-enforcement authorities were eager to cooperate with the Bureau.

"I assume," Ray said, "that you're intending to divert westbound traffic, too, Commissioner."

If Red Martin had been momentarily negligent, he was quick to correct the fault. "Can't have fireworks spraying across the road, can we?"

Johnny realized the Commissioner was addressing him. "No, sir," he said.

Red Martin grinned. "One of your new agents, Mr. Merrill?"

"Still has his diploma in his hip pocket, Commissioner."

"Stick around me if the shooting starts, young fellow, and you'll be safe." Martin chuckled. "My people insist on taking good care of me."

Several agents and troopers laughed.

Johnny flushed. They were patronizing him, dammit!

Red Martin sobered. "I assume the robbers are driving a stolen vehicle?"

"That's what NCIC says," Ray told him.

"Then we won't want it banged up any more than can be helped." The Commissioner turned to a uniformed sergeant. "Pass the word."

An agent listening to the two-way radio in his car cupped his hands. "Pinto two-door with New York plates has been spotted on the pike near exit thirty-one-A. Heading this way and barreling."

Ray and the Commissioner exchanged glances, and there was

no need for communication between them. No attempt would be made to halt the robbers before they reached the roadblock.

Someone handed Red Martin a bullhorn, and he turned on the power. "Full alert! Stand ready!"

Cigarette butts were flipped away, and in the silence that followed Johnny could hear rifles being cocked.

Ray glanced at his watch. "Two to three minutes," he said, and moved to a place beside Martin, directly behind the Commissioner's limousine, which was parked adjacent to the trailer truck.

As Johnny joined them he realized that, in spite of the Commissioner's joke, there was no more exposed a position on the road.

Some of the officers were resting on one knee, several were squatting, and a few were lying on their stomachs. None stood upright, and the rookie knew the principle he had been taught at the Academy was being observed to the letter: in a confrontation always hug the ground. Even those accustomed to firearms tend to aim high.

The wait seemed interminable, but at last the small car appeared down the Turnpike, approaching at a high speed. Then the driver became aware of the obstructions in his path, and slowed his speed while remaining on course. Certainly he knew he could not crash through the barrier, but presumably he was estimating his chance of finding some way to swerve around it.

The standard procedure was: if the driver tried to stay in motion, perhaps attempting a U-turn in order to double back in the direction from which he had come, the agents and police would shoot out his tires.

When the vehicle came within earshot Red Martin raised his bullhorn. "Halt!" The roar echoed through the hills.

At last the driver knew he had no alternative, and his tires screamed in protest as he drew to a stop a scant fifty feet short of the barrier.

"Come out one at a time, slowly," the Commissioner ordered. "With your hands up. Way up."

The trio emerged, more nearly resembling frightened schoolboys than a gang of bank robbers.

The rest was anticlimactic. Troopers surrounded and frisked the youths, relieving one of a pistol and another of a concealed switchblade. Meanwhile agents swarmed over the car, where they removed other firearms and several burlap bags, two with bank seals still intact.

Ray Merrill was satisfied that the entire proceeds of the robbery had been recovered, principally because there had been no opportunity to dispose of it. He read the trio their rights, then asked, "Where have you stored the other money you've stolen?"

The youths exchanged glances, but made no reply.

"Bank robbery is a federal offense," he told them, "so you'll be appearing in U.S. District Court. If the prosecutor is disposed in your favor, and that will depend on what I tell him about your willingness to cooperate, you might be spared as much as ten years. What you decide is strictly up to you, of course."

The driver was the first to break, and admitted that the loot taken in two previous robberies was hidden in an old well behind a North Stonington farmhouse.

Two agents and a trooper were dispatched to the scene, the robbers were taken off in separate State Police cars for booking in the federal court in Winthrop, the stolen car was moved to the shoulder of the Turnpike, and as soon as the roadblock was removed the various authorities began to disperse.

But Ray was in no hurry. "I did something wrong, although it was deliberate," he said to the new agent. "Do you know what it was?"

Johnny thought hard. "No, sir."

"I questioned all three of them together. They should have been separated and interrogated individually, but in this instance I kept them together, hoping that a slip by one would force them to talk, and that's the way it worked out. Now, then. They made a serious error in their operation that made our job easier. Would you like to guess what it was?"

"I think I know, Mr. Merrill," Johnny said. "They should have abandoned their stolen car and switched to a legitimate car with proper registration. It might have taken us longer to track them."

"Good. You're learning." Ray smiled and glanced at his watch. "Not bad for a half-morning's work, but there's time for a lot of paper shuffling before lunch. I'll spare you some of it. Take the stolen car to the Winthrop Police Department garage, check out the owner through NCIC, and make sure the local P.D.

notifies him his car has been recovered before you come back to the office."

As Johnny walked to the Pinto he understood why the Bureau placed such emphasis on ITSMV, particularly ring cases. It was bad enough that, somewhere in the United States, a motor vehicle was stolen every thirty seconds around the clock, 365 days per year. But that was just the beginning. All too often such thefts were directly connected with even greater crimes.

The capture of the bank robbers had been a tidy exercise, and ASAC Joe Butler scanned the report that would be sent by airtel to Bureau headquarters in Washington, indicated his approval by initialing the form, and sent it off to the teletype room. The new boss was off to a great start, even though he hadn't participated in the operation, even indirectly. No sooner had his interminable press conference ended than the U.S. Attorney had dropped in to welcome him to Winthrop, and now the Commissioner of State Police was closeted with him.

Oh, well. An ASAC knew how to run a Field Office while the boss acted as a front man. Joe Butler stared out at the neatly clipped grass and budding elms, maples, and oaks of the Winthrop Common, with three major churches lining one side and buildings belonging to the University filling the other. The view was one of the most attractive in town, as visitors frequently told him, but after four years in this slot he was tired of it.

He had been hoping for promotion to Inspector before the change had been made at the top, but there wasn't a chance now that he'd be moved until Dave Daniels became acclimated. Three months, if Joe was lucky. Never, if his name wasn't on the Bureau list.

Not that he looked forward to being an Inspector, a job he likened to sorting out other people's dirty laundry. He knew the Bureau was rightly proud of its unique ability to police itself, to keep its own nest clean, and that Inspectors, aided by agents drawn temporarily from other offices around the country, were the keys to the system. He wasn't keen on moving his family to Washington for a couple of years while spending virtually his whole time on the road as he made a thorough, three- or four-week study of one Field Office after another.

The demands of precedent left no alternative. One was promoted from ASAC to Inspector, who for a minimum of two years snooped and poked on internal investigations, showing favor to none. Then, if the cards were right, the last big jump to SAC, with a Field Office of his own, where he could spend the last four years of his active career before he faced mandatory retirement.

After spending a quarter of a century as a Special Agent Joe knew better than to take any move upward for granted, and if his promotion failed to materialize he could always retire next year, when he reached his fiftieth birthday. The trouble was that, with the kids grown, he and Stella would spend their time just sitting and looking at each other. He could get a job as head of security for an industrial plant somewhere to augment his generous pension, but that was no good, either. According to the reliable grapevine, too many retired colleagues who had taken the industry route regretted the move. Disciplines were so sloppy in the private sector that anyone accustomed to the precision demanded by the Bureau soon became disgusted elsewhere.

Go easy, Joe told himself. Just because a new SAC known to his peers as Old Iron Guts had moved in today was no reason to get uptight. He himself was regarded as something of a martinet by the lower echelons, so he should get along okay with Daniels, although not so well that the new boss would want to keep him in Winthrop.

The agents who had gone out on the bank robbery were drifting back into the office, so Joe decided the time had come to make his regular morning tour of the bullpen. Donning his jacket just to be on the safe side, he sauntered out of his private office, which was about half the size of the SAC's.

Two agents were just coming in through the front entrance, past the reception room, and neither looked the part. Samson Grant, at twenty-nine, was a second-office agent and the pride of Winthrop. He was black, an attorney, and a one-time All-American football player, qualifications that made him priceless in a state where racial tensions created problems for white agents who tried to deal with the black community.

Grant was holding the door for Linda Bartlett, and she was out of the ordinary, too. Now twenty-six, she was in the third year of her first-office assignment, and most of the men treated her as an equal. She looked as though she belonged in an advertising agency, and most visitors to the Winthrop Field Office assumed she was a clerk or secretary. Joe, who didn't approve of women as agents, had to admit that Bartlett was tough, unsentimental, and, according to her Academy record, well versed in self-defense.

"Samson," he said, "you missed some fun this morning. Where were you?"

Samson Grant made a wary face. "Out on applicant interviews in New Haven."

Joe knew how he felt. He was assigned to interview every black who wanted a federal job, and he had to be tired of the merry-go-round.

There was a strong hint of hostility in Linda Bartlett's attitude. "I missed the robbery roundup, too. If it matters, Mr. Butler. Which it does to me. I've spent three hours oozing sympathy at a Spanish-speaking lady—"

"The one who has a fugitive son?"

"Yes, sir. For all the good it did. Either she doesn't know where he is, which I refuse to believe, or she still doesn't trust me."

"Keep after her," Joe said.

Linda looked weary. "What else? I'll appreciate it if you'll put me down for a private chat with the new boss."

"You're already on the list, and so are you, Grant. Stick around for the rest of the morning. He's called an agents' meeting before lunch." Joe walked on to the bullpen, where he passed the word about the meeting to the supervisors and street agents. He felt reasonably certain Grant intended to complain about a lack of variety in his assignments, but he had no idea what was bugging Bartlett. He had enough trouble trying to understand Stella, and had no desire to cope with the mysterious workings of a woman agent's mind.

The voice of the boss's secretary came over the intercom. "Mr. Daniels would like to see all agents in his office, please."

There was no need to repeat the request. Those who were talking on the telephone hurriedly concluded their calls, and a supervisor who was watching a message coming in on the teletype from the Bureau in Washington left the task to a stenographer.

They crowded into the large office, filling it. Protocol made it necessary for Joe Butler to stand at one side of his superior's desk, and the supervisors stood together in the front.

SAC David Daniels was the only person in the room in shirtsleeves.

"Miss Bartlett and gentlemen," he said, "I'm sorry we didn't get together a little sooner today, but all of us have been busy. Your morning's work will produce statistics for this year's *Crime in the United States,* which is more than I can say for mine. I'm sure you've heard stories about me, but don't believe them. Let's form our individual reactions to each other. One of the great advantages of working for the Bureau is that we follow a standard *modus operandi,* no matter who sits in the catbird seat. Don't change your routines. If there's something special I want, I'll tell you about it.

"I intend to become acquainted with all of you, as well as with the agents in the Resident Agencies, and I plan to have a private chat with each of you. All of you know Mr. Butler, so I suggest you schedule our appointments through him. For the present, I have only a few announcements. You'll qualify every month with firearms instead of five times per year. I'm something of a nut on overweight, so I want everyone to schedule extra physical exams one month from now, and anyone who tips the scales more than he should will be wise to go on a crash diet. Only one other announcement. When you're earning overtime pay, earn it. Don't sit on your butts. You know the job that needs to be done. Do it. You know regulations. Follow them. That's all for now. There's time for a few sessions before lunch, so I'll start with Miss Bartlett. The rest of you are dismissed."

The agents filed out, and Linda Bartlett sat down at her superior's bidding, smoothing the skirt of her cream-colored gabardine suit.

There was a suspicion of humor in Dave Daniels's eyes as he sat opposite her. "I've been hearing about you ever since you went through the Academy," he said.

She raised her invisible guard. "Sir?"

"Some of the faculty thought you weren't aggressive enough, the way I heard it. So one of your classmates, who had been a Golden Glover, was told to pop you good during boxing. I'm told you tore off your gloves and went at him with feet, fingernails, and teeth."

Linda retained her composure. "That's a slight exaggeration, sir, but not all that much."

"I appreciate a fighting spirit. Keep it up." Dave leaned back in his chair and studied her. "You asked to see me because you're unhappy in Winthrop, Miss Bartlett, and you want a transfer."

"You must be a mind reader, Mr. Daniels. I didn't even tell Mr. Butler my reasons."

"You're suffering from a common ailment known as the woman agent's syndrome. You're tired of interviewing women and interrogating women. You joined the Bureau for action, and you aren't getting your share. I'll okay a transfer, if you insist, but you'll find a similar situation in most places. It may become a bit livelier around here for you if you'll hang on. I'm the father of three daughters, you see, and I don't believe any of you are delicate plants."

Linda looked even more attractive when she smiled. "I'll hang on, Mr. Daniels," she said. "And thanks."

"Wait until I produce such good results that you come within a millimeter of getting your head blown off. You've had no specific squad assignment, and I'm giving you none. Maybe you and I, between us, can convince the Personnel Division down in Washington that we can use a great many more women agents."

She was dismissed, and was pleased when he remained seated. She was being treated as an agent, not a woman, and that was the way she wanted it.

"Send in Agent Grant, will you?" Dave scribbled something on a scrap of paper.

Samson Grant looked more self-assured than he felt when he entered the office and sat opposite the new SAC.

"I'm informed," Dave said, "that you've had one hell of a good job offer on the outside."

"Yes, sir, I do. With a fifty percent pay increase."

"You and every other black agent worth his salt," Dave said with a sigh. "You spend five years with the Bureau, and they line up in the private sector, waiting to outbid each other for you."

"Just for the record, Mr. Daniels, I've had six years since I was graduated from the Academy."

"So I've noticed. And that causes me to hope that maybe you aren't all that anxious to leave us."

"If I could, I'd like to stay."

"Somebody forcing you out?"

"The Bureau. I'm Winthrop's token black, Mr. Daniels. I do the black applicant interviews. When an investigation is needed in a black neighborhood, I make it. When we take a black prisoner, I interrogate him. I can't persuade the supervisors to forget the goddamn color line."

"They follow the course of least resistance," Dave said, "partly because you'll get better results with a black suspect than a white agent can achieve."

"Now you know why I'm thinking of getting out, Mr. Daniels!"

"I knew before you told me. We face a nasty problem, Grant, and it isn't just here. Our standards are so high, intellectual and educational as well as physical and moral, that it isn't easy for members of a minority that has been suppressed to qualify as Special Agents. There won't be any black S-A-Cs during the rest of my active career, but you'll see them in your lifetime."

"My grandfather was a Pullman porter, Mr. Daniels, and my father was a small businessman who scrimped to put me through college and law school. Waiting doesn't come easy."

"Do you think I waltzed into this job of mine overnight?"

"No, sir."

"Do you know how to solve the problem of giving Special Agent Samson Grant greater job opportunities?"

"Not offhand I don't, Mr. Daniels."

"As it happens, I do. There's a promising young black in the new agents class that's being graduated from the Academy in another two weeks, and the Personnel Division has promised me I can have him. So we'll turn him loose on the sludge assignments as soon as he's capable of handling them—jobs that no white agents do, remember—and that will free you for other work. If you're willing to wait."

Samson Grant grinned broadly.

Dave rose and extended his hand. "It's a deal?"

"Hell, yes! I mean—yes, sir." There was a spring in Grant's step as he went out.

Two rebellions squelched, at least temporarily. Not too bad a start. Dave flipped a switch that connected him with the agent on duty in the communications center. "Daniels. Anything hot on the teletype?"

"No, sir. Just routines, although there's been a new bombing near one of the United Nations missions in New York. Nobody hurt."

"I guess New York can handle it without help from us. I'm going to lunch, and so is Mr. Butler." Common sense dictated a lunch engagement with his first assistant, but there was more to it than that. Two Assistant Directors at the Bureau had requested Dave, off the record, to make a private analysis of Joe Butler's capabilities and report within a month whether he was qualified for promotion to Inspector. With that project under way he could start concentrating on the case loads being carried by each of his supervisors and start learning what was happening in his new bailiwick.

Pete's Bar & Grill was located two blocks from the Winthrop Federal Building, in a neighborhood of pawnshops, small stores, and discount houses. Inside and out it resembled a score of other eating and drinking establishments in the area, and was large and comfortable, with a slightly seedy air. But it was cleaner than most, the chef knew his business, and the proprietor was generous in his servings of both food and liquor. As a result Pete's had been the unofficial FBI mess for more than ten years.

Other law-enforcement people knew it, and detectives from the Winthrop Police Department sometimes ate there, too, as did off-duty State Police troopers. The city's hoodlum element was conspicuous by its absence, and Pete, who encouraged the FBI trade, was the only restaurateur in the district who had never been robbed. His clientele was quiet, distinguished by few big spenders, but the proprietor was aware of the advantages he enjoyed.

Raymond Merrill entered, exchanged a word with Pete, and waved to the bartender as he made his way to a booth at the rear of the establishment. A dozen agents greeted him, the younger men looking self-conscious because there were drinks on their tables, but Ray was conveniently short-sighted, expecting the same courtesy in return.

He seated himself, glanced at his watch as he lighted a cigarette, and knew that Linda Bartlett would join him in no more than three minutes. They had formed the habit of meeting at Pete's every Monday and Friday, sometimes dropping in for a drink after work, too. Ray realized some members of the staff were gossiping, but he shrugged off the talk. Whispers were inevitable when a woman agent was involved, but he was a bachelor again, entitled to meet anyone he pleased. Besides, his relationship with Linda was innocent enough. There was a fourteen-year difference in their ages, and he thought it unlikely that they would ever become intimate.

They had the Bureau in common, but little else in their lives was similar. In fact, he shuddered when he thought of her idea of a weekend, wearing jeans and roaring around the countryside beyond the Winthrop suburbs on a motorcycle. In Mr. Hoover's day there had not only been no women agents, but no one in the Bureau, not even a young clerk, would have dreamed of riding a motorcycle. Ray preferred fishing, and hoped he could interest Linda in the sport. She had promised to go out with him, so that was a beginning.

She slipped into the booth, seating herself opposite him, and her smile was apologetic. "Sorry, but I couldn't get away from the S-A-C. Have you ordered?"

This phase of their conversation followed a standard routine. "I was waiting for you," Ray said.

"But this is a workday. I really shouldn't have a drink."

"I'm having a Manhattan, Linda. You do what you please. I can promise you that if there's a bank robbery this afternoon, I won't assign you to it."

"Well, I'll just have one, then."

Ray signaled to a waiter, who had already placed the order, and quickly brought two Manhattans to the booth.

They clinked glasses in an old-fashioned ritual.

"How did it go with the new boss?" Ray wanted to know.

"He's promised me more action. We'll see if he means it."

Ray was unfailingly surprised by her desire for greater excitement in the field. But her attitude was no pose; if her mad motorcycling was any criterion, she actually relished physical danger.

"I've got to say one thing for Mr. Daniels. He had looked up my record, all the way back to the Academy."

"That's encouraging."

Linda placed her elbows on the table and leaned forward. "You know more about him than you've told me."

"Not really. You hear about different S-A-Cs from some of the old-timers, but then you form your own judgments."

"Tell me."

"Everybody agrees he's informal and tries to give you a break. Doesn't stand on ceremony. Like his seeing us in shirtsleeves today. That was a signal. But anybody who judges him by surface things will end up in either New York or Butte, Montana." Both offices were regarded by most agents as the least desirable.

"He struck me as tough," Linda said.

Her intuition was remarkable, Ray had discovered. Sometimes it took a male agent hours of plodding to work out what she knew at a glance. "Well, I sure wouldn't want to cross him. Or fail to produce for him."

Their waiter appeared with a second round of drinks.

"Oh, dear," Linda said. "I was going to eat the omelet, but now I'll have to take the small salad."

"With a figure like you got, Miss Bartlett, you don't have to worry," the waiter said.

"Ha! Small salad. With low-calorie dressing."

Ray waited until the waiter moved out of earshot. "Is the boss assigning you to a squad?"

Linda shook her head. "No, he wants to shoot me in wherever there may be a need for me."

"Too bad. I could have used you." He started to offer her a cigarette before remembering she didn't smoke. "I begin to get the pitch."

"I don't."

"That's because you weren't around when Mr. Hoover was still the Director. You tell the boss you want more action, and he gives you a seat on a trapeze, so you can drop off anywhere. Except there's a catch. Some capers aren't suitable for women."

Linda's temper flared. "Don't you start handing me that line, Ray Merrill!"

He grinned at her, then summoned the waiter to order baked meatloaf with mashed potatoes and gravy, which he knew he'd regret. What the hell, he had no appetite when he ate alone, and was underweight.

"You may be as big a male chauvinist as I think you are!"

Ray held up a hand. "Let me finish. There are other cases where you could do a whale of a job. I suspect what the S-A-C was doing was urging you to develop a case of your own."

"Just like that—out of thin air? Find myself a nest of spies in the Department of International Relations at the University, maybe. Or dig up a kidnapping that hasn't yet been reported."

He drained his glass. "Maybe I can help. We'll watch the airtels and P.D. reports in the next couple of days, and let's see what we find."

Linda placed a hand over his for a moment. "You're a dear." He was, too, and she had to smile when she remembered she had been afraid of him, when she had first come to Winthrop, because he appeared so hard-boiled. His divorce had shattered him, he desperately needed a promotion to restore his ego, and it wouldn't hurt him to spend a night with a woman. She thought enough of him to be that woman, but was afraid he'd then imagine himself in love with her, which would cause too many complications.

Ray became embarrassed and withdrew his hand. "Something juicy will come along soon, never fear. Big cases always develop in cycles, and we're due for a fancy caper. You'll get the first."

2

The first major change in routines made by the new Winthrop SAC was the posting of a Special Agent on the late-night lobster shift. Previously the staff had been rotated on the day and evening shifts, with a senior clerk remaining on duty from midnight until 8:00 A.M. This was considered satisfactory in most Field Offices, particularly when the clerks chosen for night duty were ambitious young men, eager to be accepted for Special Agent training. No one in the higher echelons forgot that twenty percent of the agents had risen through the ranks.

But Dave Daniels had his own firm ideas on the subject. "If something important breaks late at night," he said, "I want someone in the office with enough authority to start the ball rolling even before he gets in touch with Joe Butler or me."

To the surprise of no one Johnny Hedley, the junior agent, was given the dubious honor of inaugurating the new system, and it was made clear to him that he would not be relieved of his regular duties for the assignment. All agents were required to put in obligatory overtime work each week in order to qualify for a payment of $3,000 per year that they received in addition to their regular salaries, and Johnny's night stint would be counted as overtime for the week.

When the evening shift departed he was locked into the office for the night. The bombproof, fireproof double doors at all entrances were locked and bolted, and the sophisticated electronic devices that gave ample advance notice of the approach of an intruder were switched to full alert. Federal security guards, augmented by a special squad from the Winthrop Police Department, were on patrol outside the building and in the lobby, so the Field Office was as safe as the ingenuity of experts could make it.

But there were additional precautions that Johnny was required to observe. He made certain that the special lock on the metal door of the arsenal, its combination known only to a few, was sealed. He went from office to office, checking papers left on desks to insure that all confidential documents had been placed in safes for the night. Then he tested desk drawers and file cabinets to see if they, too, were locked.

Only when he had taken each of the steps prescribed in the *Manual* did he go to the communications center, where he read the messages coming in on the teletype machines. The State Police were picking up the usual drunks on the highways, local police departments were reporting run-of-the-mill muggings and robberies, burglaries and barroom fights. The night promised to be quiet.

Johnny turned up the volume of the bells that would be activated electronically if important bulletins came through on the machines. Then he removed his jacket, necktie, and shoes, and at 1:30 A.M. he stretched out on the cot in the communications center for a nap. Older agents had been known to complain that the clatter of the teletypes, the dusty office smells, and the lack of fresh air made it difficult for them to sleep, but Johnny encountered no such troubles. In almost no time he dozed.

The buzzing of the telephone on the table beside him roused him at 2:24 A.M., and even as he reached for the instrument he checked to make certain the device that would record the conversation was in operation. More often than not, veterans had told him, calls at this hour came from nuts or drunks, but occasionally something of value turned up, and Johnny had been instructed to take no chances.

"FBI," he said.

"Is this the Winthrop headquarters?" The man at the other end of the line had a deep voice and sounded sober.

"That's right."

"I want to talk to the top guy."

"You're speaking to him," Johnny said, wide awake by now.

There was a moment's hesitation before the man spoke again. "You know Hernando Reyes Gomez?"

"Who?"

The name was repeated.

"Offhand I can't place him," Johnny said. "Should I know him?"

"You better know him, buddy." The voice sounded ominous.

Johnny had been taught how to handle anonymous informants in an Academy course, but this was his first opportunity to practice what he had learned. Assuming, of course, that this was something more than a nut call.

"Hernando Reyes Gomez isn't your friend," Johnny said.

The man's derisive laugh was hoarse.

Johnny made an effort to speak casually. "What's he done to you?"

"Nothing to me, buddy. This is one cat who won't get his fingers burned."

"Why don't you like him?"

"Because he's a no-good, two-faced bastard!" The intensity of the man's voice was startling. "He promises to pay off when you deliver for him, but he makes excuses."

"He sounds pretty rotten to me," Johnny said. "What was delivered to him that he wouldn't pay for?"

Again the man hesitated. "Just you remember his name," he said, and rang off.

Johnny followed the standard procedures. The name of Hernando Reyes Gomez did not appear on the Bureau's *Wanted* list, the State Police list, or the weekly survey of local police departments. Lacking a birth date or other identifying data, he could not query the memory bank of the National Crime Information Center.

He had no way of knowing whether the call had been significant or merely the attempt of a disgruntled citizen to get another into trouble. Speculation was useless, so he confined himself to facts in the one-paragraph summary of the conversation he wrote on the night sheet.

Returning to the cot, Johnny found it difficult to go back to sleep. Perhaps the phone call had been meaningless, and an old-timer would have put it out of his mind. But this was his first experience of the sort, and if he ever came across the name of Hernando Reyes Gomez he would remember it.

Samson Grant had an hour to kill after giving testimony in a Federal District Court trial in Winthrop, so he dropped in at the city police headquarters. The desk sergeant greeted him with the respect that local police officials customarily showed for Bureau representatives, but the lieutenant of detectives was on more familiar terms with him and, after slapping him on the back, thrust a carton of coffee at him.

"Slumming today, huh?" the lieutenant asked.

Samson shrugged. "I may be recalled as a witness by the defense at the courthouse, so I've got to hang around town until lunchtime. What's new, Bill?" Not waiting for a reply, he began to leaf through the detectives' daybook.

"You won't find anything much in there," the lieutenant said. "Earlier this morning we thought we'd get your new boss off to a good start with a kidnapping, but it blew up faster than it developed. Rich kid disappeared from home, but she called her parents. Seems she was running away somewhere with a boyfriend."

Samson smiled, but wasn't interested.

"Come to think of it, we may have a lead on something for you. Are you in on stolen motor vehicles?"

"I'm in on everything," the Special Agent said.

The lieutenant went to the door of his office and shouted to an assistant, who brought him a sheaf of reports. "If you think there's anything in these, I'll have them photocopied for you."

Samson glanced at the reports of stolen motor vehicles, flipping them over as he sipped his coffee. He looked bored as he scanned each sheet, but his eyes brightened, and he grinned at the detective. "White man," he said, "you may have the makings of a ring case."

"You're welcome, black man," the lieutenant said.

"Six Buicks and Mercury Monarchs stolen within the same twenty-four-hour period. None of them more than two years old. Not coincidence."

"We don't often see that many medium-priced cars disappear at the same time."

"Right," Samson said. "They're harder to unload than the small cars." There was no need for him to remind the city detective of the maxim that the higher the price of a stolen car, the greater was the risk taken by the thief. "Any leads?"

"Not yet. We've sent full teletype reports to NCIC, and we've alerted the State Police, but that's about all we can do."

"What about NATB?" Samson wanted to know. The National Automobile Theft Bureau was a private organization, jointly owned and operated by the major insurance companies, and was valuable in disseminating information.

"We've notified their Winthrop office. The Connecticut representative will be dropping in later today, as he always does, so we'll fill him in on anything else he may want to know."

"I'll take those photocopies, please." Samson's air of lethargy had vanished. "Our ITSMV supervisor will want a look. And, Bill, if any more Buicks or Monarchs go down the drain, call the information in to us, will you?"

"Glad to oblige," the detective lieutenant said.

Linda Bartlett was no stranger to car auctions, having visited all four held in Connecticut during her year of indoctrination training. But people from the Resident Agencies were assigned to them on a regular basis, so she wasn't all that familiar with them, either.

The lot at Plymouth, about twenty-five miles inland from Winthrop, was the largest in the state, covering a tract of thirty acres, and on the one day each week when an auction was held it became a madhouse. Hundreds of cars were being moved from one part of the lot to another, seemingly at random, some under their own power and others on trailer trucks. Men armed with clipboards and ballpoint pens swarmed over them, inspecting paint jobs, poking at interiors, listening to engines.

Linda needed no one to tell her the point and purpose of an auction, a phase of the automobile industry little known to the public. More often than not, dealers who sold new cars took old cars in trade; when those second-hand cars weren't moved, they were taken to an auction, which functioned as a gigantic exchange. A dealer who was enjoying a brisk sale of low-priced two-door sedans would buy more of them, while another, whose luck with sports cars was good, would stock up on them.

The rules were simple: the potential buyer made his bid, which the potential seller either accepted or rejected. When a bargain was struck, one or more cars changed hands, with the proprietors of the auction taking a modest fee for their part in the transaction. Sellers were required to provide clear, legitimate titles of ownership, and the State Department of Motor Vehicles was duly notified. The procedure was simple, on the surface, but the FBI had reasons of its own for taking an interest in the auctions.

As Linda knew, many of the cars offered for sale at an auction came from other states, and cars from the so-called nontitle states caused the headaches. In order to obtain a title in these states, the owner of a car was not required to provide a Vehicle Identification Number, which made it easier for sellers of stolen cars to do business without fear of detection. Until recently neighboring Massachusetts had been a nontitle state. Neighboring New York was still in that category, which meant that uncounted thousands of stolen cars made their way from New York to Connecticut for resale each year, each of them accompanied by a simple "sales slip" that was easy to forge.

Linda drove her Bureau car past long rows of trailer trucks and tractors as well as passenger vehicles. She was invading a man's world, and was prepared for the hostilities and snubs she would face. Ray Merrill had suggested she develop a case on her own initiative, however, and an agent who took the time and made the effort was certain to run across something shady at an auction. It would do no good, to be sure, to locate an odd stolen car here or there. Because of a lack of manpower the Bureau no longer handled such cases, concentrating instead on the multiple thefts known as ring cases.

Linda parked outside the single-story red brick building bearing the legend LARIGIO BROTHERS—CAR AUCTION. The main room was crowded with men seated in clusters at tables and desks, and she felt rather than saw them pause long enough in their negotiations to place her under steady scrutiny. She hated being eyed en masse. Only her somewhat bulky shoulder bag was out of place, but that couldn't be helped; it contained a secret compartment in which she carried her regulation .38 with a two-inch barrel, a special weapon issued to women agents.

"I want to see Mr. Larigio," she told a male secretary.

The man turned to a group in the corner. "Carlos," he shouted, "the lady wants to talk to you."

A short man wearing a hat, with a cigar stub clamped between his teeth, separated himself from the group and looked Linda up and down as he sauntered toward her. "We just sell to dealers," he told her.

She replied by showing him her Bureau credentials.

Carlos Larigio was stunned. "You're FBI, lady?"

Linda smiled and nodded.

"I didn't know they had broads for agents. You know Fred Cross from Hartford who comes here sometimes?"

"I know him." She gave the man a chance to recover from his surprise.

"What can I do for you, ma'am?" Larigio paid her the ultimate compliment of removing his hat.

"Give me a desk in a private corner somewhere, and let me see carbon copies of the day's sales, if you don't mind."

"My pleasure, ma'am." He led her to a small, unoccupied desk, which he dusted by waving his hat across it.

"I'll be obliged to you," Linda said with a sweet smile, "if you don't tell anyone my identity."

"Sure, lady!" It would do his business no good if the word spread that a woman agent from the FBI was snooping on the premises.

Linda accepted a thick stack of sales contract carbons and went to work, painstakingly scanning each for possible discrepancies. Three long years had passed since her Academy instructors had stressed in lecture after lecture that proper investigative techniques consisted of slugging, keeping watch for tiny details that laymen might miss. There was no magic in FBI techniques, and as she had learned in the field, no substitute for hard, grinding labor.

Automobile dealers were by nature gregarious, and the attractive blonde in the corner provided a natural magnet, but those who wandered to her desk and tried to strike up conversations with her soon changed their minds. None were certain of the reasons, but something in her clear, blue eyes caused them to seek conviviality elsewhere.

Linda didn't stir for almost four hours, and when she finally rose to her feet a watchful Carlos Larigio hurriedly joined her. "We're serving sandwiches and coffee pretty soon," he said. "You're welcome."

"Another time, thanks. Where can we talk?"

He was apprehensive as he led her into a private cubicle. "You can ask Freddie Cross about my brother and me. We run as clean an auction as you'll find anywheres."

"I don't doubt it, Mr. Larigio." It was easier for Linda to be soothing than it would have been for a male agent. "What do you know about Premier Cars of the Bronx, New York? A Hunts Point Avenue address."

He shoved his hat toward the back of his head and pondered.

"They sold four Ford Granada sedans here this morning, all of them less than six months old." She showed him the carbons of the sales receipts.

"Oh, yeah. These cars were good buys. I never met the fellow before, but he said something about having to go out of business. Anyway, they were snapped up."

"I don't wonder. A thousand dollars off the list price for what's practically a new car is quite a bargain. Do you mind if I use the telephone?"

"Help yourself, ma'am. And I'll bring you a chicken sandwich. Just in case you change your mind about eating." He bustled off.

Linda called the Field Office and asked for Raymond Merrill. "Do me a favor if you aren't busy, Ray. I have Vehicle Identification Numbers for four cars, and I'd like you to run them through NCIC for me."

"No sweat." Ray took down the numbers.

Larigio brought Linda a sandwich, a mug of coffee, and, as a special treat, a paper napkin.

In less than a minute Ray was on the line again. "No dice, Linda. They're all clean."

"Something is fishy," she said, "but I can't quite put my finger on it."

"Well, come back to the office when you're finished, and I'll buy you a drink as a reward for your supersleuthing."

"Thanks, boss." Just this once she'd like to show Ray she could develop a case on her own.

Larigio was hovering within earshot.

Linda ate the sandwich, trying to determine what it might be that made her uneasy. Still unable to identify it, she joined the owner of the auction. "Are those Granadas still on the lot?"

"Sure. They won't be moved until we close at three."

"You don't imagine the new owners would object if I look at them?"

"They'll be glad to cooperate, ma'am. They do business with us all the time, and they're legitimate dealers."

"I'm sure they are." She walked beside him as they headed onto the lot.

Larigio took her to a row of cars that looked new.

Linda was impressed. All four sedans were in perfect condition, outside and in, and in the second-hand automobile industry were known as creampuffs.

She checked the New York sales slips, none of which listed a VIN. But the numbers were listed on the Connecticut sales forms, as required by state law, and when she checked these against the number plates on the dashboards of the cars they tallied.

At first glance the VINs seemed legitimate. At the left side of the panel was the Ford script, "F," followed by a single number indicating the year in which this model was produced. All four showed the current year. Next came a letter that showed the symbol for the plant where the car had been assembled. The next two numbers indicated the series and body-style symbols. All checked out with the Motor Vehicle Identification Manual published by the National Automobile Theft Bureau. She paid little attention to the last numbers in the series, the sequential production number of each car, which started at each Ford plant with 100,001, regardless of the body style or engine.

Well, there was no escape: she'd have to get herself grubby, so she climbed under each car and, with the aid of a flashlight, wrote down the secret identification number, which on this particular model of this particular car was located on the inner fender panel.

Carlos Larigio had seen Fred Cross and other FBI men climb under cars and look in odd places for the secret identification numbers placed there by the manufacturers, but he had never dreamed he would watch a woman doing it. "Are you okay, lady?" he asked as she emerged.

Linda stood, dusting her hands and brushing off her dress. Aside from a slight snag in the left leg of her pantyhose she had escaped damage. "Just fine, thanks."

He peered at her anxiously. "Are these cars legitimate?"

"They appear to be. Strictly unofficially, Mr. Larigio, I wonder if you'd do the dealers who bought these cars a favor. I've found no indication that any one of the four is stolen, but the dealers might be wise if they held these cars on their lots for about forty-eight hours before they dispose of them. Okay?"

"Fair enough, ma'am." What really stunned him was that she seemed to know her business.

Linda spread the data she had accumulated on Ray Merrill's desk. "I'm going on a blind hunch, nothing more," she said. "I've sent a telegram to the Ford Motor Company, followed by a letter of confirmation, requesting the sales records of the four Granadas."

"If they're busy in Detroit it could take a long time for that information to come through," Ray said.

"I know. So I'd like permission to send an airtel to the New York Field Office. I'd like a rundown on Premier Cars in the Bronx."

He could remember showing the same eager determination in the development of a case, and felt a pang of regret. That had been a long time ago, and these days nothing mattered all that much. "There's been a whole series of bombings down in New York this past couple of weeks," he said. "I don't think the Assistant Director in Charge there will appreciate a nuisance request."

"I'm sure the whole Manhattan staff hasn't been assigned to their bomb squad."

Ray looked at her, then laughed. "You win. Send your airtel."

"Thanks, boss." Linda rose and gathered her papers.

"I'd hate to be a crook and have you gunning for me. Or your husband, staying out late some night to drink with the boys. The poor slob wouldn't stand a chance."

"Fortunately for members of the so-called master sex," Linda replied in the same light vein, "I'm not planning on marrying anybody."

"You will, eventually."

"I suppose."

"Somebody in the Bureau," he said, his words halting her at the door.

"What makes you think so?"

"Statistics. Seventy-three percent of women agents who have married to date are married to fellow agents. And most of them stay in service."

"I'm relieved to hear it," Linda said, "since I have no intention of retiring just yet."

Ray watched her as she went off to the communications center to send her airtel to New York, and he admired the way she moved. Watch it, he warned himself.

He had to admit his personal interest in her was growing, and he knew the reasons. After the dismal failure of his marriage to a woman who had been unable to tolerate his erratic hours, the demands of his job, and the frequent transfers, it was a relief to spend time with a girl who needed no explanations, who understood his way of life. But the relationship would end right there. He couldn't allow himself to forget that Linda Bartlett was fourteen years his junior. And ambitious. There was no reason on earth she'd tie herself to a has-been, a supervisor of forty whose chances of promotion were slim and who would be retired at the convenience of the Bureau when some bright-eyed Inspector in Washington studied his record.

A buzz sounded, and a light on Ray's miniature switchboard glowed. He pushed a switch. "Yes, sir?"

"If you aren't too busy," the SAC said, "I'd like a word with you."

Ray straightened his necktie and hurried to the office of the new boss.

Dave waved him to a chair. "I've been going over various figures, and I wonder why bank robberies in the state have doubled in the past six months. Do you have any idea?"

"I can take a pretty good stab at it, Mr. Daniels. The robberies perpetrated by professional thieves have held steady, neither rising nor falling very much. Most of the increase has been caused by kids getting into the field. Brainless youngsters read about a gang of their own age pulling a stunt at some bank, so they do the same."

Dave studied him. "How do you like the Winthrop office?"

"Just fine, sir. This is my fifth in sixteen years, and I feel at home here." Ray wondered if the ax was about to fall.

"I gather you had some domestic problems."

"They're behind me." Ray didn't realize it, but his voice became firmer.

Dave smiled. "Are you satisfied with your present spot?"

The answer required care. "I'd like to set a better record before I switch to something else."

"Good, but that isn't what I meant. Some agents prefer to spend their entire careers on the street. Others are happy for life in a supervisor's slot. What about you?"

Ray decided to shoot the works, and to hell with diplomacy. "I'd give damn near anything to be sitting behind your desk, Mr. Daniels."

The SAC's expression was unfathomable. "How long has it been since you've had a brush-up course at the Academy?"

"Eighteen months."

"So you're due."

"Yes, sir. But if you don't mind, I'd like to get a big case or two under my belt before I go off to school again." Ray was astonished by his own reply. An Academy course for prospective ASACs was precisely what he needed on his record if he hoped to win a promotion. Not that the two weeks of schooling would guarantee a move up the ladder, but it was a necessary step. And he found himself sidestepping, procrastinating. Because he was afraid of failure, afraid he couldn't handle the responsibilities of a bigger job.

What had happened to his self-confidence? Certainly a sour marriage hadn't robbed him of it. Or had it? He hated to think he was hesitating because he'd become middle-aged on his last birthday and the Bureau was a place for young, vigorous men.

Whatever the cause of his confusion, the new SAC seemed to understand. "I won't rush you, Merrill," he said. "Take your time, and let me know when you're ready."

The ASAC was in personal charge of new agent training, so Johnny Hedley wasn't surprised when he was summoned to Joe Butler's office. He thought he knew what was coming, and tried to anticipate it by opening the subject himself.

"I'm trying to follow up that anonymous telephone call of last night, Mr. Butler," he said. "I'm checking out names in the city directories of Winthrop, Hartford, New Haven, Bridgeport. All the bigger cities. And I'd like to query the local P.D.s to see if they have any record of the guy."

Joe Butler shook his head. "Don't."

"But—"

"In the first place, you're wasting time, not only your own, but that of police officers in understaffed departments. In the second place, and this is even more important, you don't want to be guilty of harassment."

"How could I, sir?"

The ASAC had been preaching the same theme to new agents for years. "You don't know what motivated last night's call. A squabble between neighbors, a fight over a woman, anything. Local cops take a request from the Bureau seriously, and we don't want to give some law-abiding citizen a possible black eye."

"I realize all that," Johnny said. "But according to what I've learned, a great many tips on criminal activities come to us in anonymous letters and telephone calls."

"No doubt about it, and I'm sure you can cite the actual percentages. In this instance, though, there's been no charge of specific wrongdoing, no indication that the man mentioned to you on the telephone has broken any law. So just sit tight. I'm not telling you to throw the name into a file and forget it. Keep your eyes and ears open, and if the subject is engaged in criminal activity he'll pop to the surface again, sooner or later."

"I see."

"I hope you do," Joe Butler said. "Because the basic principle of all law enforcement, and especially the investigative end, can't be taught at the Academy or any other school. It's called patience. Every day of every year you'll be working for the Bureau you'll be putting jigsaw puzzles together. Sometimes they'll fall into place in a hurry, but that doesn't happen very often. Mostly you'll be fitting tiny bits and pieces into recognizable patterns. People make mistakes, you see, including Special Agents. Our one advantage over the criminals who try to outsmart us and outfox us is that we can afford to exercise patience, and they can't. Sooner or later they slip, and we nail them."

"Yes, sir," Johnny said, and headed back to his own desk.

Joe Butler waited until the day crew had gone for the night and the agents, clerks, and stenographers on the evening shift had settled into their regular routines. Then, armed with the red-tab file, he went into the office of the SAC for the roundup session that every Field Office head demanded before going home to a waiting bourbon and water.

Dave, who was speaking on the telephone, waved him to a chair.

The ASAC noted that he was using the direct Washington line.

"I'm already getting calluses on my tail, Mr. Henry," Dave said. "So I seem to be breaking into the job just fine. No, sir—no problems I can't handle. Yet. I sent External Affairs the clippings of my press conference, with an extra set for Mr. Kelley and another for you. I think the dust will settle by the end of the week, and I'll give you a comprehensive report then. There's nothing urgent at the moment, except that New York is short-handed because of the bombings there, and wants to borrow a half-dozen of our people for a few days. That's fine with me, if it's okay with you. Yes, sir. I'll draw a couple of RAs from Hartford, and one each from some of the smaller offices. And you can tell New York I'll expect them to return the favor when we get into a jam." He replaced the telephone in its cradle, stretched, and lighted a cigar. "What's new, Joe?"

The ASAC handed him a typed list of names. "These are the agents we'll send to New York tomorrow, if you approve."

"You know the personnel better than I do." Dave initialed the order.

Joe took a paper stamped *Confidential* from the folder. "The surveillance on that visiting lecturer in Slavic languages at the University hasn't turned up anything. We've had him under the microscope for almost two weeks, and it looks like a dud case to me."

"Have you had a tap on his phone?"

"No. I didn't want to ask for a court order without something solid, and we haven't found it."

"Do you recommend we drop the case?"

"Yes, sir."

"Okay, I'll sign the recommendation, and leave the final decision up to Washington. Next?"

"Ralph Camarra showed up in Fairfield County today."

Dave hitched forward in his chair. Camarra was the head of one of the leading organized crime families, and anything he did was of interest to the Bureau. "Any details?"

"He was visiting old Sam Bonetti, who retired to a farm outside Weston about seven or eight years ago."

"I chased Bonetti for a long time, and I think that prison hitch he served cooled his enthusiasms a bit. I'm inclined to believe his retirement is genuine."

"Well," Joe said, "this may have been a purely social visit Camarra was making. We don't know. He may like the spaghetti sauce the Bonetti cook makes."

"You've ordered the Fairfield County RA to keep a close watch on the Bonetti house?"

"Yes, sir. Day and night, as long as Camarra is there. It's an enormous drain on manpower to maintain that kind of surveillance, of course, but we have no choice."

Dave blew a cloud of smoke at the ceiling. "There's no point in asking the court for approval of a tap. People like Camarra and Bonetti have been around too long to say anything of significance on the telephone. You might let our agents show themselves outside the Bonetti house, Joe. That could shake Camarra up a bit, and at the least it might spur him into getting out of our territory."

Joe smiled. "In a way we're lucky here, Dave. This state is a no-man's-land between the New York Mafia and the mob that operates out of Providence and Boston."

"The day they start moving into Connecticut in strength,"

Dave said, "I'll have to ask Personnel for an additional ten or fifteen agents."

"That's about it. Except." Joe Butler stiffened. "Except for a purely personal matter. I'm prepared to offer you my resignation, Dave."

The SAC stared. "But you're not eligible until next year."

"I know."

"I had no idea you wanted to get out, Joe."

"I don't. I've been hoping for a promotion to Inspector, but I've got to forget all that."

Dave rose, closed the door, and took a bottle of bourbon from the bottom drawer of his desk. He uncapped it, then reached for two glasses that stood beside his water carafe. "Help yourself."

"Thanks." The ASAC poured himself a stiff shot.

Dave measured a splash into his own glass, then added a generous quantity of water to it.

They toasted each other in silence.

"Want to talk about it, Joe?"

"Not really. I want to give you a clear road so you can bring in an assistant of your own choice—"

"I can do that without your resignation. And just a year before you can take early retirement."

"I guess you'll have to know, Dave. Remember the bank robbery that got your administration off to a fast start yesterday? Well, one of the boys gave a false name, but his real identity was revealed today. The State Police have been keeping quiet—as a favor. But they can't sit on it much longer. The stupid boy happens to be my son."

Dave Daniels liked to regard himself as shockproof, but he was stunned. "My God! I'm sorry."

"Not half as sorry as I am. I had to tell you first. Now I'll call Mr. Kelley and then I'll clean out my desk."

"Like hell you will. I'm not accepting your resignation, Joe."

The ASAC's face worked painfully. "I can't stay in the Bureau when my own kid is a member of a gang that's robbed three banks in a week!"

"How old is he?"

"Nineteen."

"Old enough to take his own punishment, then, without crippling his father. When did you find out about all this, Joe?"

"Commissioner Martin called me a couple of hours ago. I suspected something, I didn't know what, but I had no idea it would be this bad."

"Have you spoken to your wife?"

Joe Butler's face became grim. "I've been saving that pleasure until I get home tonight."

Dave knew better than to intervene in an obviously delicate and tense domestic situation, but his own duty was clear. "This thing has just hit you, and you're crazy if you do anything hasty. You've been in the Bureau almost as long as I have, Joe. You can't throw away your career. And your retirement security."

The ASAC averted his face. "I'm not going to cry for anybody's sympathy. The boy has my blood in his veins and my name. So I'm finished in the Bureau."

"You're wrong. It isn't accidental that I'm familiar with your record. Four commendations from Mr. Hoover. Two from Mr. Kelley. You're a dead cinch to make Inspector either this year or next, Joe."

"The only Inspector in the Bureau with a jailbird for a son? I think too much of the FBI for that!"

"The Bureau," Dave said, his voice hardening, "thinks too much of highly qualified personnel to let you resign without putting up a fight to keep you. Are you suggesting you're going to try to get your son off with a suspended sentence?"

"Never! I've seen the way he's been drifting. For years. Now I'm going to insist that he go to trial. As a first offender he'll get five to ten, and if it's the last thing I ever do I'll see to it that he goes to prison. No matter what happens at home."

Dave tried to place Mrs. Butler, but couldn't remember anything about her other than that she was one of those vaguely pretty Bureau wives who faded into the background at parties and receptions. "Look, I'm going to make this official. Under no circumstances will I accept either your resignation or your suspension from duty. I'm new here, I need your help, and I'm damn well going to have it. That's an order."

The habit of years was even stronger than Joe's shame and outrage. "Yes, sir."

"You can call Mr. Kelley tomorrow morning. I know you'll

want to tell him all this yourself, but you need time to pull yourself together. Okay?" Dave had no intention of mentioning that he intended to speak privately to the Director first.

The ASAC nodded.

"I know how you must feel, Joe, and I can only assure you that I stand behind you and with you, all the way. So will the whole Bureau. You ought to know after all these years that we look after our own!"

"That's one reason I feel so awful. Do you realize that only because it was your first day in this office that I didn't go out on that robbery myself yesterday? If I had, I swear to you, I'd have put a bullet between that kid's eyes."

"Then it's fortunate you weren't there." Dave gestured toward the bottle.

"No more, thanks. I don't dare." Joe heaved himself to his feet.

"For whatever consolation this is," his superior said, "a lot of good people have seen their kids go sour. Senators, doctors, prominent athletes, industrialists, bankers—all kinds. You've watched it again and again, just as I have, and you know how tough it is to buck a peer group influence. Once a kid falls in with a bunch of smartasses who throw morality out the window, there isn't much a parent can do to haul him into line. So don't blame yourself."

Joe nodded, but it was plain, as he made his way out of the office, that he hadn't really listened.

Dave believed his assistant would regain his equilibrium, in time, but meanwhile he needed a professional challenge that would occupy his mind and convince him he was carrying his share of the load. Reaching for the Washington line so he could tell Director Kelley the news, Dave promised himself he would make a study of every active case in the Field Office file. He'd have to find something that would take Joe's mind off his own nasty problem.

3

When Joe Butler walked into the house he knew at a glance that Stella had heard; her eyes were red-rimmed, her mouth was compressed, and her back was rigid. She had tried to adhere to their normal routines, however, and a pitcher of Manhattans was chilling on the bar. He had to admire her for the effort she had made, even though this was no night for drinking.

They embraced, clinging to each other for a moment, and he patted her shoulder, wishing he had the facility to express his feelings in words. But he had always been an action man, and he was too old to change.

He poured Stella a drink, making sure a couple of ice cubes landed in her glass.

She pushed back a mass of thick, dark hair, and her first words revealed her anguish. "Why did Joey do it?"

He sat opposite her and tried to reply calmly. "Suppose my father was in law-enforcement investigative work for the government, and suppose I hated him. How could I give him the finger? Easy. By breaking the law in the most spectacular way possible. Making sure I'd get a lot of publicity that would pile ashes on his head."

Stella's hand trembled as she lighted a cigarette, but even now her grooming was impeccable, and she was indicating in her own way that she wouldn't allow herself to fall apart. "But he doesn't hate you, Joe. He admires you."

"I can tell."

"It's true. Ever since he was old enough to talk he's bragged that his father is an FBI agent."

"Three banks in less than a week, Stell. The real tipoff is that all the money has been recovered. Joey and his pals were doing it for kicks, not cash. So I damn well know this was his way of thumbing his nose at me."

A deep sigh shook her slender body. "Have you seen him?"

"I have no intention of seeing him. I'll make arrangements for you to visit him anytime you want to go, of course."

"What's going to happen, Joe?"

"He and his chums will be arraigned later in the week. I'm asking the U.S. Attorney, as a favor, to recommend that they be held without bail."

"No, Joe!"

"When they come to trial, I'm prepared to go on the witness stand and urge the judge to give them the maximum sentence."

Stella looked at him for a long time. "Joey is your firstborn. Do you hate him that much?"

"I could shake him until his teeth fall out, but I don't hate him, Stell. That's the crazy part of it. I love the little monster."

"If only you hadn't been so strict with him all these years—"

"Hold on. One thing you and I aren't going to do is start a tennis match. If I hadn't been so tough. If you hadn't been so indulgent. Before we know it we're both shooting recriminations from the hip, and that solves nothing. I won't have it."

Common sense told her he was right, and she tried to stifle her hostilities toward him. "I should think," she said, speaking with deliberation, "that a man in your position could get Joey off lightly if you chose to exert yourself. But you say you're going to ask the court to throw the book at him. Why, Joe?"

"Simply because I am in my position. A quarter of a century with the Bureau. An executive job, with a reasonably good chance of moving still higher."

"At Joey's expense?"

"In spite of him! You know the shellacking the Bureau has had in the newspapers and on the air this past year. Some of it deserved, some of it because this is open season on us after years of nothing but praise."

"I don't see the connection."

"Then let me finish," Joe said. "How would it look to the public if the Assistant Special Agent in Charge of the Winthrop Field Office uses whatever influence he supposedly possesses to get probation or a light sentence for his son? Wham! Another black eye for the Bureau. Every major newspaper in the country would tear the FBI apart, and that's something we don't need."

"So you're putting the Bureau ahead of your son." There was weariness in her voice; he had always put the Bureau first.

"My salary has paid for our food and clothing and housing. And Joey's education. I'm making more than thirty thousand a year right now, and that's not peanuts."

"Surely you must have family loyalities!"

Joe tried not to let his exasperation show. "What I do for a living isn't just a job. I could have gone with a law firm after I got out of school. Or I could have become a cop, if that's what I'd wanted. Instead I went with the Bureau. Of my own free will. I never wanted anything else."

"I know," Stella said.

"I realize it hasn't been easy on you and the kids. Tearing up roots and moving to another town every few years. Being careful when you've made friends. Putting up with my crazy hours and never knowing when I'll be coming home."

"I've tried not to complain."

"You've been pretty terrific all these years, Stell. Well, you know the rules. We can't live like ordinary citizens. The Bureau—"

"Always the Bureau!"

"Right. A Special Agent has to be clean, and so does his family."

"Like Caesar's wife," she said, but saw he didn't understand.

"I have two choices, and there's nothing in between," Joe said. "I can keep my job, hope this mess doesn't hurt me too much, and maintain my integrity—and the Bureau's—by trying to observe the letter of the law. Or I can resign and give up my pension. But even then I wouldn't try to get Joey off. I've never in my life coddled a criminal, and I'm not going to start now!"

A stenographer brought Supervisor Raymond Merrill a cup of coffee as he went over the previous evening's log, and he was just settling in for the day when Linda Bartlett came into his office, waving an airtel.

"We've hit paydirt," she said. "New York advises in an overnight message that there is no such place as Premier Cars on Hunts Point Avenue in the Bronx. Those Ford Granadas that went through the Larigio Brothers auction came from a phony source."

She was one of the few women he had ever known who looked attractive first thing in the morning. "Sit down," he said, "and let's check a few basics before we get excited. You went over the Vehicle Identification Numbers of the cars?"

"Yes, sir. I put them through NCIC, and they were clean."

"You're certain there was no tampering with the original VIN plates?"

Linda hesitated. "To the best of my knowledge they were okay."

"Step number one. I'll have an expert go over the cars." He reached for the case file she handed him and studied it. "You say here the New York registrations were legitimate. You're positive of that?"

"Almost," she said. "If they were forgeries, they were very clever forgeries."

"I'll have the titles double-checked, too. I want to see the S-A-C about all this. Meantime, send an airtel to the Detroit Field Office—no, on second thought, phone them. Ask them to put the heat on Ford Motors to find out the Secret Identification Numbers files on those cars and discover who the legitimate owners were." He rose, his coffee forgotten, and headed toward the front office.

As Linda walked back to her desk Special Agent Sid Benjamin stopped her.

"No woman," he said, "has the right to look as pleased with herself at this ungodly hour of day as you do."

"I may have stumbled into an ITSMV ring case," she said.

Sid made a wry face. "There's nothing duller than stolen cars."

Linda sniffed. "We aren't all such hotshots that we're assigned to the extortion, missing persons, and hostages squad." She swept past him and went to her desk to call Detroit.

Sid was one of the Bureau's new breed, and proud of it. His clothes had flair, his black hair hit his collar, his sideburns were thick, and he had grown a mustache, not for an undercover assignment, but because he liked the way it looked on him. At twenty-eight he had spent five years in the Bureau after distinguishing himself as a track star and boxer at a state university, and in spite of his reputation as a swinging bachelor he was held in universal respect, even by his superiors. He had killed two men in line of duty, and unfailingly volunteered for dangerous assignments.

Not that Sid Benjamin enjoyed taking risks any more than the next agent, but he was proving something to himself, his colleagues, and Bureau headquarters. In the days of the old regime not many Jews had found an FBI career attractive, but that was changed now, and Sid thought of himself as a pioneer, a pacesetter. He was living proof that rumors of anti-Semitism in the Bureau were not true. And he was a valuable addition to any staff, as he well knew. He had mastered both Spanish and Italian, and his facility with languages, combined with his coloring, enabled him to pass as a Mediterranean or even a light-skinned Latin American. He was good at his job, he knew it, and as he liked to observe, there was nothing wrong with that.

Ray Merrill hurried through the bullpen and stopped at Sid's desk. "Come into my office for a minute, please."

Sid hitched up his .38 and followed the supervisor.

"The S-A-C has loaned you to me. Temporarily if we hit a dead end. Longer term if we develop a case." Ray brought the agent up to date. "Now, I want you to team with Bartlett—"

"There's nothing I'd like better."

Ray glared at him. "Check the VINs on those cars to see if there has been tampering. And go over the titles carefully. Then I want you to talk to Samson Grant about a raft of Buicks and Mercury Monarchs that have been stolen lately. You may or may not be able to establish a connection between the two, but it's possible."

"Anything is possible, Mr. Merrill," Sid said, "but I don't see how the two tie together."

"In the fourteen years I've worked on ITSMV," Ray said, "I've learned that when two or more ring cases start to develop simultaneously, they usually turn out to be one ring."

Sid knew he deserved the rap across the knuckles. "Sorry, Mr. Merrill. It's too early in the day for jokes."

"Call in if you run across anything interesting. By the time you get back we may have some information from Detroit."

Sid went to Linda's desk and waited until she completed her call. "Honey," he said, "freshen your lipstick and pull up your stockings. You've won the jackpot."

She raised an eyebrow.

"An all-day date with me."

A short time later, after they received final instructions from Ray, they started out in Sid's Bureau car to visit the various dealers who had purchased the Granadas whose origins were a mystery.

"I must have missed something when I examined those cars," Linda said.

"Not necessarily." Sid hit the Turnpike and increased his speed.

"Well, we know the dealership doesn't exist—"

"The gent who sold those cars cashed the checks he received. Samson Grant is looking into that angle, and may come up with something."

"Maybe the VINs were transferred from clean cars. Maybe the registrations are fakes and won't hold up."

"And maybe," Sid said, "the moon really is made of green cheese, no matter what the astronauts tell us."

"That's supposed to be funny, but it went over my head."

"Never try to outsmart a bunch of crooks at the beginning of an investigation. Wait until you've gathered the facts, honey, and then you'll know what direction to take."

Linda resented his patronizing air. "To you," she said, "I'm not 'honey.' "

"There's a cozy motel a few miles down the road. We might stop there for an hour, and I'll make you eat those words."

"It appears," she said, her voice frigid, "that you've never before had a woman agent as a partner."

"I haven't, now that you mention it"—Sid was unabashed—"but I'm thinking of asking the Ay-Sack to make this a permanent assignment."

"I carry the same credentials you carry," Linda said. "I want through the same Academy. I'll match the marksmanship of most agents with a pistol or a rifle. Not you, maybe, because they say you're something else. And I'll take care of myself in hand-to-hand combat. I happen to be a Special Agent, Mr. Benjamin—"

"I don't doubt it."

"—and I am not a quick lay."

"What a pity. I was hoping you were both."

In spite of her indignation Linda laughed. "You're incorrigible."

"That's the nicest compliment any blonde has given me in months." He was silent for a moment, then sobered. "What's the pitch on the Larigios?"

"They're top drawer, and honest. The Bureau has checked them out a half-dozen times, most recently a couple of years ago, and their record is impeccable."

"Depending on what else we find, we may drop in on them for a chat. Have you had much ITSMV experience?"

"A few cases."

"Well, this one smells complicated. And big."

"Your nose working overtime, Sid?"

"Not mine. Ray Merrill's. I could tell by his attitude, and I believe in playing along with a veteran's sixth sense."

They left the Turnpike, and soon arrived at the lot of a dealer who had purchased two of the cars in question. There, with Linda keeping salesmen and other employees at a distance, Sid went to work. Armed with a hammer and screwdriver, he gently tested the Vehicle Identification Number plates, and found they had been riveted and sealed in place. Then he took a small machine known in the Bureau as a "metal X-ray kit," and tested to see if an entire section of the dashboard had been substituted for the original.

"Nobody has tampered with the VINs of either car," he told Linda. "Let's see what we can find in the papers."

They repaired to the office of the nervous dealer, where they subjected the New York State registrations of both automobiles to a careful scrutiny. The ink did not smudge, the printing was clean, and the watermark matched that of true registrations.

"Barring a full laboratory test, which we may want," Sid told the dealer, "these look legitimate. Where are the New York plates?"

"The fellow who sold me the cars removed them," the dealer said. "He made a point of assuming responsibility for turning them in."

Linda and Sid exchanged a glance.

"Are you certain these cars are stolen?"

"All we know for sure," Linda said, "is that they were sold to you by a nonexistent dealership."

The man became even more upset. "I gave him a check for six thousand!"

"You can be sure it's been cashed." Sid was sympathetic. "For your sake, I hope this turns out okay. If it doesn't, are you covered by insurance?"

"I can see a long hassle ahead with the insurance company."

"Keep your chin up," Linda said. "We have nothing definite one way or the other yet, but we'll keep you informed."

"Meanwhile," Sid said, "we hope you'll cooperate by keeping these cars off the market. If necessary we'll get a court order and impound them, but it'll be easier for everyone concerned if you'll play ball with us."

"You can depend on it," the dealer said. "I run an honorable business, and I'm as anxious as you are to see this situation cleared up."

The two agents did not speak again until they had returned to Sid's car and started off for the lot of the next dealer.

"If those cars are hot," Linda said, "I don't see how he can collect from his insurance company."

"He can't. He'll have a six-thousand-dollar hole in his pocket, and there's no way he can recoup the loss. That's what happens when honest people unknowingly buy stolen cars. They get burned."

Merrill took the call from the Detroit Field Office, then made another, longer call before hurrying to the office of the SAC. Dave Daniels listened to his detailed report, occasionally asking a question, and after dismissing him made a call of his own to the Assistant Director in charge of the New York Field Office.

Finally he summoned his ASAC, to whom he had not spoken that morning.

Joe Butler looked as though he had spent a sleepless night. "My wife went to the federal lockup this morning, but the kid wouldn't talk to her. Which doesn't surprise me. What could he say?" He sank into a chair, then brightened somewhat. "I called Mr. Kelley, and he was tremendous. The Bureau won't accept my resignation."

Dave pretended pleased surprise.

"He also made it plain that the Bureau is big enough and strong enough to take a foul-up like this in its stride. He has no objection if I want to help my son, hire a lawyer for him, or whatever. And he said he'd talk to you about the idea of holding a press conference."

"He called me. And there's no need for you to subject yourself to the torture of meeting the press. I'm going to call in the reporters myself, give them the facts straight, and lay it on the line that the Bureau doesn't intend to throw any spanners into the wheels of justice. What you do or don't do as a private citizen is your right, and is irrelevant to your position here."

"Thanks, Dave." Joe's voice was husky. "And thank Mrs. Daniels for calling Stella last night. I'm not sure we could hack it on our own."

The moment had come to change the subject, and Dave became crisp. "Ready to go to work?"

"I'd love it!"

"Good. I want you personally to ride herd on something that's growing and could become very big." Dave brought him up to date on the developing automobile case. "Benjamin and Bartlett have visited all three dealers who bought the Granadas and can find nothing illegitimate. They're heading back to the office right now."

"Curious," the ASAC said.

"It's about to get even more so. Ray Merrill has heard from Detroit. Ford Motors checked the Secret Identification Numbers and found that these four cars were part of a block of seventy-five sold less than three months ago to All-American Car Rentals. Ray has just spoken to their headquarters, and has learned that these were four of twenty new cars sent to their lot at JKF Airport."

Joe stared into space, shaking his head. "That makes no sense."

"There's more confusion to come. I take it Merrill is sound?"

"None better on ITSMV."

"Well, he insists there's a connection between this case and the stealing of a half-dozen Mercury Monarchs and big Buicks in Winthrop during the past few days. He can't prove it, and he doesn't even have a logical reason, but he says he feels it."

"I'd be inclined to play his hunch."

"Play away," Dave said. "I've now spoken to the New York Field Office, and they're so jammed up on their bombings that they're happy to let us invade their territory. How does that sound?"

"I always like it when we can run our own show." Joe's professionalism overcame his preoccupation with his own problems. "First, I'd like to send Benjamin and Bartlett down to Kennedy Airport. They make a balanced team, and maybe they'll dig up something."

"Fine."

"At the same time, I'll alert the whole office, and maybe some of our informants can come up with a few scraps. Samson Grant won't like going to his sources in the black community since he's tired of being identified as a bridge between them and the Bureau, but it can't be helped. We can make it up to him later. I also want to bear down on the Latin American communities."

Dave was surprised.

"In this state, at least, Spanish-speaking people have been involved in more than half of the ITSMV ring cases had in recent years, so I want to play the percentages."

"Make your own decisions, Joe." Dave was relieved by the way he was taking hold. "All I ask is that you keep me informed."

"Right, sir. I see this case as a graduate course of instruction for young Hedley, so I'll perch him on Merrill's shoulder and use him as a swing man as situations arise. Not that we'll get much mileage out of him, of course, but he'll learn plenty." The ASAC stood, and although he looked gaunt, he still managed a smile. "This one can be fun."

His secretary told him that Linda Bartlett and Sid Benjamin

had just returned from their trips to the various dealers, so he summoned them and Ray Merrill to his office.

"I've just told them the situation at All-American Rentals," Ray said.

Linda smiled. "It's crazy."

"You and Benjamin will have a chance to find out whether it is or not," Joe Butler said, and gave them their new assignment. "Grab some sandwiches and eat them as you drive down to JFK, and you should be back in Winthrop by early evening."

Ray felt a pang of regret as he realized his lunch date with Linda was cancelled. Oh, well. Bureau business came first, but he was almost sorry he had teamed her with the jaunty Benjamin. "If you get any leads," he told the couple, "call me from the airport. Don't wait until you get back here to make your report."

His request was a trifle out of the ordinary, and they looked at him.

Ray felt slightly foolish, but couldn't back down. "I think I may have the explanation for all this mystery, but I'd rather not mention it. Just in case I'm wrong, it could throw you off the scent." Aware of their full attention, he became self-conscious. Then, suddenly overcome by feelings of uneasiness, he refrained from adding that, if he was right, this could be the biggest ITSMV ring case in years.

The dragnet was cast.

In Hartford an inconspicuous two-door sedan rolled through a tenement district of the East End, finally pulling into the paved lot of a one-story brick establishment that advertised itself as an automobile body repair and paint shop. The overhead doors were open, and a half-dozen employees were lazing through their afternoon's work on three cars. None paid any attention to the man in his mid-forties, somewhat more slender and athletic than most of his age, who pocketed his car keys and strolled in.

"Is your boss around?"

A man gently pounding a fender into shape jerked his padded hammer in the direction of a tiny, cluttered office.

There was a hint of fear in the eyes of the sweater-clad proprietor when he saw his visitor, but he gave no other sign of recognition.

"I'm thinking of having my car repainted. Another color, perhaps. I wonder if you could look at it and give me a rough estimate."

They strolled together to the sedan parked in the lot, and the proprietor did not speak until they were out of earshot of his hired help. "I've been clean all this last year, Mr. Giles, honest to God! I promised when you got me off on probation that I wouldn't touch another hot car, and I've kept my word."

"I'm sure you have, Tony, so don't get excited." The Resident Agent's voice was soothing. "I'm just hoping you can do me a little favor, that's all."

The proprietor's relief was infinite. "Sure, Mr. Giles, glad to oblige whenever I can. You know me."

What the agent knew was that the man wasn't quite as clean as he pretended. He was no longer actively engaged in altering the appearance of stolen cars, it was true, but he still maintained his connections in the half-world that served thieves of motor vehicles, so he had his uses. The Bureau made no secret of its interest in him, and consequently his arm needed only a slight twist to obtain his cooperation. "Hear anything interesting in the way of gossip lately?"

"Nothing, Mr. Giles!"

"You wouldn't happen to know about some slick operators who have been unloading Ford Granadas?"

The body shop proprietor shook his head.

"I don't suppose you've run into anyone who'd like a disguise job done on Mercury Monarchs or big Buicks?"

"I never see any of the old crowd."

"You might want to look up some of them, Tony. You never know when you can pick up a little gossip here and there. You know my number. Call me from a pay booth." The agent opened his car door, then spoke loudly. "Thanks for your estimate. I'll keep it in mind and get in touch with you."

In New Haven another car headed out Whalley Avenue and drew to a halt in a gas station, beyond the pumps. "What do you charge for a new battery?" he asked the attendant.

"I'll have to get Frank."

After a short wait a tall man in coveralls appeared, wiping grease from his hands with a rag.

The agent wasted no time. "Frank," he said, "I want you to dig up whatever you can on Granadas, Buicks, and Monarchs. The sooner the better."

"Any cash in it for me?"

The man from the FBI shook his head. "No, but the U.S. Attorney will be pleased to hear you're cooperating, Frank."

"How long are you guys going to keep me on the griddle?"

The agent's smile was pleasant. "That's no way to talk. Why, I thought you'd be grateful to us. You still run your business, you still breathe free air. You know how long your marriage will last if you end up in the clink, Frank. That wife of yours is too cute to run around alone for very long."

"I'll put out feelers," the gas station man said in a surly voice.

"Lots of feelers," the agent said. "The juice has been turned up high for this one."

In Bridgeport a car drove through the factory district into a Puerto Rican neighborhood, parking in front of a small grocery store that pecialized in tropical fruits and vegetables. Several boys playing stickball in the street showed a momentary interest in the driver and his vehicle, but relaxed again when they saw that he, too, was a Puerto Rican.

He sauntered into the store, made his way to a rear counter, and inspected the contents of several bins while the heavyset woman in charge attended to the needs of another customer. Eventually she joined him, and they were alone in the store.

"Are these breadfruit fresh, Mrs. Fazzina?"

"I guarantee it, Señor. Flown in from the islands just this morning."

"I'll take this one, please. Mrs. Fazzina, there's a chance Juan can be home even sooner than you've hoped."

"You think so?" She rubbed her hands together in a curious gesture, as though washing them.

"Oh, I know it," he assured her. "The parole board was very grateful for the information you gave us when Marcos was hiding out."

She looked around apprehensively, even though no one else was in the store.

"Help us again, and I guarantee you that Juan will be behind this counter with you before summer. Put on the pressure for this one, Mrs. Fazzina. Find out where a good customer can pick up a new Granada in a hurry. Or a Monarch or big Buick less than two years old. Get back to me fast, and you can start fixing Juan's welcome home feast."

In Winthrop the Field Office was located only six blocks from the port district, so Samson Grant walked to a waterfront bar owned by a black couple and frequented by longshoremen and merchant seamen from many countries. In the harbor a tanker was discharging oil into the huge, flexible mouth of a pipe, and a freighter flying the Liberian flag was unloading cargo at a nearby wharf.

Eight or ten men were clustered together at one end of the bar, the Americans watching an early-season baseball game on the television set in the corner, the foreign sailors scrutinizing the barmaid-proprietress, whose tight-fitting, knitted minidress left little of her figure to the imagination. What they didn't know was that, at the first sign of trouble, all she needed to do was press a buzzer beneath the bar ledge, and her husband, a former professional wrestler, would cool the sailors' ardor.

Samson went to the unoccupied end of the bar, sat on a stool, and ordered a beer. The other customers paid no attention to him.

The barmaid slid his stein to him, then lingered nearby, drying glasses.

"Claudia," Samson said, "that outfit is old-fashioned. You need some new clothes."

The young woman shrugged, her scarlet mouth forming in a slight pout.

"How's Henry these days? Staying off the sauce?"

"He's doin' pretty good," she said, "but you know Henry. Just like you know why I can't dress up like I want. Every time we get a little cash, out of the register it goes."

"I remember that fur jacket you were sporting all winter. There's more where that came from."

The barmaid inched closer, but did not look at him. "What you got in that handsome head, sugar?"

"All kinds of thoughts." It took discipline not to make a pass at her. "There's a nice bundle floating around, waiting for the right information."

"Like what?"

"Whether any freighters are picking up automobiles here for shipment to the West Coast, Alaska, or some foreign country."

"That's easy," Claudia said, flashing him a self-confident smile.

"I'm just warming into it. Not just any old cars. Granadas. Big Buicks, Mercury Monarchs. None more than a couple of years old."

Her false eyelashes fluttered. "That's gettin' a little tougher, sugar."

"What's more," Samson said, his voice firm, "I'll need this information at least twenty-four hours before the freighter sails. Come to me after she puts out to sea, and you'll be wearing that same old dress into the hot weather."

The barmaid glared at him. "Anybody ever tell you that you're just plain mean?"

Samson shrugged. "It isn't my money to throw around, Claudia. I follow orders. Like everybody else."

"Well, I'll try."

"I'm sure you will, and you'll get results. I have confidence in you."

She was mollified and leaned closer, her elbows on the bar. "Henry is on his way again, sugar. I know the signs, and in a couple more days he's goin' to be spaced out. Drop around at closin' time day after tomorrow, and I'll show you some real action."

"I'll see you before then," he said, evading the invitation. "The heat has been turned onto this assignment, so don't you let me down."

"When I go for a man I never let him down," Claudia said, moving off to the other end of the bar to take reorders.

Samson took a token sip of his beer, but left his stein almost full as he put some money on the bar and walked out. He had to put out feelers in three other bars, a diner, and a dance hall before the end of the day.

At Field Office headquarters Supervisor Ray Merrill continued to organize the operation, sending out airtels to Field Offices in nearby states asking for their cooperation. Then, when he finally had a moment to spare, he summoned Johnny Hedley.

"Hedley," he said, "you're going to be part of the team that digs into this ring case."

The new agent beamed.

"I'm starting you off with a drudge job. Go through the want-ad sections of the newspapers, and see if any individuals are putting up Monarchs and Buicks for sale. Less than two years old, and keep an eye on the prices. If you find any offered for very low amounts, it may be a tip-off."

Johnny was being handed a clerical assignment, and concealed his disappointment. The instructors at the Academy hadn't been fooling when they had said that a large share of investigative work consisted of interminable paper shuffling. "The Winthrop newspapers, Mr. Merrill?'

"Winthrop, Hartford, New Haven. New London, Bridgeport, Stamford. Danbury, Waterbury, Meriden. And so on. All the major press outlets in the state. Offhand, I'd say about eighty or ninety of them. Beginning with yesterday's papers."

It occurred to Johnny that he would be doing nothing but wade through want-ad sections while more experienced agents had all the fun. But only one reply to the order was expected of him. "Yes, sir," he said.

Ray averted his face to hide his smile, and then went off to the ASAC's office.

"Do you have the list of All-American Car Rental outlets yet?" Joe Butler wanted to know.

"Yes, sir. One hundred and seventy-four cities. Their operations are more extensive than I realized."

"Okay," the ASAC said. "That means just about every Field Office in the country will be involved."

"Looks that way."

"Send out a blanket airtel requesting a priority check of every All-American branch, and make sure they send us an inventory of the actual cars they have in stock. When we visit the main office of All-American we'll check their figures against our figures."

"I'll bet you a lunch they don't jibe, Joe."

"You're on, and if your hunch is right, we're off to a good start."

"I've got to be right," Ray said. "All the patterns of a classic ring case are present, with one new twist. An angle so clever that

I'm just surprised no gang of car thieves ever thought of it before now."

Linda Bartlett and Sid Benjamin spent the better part of an hour loitering near the All-American Car Rentals booth at the International Arrivals Building at John F. Kennedy Airport, the largest of the booths there and the clearing center for the smaller outlets. Then, after observing the operation, they went to the office at the rear, where they presented their credentials to the manager and began to question him.

"How close a check do you maintain on the cars in your lot?" Sid asked.

"Well, we try to get a comprehensive figure at the normal end of each workday. Around six o'clock. But it isn't easy. That's one of the busiest times of day, and cars are piling in and out of the lot at a pretty fast clip. What's more, many of those being turned in at the terminals of the individual airlines haven't been brought into the main lot yet."

"In other words," Linda said, "You never do get an accurate breakdown."

"I wouldn't say never." The manager smiled, but was troubled. "That's pretty broad. But I'll admit that it isn't easy to come up with a precise figure. Remember, there are cars constantly heading in and out of more than twenty separate terminals, and sometimes that lot is a real madhouse."

"Who makes up your inventories?" Sid wanted to know.

"When I can, I do it myself, which isn't very often. Usually my assistant does it." The manager gestured in the direction of a middle-aged woman who occupied a tiny office adjacent to his.

"Let's get her in here, too," Linda suggested.

The manager summoned the woman, who was frightened when the visitors were identified as FBI agents.

"You have nothing to fear," Linda told her. "We're just trying to understand your routines."

"I never make out an actual list of the cars in the lot," the woman said. "That would take up all my time. Don't forget, there are dozens that move in and out every day and every night. Usually twenty-four hours a day."

"Show us your inventory," Sid suggested.

She went off to her own office, returning with a clipboard, to which a stack of pink slips was attached. "This one is for incoming cars," she said. "When a customer turns in a rental, this slip—which is a copy of his contract—is sent over to me from the terminal where he turns it in. And this," she continued, indicating a board with green slips attached, "is our record of outgoing cars. The bottom copy of the contract."

"What happens if one of these slips gets lost or misplaced?" Sid asked.

The woman became prim. "I make an effort not to lose them."

The system was slipshod, but the agents refrained from expressing their opinion.

The manager became defensive. "We have a turnover of between three hundred and fifty and four hundred car rentals per day at the airport," he said. "That's a lot of cars. We try to vacuum them, empty ashtrays, and check them for packages or other belongings a customer may have left behind. We advertise that we perform these services. I wouldn't want you to quote me, you understand, but when we're in a rush a car often goes out again as fast as it comes in."

"So you don't really know how many cars you have on hand at any given time?" Sid persisted.

"We do the best we can with the personnel we have available," the manager said. "I've sent memo after memo to the main office, requesting more help, but I don't get it. So I've got to make do with what I'm given, and sometimes that isn't easy!"

Linda's smile was calming. "We aren't here to criticize you or your staff. I'm sure you didn't invent the way your company chooses to do business."

"I do what I'm told," the manager said. "But our system isn't unique. All the major car rental outfits operate in pretty much the same way."

Sid nodded, then turned to the assistant. "Do us and yourselves a favor. While we're here, please, make a complete inventory for us, including those indicated by your in-and-out slips. Trace every car that's come in, gone out, or is sitting in the lot. Then check that list against the number of cars your records indicate you *should* have."

The woman looked at her superior.

"Do as the gentleman suggests, Mrs. Brennan. If you please."

It was obvious she was disgruntled. "This will take me an hour, and our service will suffer." She returned to her office in a huff.

"We believe," Sid said to the manager, "that you've lost a number of cars to some thieves who have been operating on a system of their own. A very simple system."

"That's hard to believe!"

The agent ignored his indignation. "The big question right now is how many cars you've lost. We have reason to suspect that at least four of your new Granadas were taken."

"I'd like to know how it was done, if you don't mind."

"We'll illustrate," Sid said. "Follow us out to your counter. Watch, and we'll show you step number one."

He and Linda left the office, then waited until the manager came up behind them. Sid nodded, then stood at the counter until one of the two busy clerks could attend to him. "What kind of cars do you have here, Miss?" he asked.

The clerk fell into conversation with him.

As he inquired about rates, Linda came up beside him, pretending she didn't know him, and while he continued to occupy the clerk's attention she quietly picked up an All-American contract form, folded it, and dropped it into her shoulder bag.

"Could I have a list of your branches around the country, please?" Sid asked the clerk.

As the girl turned away for a moment, Linda reached out to the wallboard on which sets of car keys were hanging, scooped up a set, and walked away.

Then she and Sid followed the shaken manager into his office.

"We have the contract and the keys," Sid said. "Now comes step two." He began to fill in the form. "I use a phony name and address. Then I may dream up a nonexistent credit card number—"

"That wouldn't work," the All-American manager said. "We make a thorough credit card check before we release a car on one."

Sid disliked the interruption, and his voice became a little louder. "Preferably, however, I indicate that I made my initial deposit in cash. Since the whole thing is made up, it doesn't cost me anything, no matter what I put down. Then I list several hotel chains and department stores as credit references. Next I add the make and model of car. Now I fake the clerk's signature at the bottom. You don't happen to use a stamp, or a seal, as some of the car rental companies do, but that's a minor detail. If you did, we could steal that, too." He completed the form, and stood. "The end of step number two. Ready for the last?"

"I know what's going to happen," the manager said, "so I'm afraid to watch."

"Come along," Sid urged. "This will be instructive."

The trio left the office, walked out of the building, and crossed the inner ring of streets to the All-American lot. There, with Sid and the manager lingering in the background, Linda presented the falsified contract and keys to an attendant, who went off into the lot to find the appropriate car.

Five minutes later she sat behind the wheel of a new Chevrolet. Nothing prevented her from driving off, but she informed the bewildered attendant that she had changed her mind and didn't want to rent an automobile.

The manager was silent as they made their way back to his office.

"There you have it," Sid said. "Not only have we stolen one of your cars, but nobody knows it. If we're stopped on a highway or in traffic, we have a seemingly valid rental contract. It may be many days before you learn the contract is phony and that one of your cars is missing."

"Weeks," the glum manager said. "If ever. What with the combination of cash and credit cards, our bookkeepers have a hell of a time, and the error of a few dollars in the accounts would be very difficult to detect."

"On the phony contract," Sid said, "I wrote that Buffalo was my destination, so you could ask your Buffalo branch—theoretically—to notify you when the car arrived there. But suppose I were a legitimate businessman who had filled out a legitimate contract. Let's say I marked down Buffalo as my destination because that was where I intended to go. But my boss decided subsequently to send me to Rochester instead. A car rental company must be flexible and allow the customer the privilege of making changes if it hopes to stay in business. So I'm allowed to alter my plan and go to Rochester instead. I never turn up in Buffalo."

The manager looked blank.

"What my associate is trying to point out," Linda said, "is that there's no way you can forcibly trace a rented car from point A to point B."

"Quite so, Miss. That's one of the major headaches of the industry."

The assistant came in, looking shaken. "Excuse me, Mr. Carr," she said. "But this is terrible. I have a lot more checking to do, but so far I've discovered eleven cars missing. At least no carbon has come back to me indicating they were taken out legitimately."

"All of them Granadas?" Sid asked.

Mrs. Brennan nodded. "How did you know?"

"I guessed," the agent said. "May we have the Vehicle Identification Numbers and other details?"

"I'll photocopy them for you," the crestfallen woman said, and left hurriedly.

The manager looked stricken.

"I hate to do this to you," Sid said, "but I'm afraid this situation will grow worse before it gets better. Let's say I'm driving an All-American car, and I arrive at Kennedy Airport to catch a plane. Traffic has been heavy, and I'm pressed for time. I pull up in front of a terminal. Maybe you have an attendant in uniform there, and maybe you don't. But I have no intention of missing my plane. So I leave the car in the driveway—with the keys in it, because the cop on duty there insists. Maybe the car will have to be moved if some big buses pull in. I turn in my contract, pay for the car, and go on to the airplane. Got it so far?"

"That sort of thing happens all the time," the manager said.

"I'm a punk who hangs around the airport," Linda said. "I've been keeping a lookout for just such a car. When the customer goes into the terminal, I get into the car and drive off. I turn it over to a criminal syndicate, and they pay me a few dollars in return. Easy money for me, cheap for them."

"Meanwhile," Sid added, "All-American loses another new car."

The assistant returned, carrying photocopies of the records of all eleven missing vehicles.

Sid checked his own list. "Thanks very much," he said, his voice hard. "Is there a phone around here I can use?"

"Help yourself," the manager told him, diplomatically going off to his assistant's office.

Sid called the Winthrop Field Office, and in a moment Ray Merrill was on the line. "We've struck a gusher, Ray," Sid told him. "The four cars that showed up at the auction definitely were stolen from the All-American lot at JFK. And while I'm at it, let me give you the VINs and other identification data on seven other new Granadas that have also vanished here."

"I'll put a stenographer on the line," Ray said, "but don't hang up when you're done. I'll want to talk to you again."

Sid dictated the information.

Then the supervisor came back on the wire. "I've just been talking to the Ay-sack on the intercom," he said. "You and Bartlett are to go straight into New York City and see the president of All-American. His name is Fitzgerald. Tell him what you've found out, and get his pitch. And don't make any secret of the fact that we're launching a full-scale investigation."

"Any mud on his feet, Ray?"

"Could be, although I think it unlikely. We've given him a fast once-over, and he looks clean. Which doesn't necessarily mean that he isn't robbing his own company blind, but I wouldn't advise leaning on him. Not at this point."

"Do you want us to call in again today?"

"Only if you come up with more information that's very hot. Otherwise it will keep until morning."

Sid and Linda left the airport and drove in to Manhattan. "Maybe I'm not going to mind an ITSMV assignment after all," he said. "This case is becoming interesting."

All-American headquarters occupied several floors of a midtown skyscraper, and an assistant to the president appeared in the reception room. "Mr. Fitzgerald is very busy this afternoon," he said. "I wonder if I can help you."

"I imagine you can," Sid Benjamin said. "But we want to see your president. Personally. Today."

Linda thought he was being unnecessarily tough, that the

least he could do would be to offer an explanation of the reasons they had come here. Obviously he preferred results to goodwill.

In a short time they were shown into a paneled, corner office filled with overstuffed furniture.

The silver-haired James Fitzgerald made an effort to be pleasant, although it was plain he resented the intrusion.

"We're sorry to barge in on you without an appointment," Linda said, "but our business is so important to All-American that we felt sure you wouldn't want it to wait."

Sid broke the news bluntly, telling the head of the car rental company that eleven new Fords had disappeared from the Kennedy lot, and that four of them had shown up in Connecticut. "Your people out at the airport turned up this number on short notice," he said. "A more careful check may show that even more have been stolen."

Fitzgerald remained unruffled. "We'll report these losses to our insurance company immediately," he said. "Thank you."

"This is just the beginning," Sid told him. "I'm sure you'll want to query all of your branch offices around the country. What's happened at one could be happening at others, too. That's the way rings of car thieves operate."

"In the meantime," Linda added, "the FBI is making its own investigation. We'll be visiting all of your branches ourselves."

"You people don't leave much to chance," Fitzgerald said with a smile.

"Not when we can help it," Linda said.

"All-American will help you in any way we can, and we're grateful for your intervention, as I'll tell Clarence Kelley in a letter I'll get off to him today."

Sid had no intention of being dismissed. "We showed your airport manager how easy it is to steal one of your cars," he said. "You may find his report will help you tighten your rental procedures."

"I'll turn it over to the consultant firm we've hired to recommend an improved system," Fitzgerald said, and sighed. "I hope I don't sound indifferent, but our situation is very difficult. We're one of four major car rental companies, and the competition we face is pretty fierce. When one company makes it easier and simpler for a customer to rent a car, the others are forced to do the same. All of us are fighting and scrabbling for the customer's dollar, and the company that adds tough safeguards to the rental procedure may find itself out of business. In almost no time."

"But there's no telling how many new cars you may have lost through slipshod methods!" Linda said.

"I realize it, believe me," Fitzgerald said, and looked weary. "We buy many hundreds of cars every year, and if only ten to fifteen percent of them are stolen we consider ourselves fortunate."

Sid was astonished. "You expect to have fifty to one hundred cars stolen every year—just to pick a number out of nowhere?"

"Of course. That's normal in our industry. We pay whopping insurance fees, and the insurance companies will pay us off. So our actual losses are relatively slight, other than that we're forced to shell out in premiums."

The agents stood. "We'll keep you informed as our investigation progresses," Sid said. "At least we can tell you the specific cars you've had stolen."

"All-American would rather wash its hands of that aspect of the matter," Fitzgerald said. "We prefer that you notify our insurance company. They're making good to us, so they're the ones who'll benefit by any recoveries."

Linda did not speak until they reached Sid's Bureau car. "That was the most extraordinary interview!"

Sid switched on the engine. "He was ripped off. He lost at least eleven new cars, maybe several times that number, but he didn't want to be bothered."

"Tell the insurance company. He said it in so many words."

"I'm not surprised," Sid said. "That's the nature of the car rental industry."

"Then it serves them right if they're robbed." Linda was thoughtful. "I kept wondering if the distinguished Mr. Fitzgerald gets a personal kickback from the auto theft ring."

"I'm inclined to go along with Ray Merrill. Possible, but unlikely. As Fitzgerald told us, he anticipates the loss of a certain number of cars every year, so he doesn't throw a fit when he loses them. He has an insurance crutch, and he uses it. Oh, I'm sure the Ay-sack will have Fitzgerald examined under a microscope, just as a matter of normal routine, but I'll be surprised if that investigation turns up anything."

"Too bad."

"You're annoyed."

"Yes, I am. The stolen car racket is one of the most vicious in the country. It's something that hits at every citizen. I never knew Mr. Hoover, coming into the Bureau when I did, and I'm no fan of his. But I remember reading something he wrote years ago to the effect that a family's automobile, next to their house, is their most valuable possession. People need protection from rip-off artists, and I was hoping we'd get more from the head of a big rental agency than a shrug of the shoulders."

"We were given the kind of reception I thought we'd get," Sid said, "so I'm not disappointed."

Linda was still upset. "Well, I am!"

"From the looks of it, this is going to be a complicated case. Nothing simple like targeting the president of the rental company."

"Apparently."

He pulled to a halt at a traffic light before turning onto the East River Drive, and looked at her. "We haven't done badly in one day. What more do you want?"

"Too much, I guess. A bunch of crooks behind bars."

"All in due time." Sid paused. "What you need, honey, is a stiff drink."

"You're absolutely right!" She was slightly surprised by her own reply.

"Here in town, or on the way up?"

"New York depresses me," Linda said, echoing the sentiments of so many Special Agents. "Let's wait until we reach Connecticut, and by that time I'll be ready for a double."

Life, Sid told himself, was looking up. Definitely.

4

"A Special Agent must be malleable in his approach and his techniques," J. Edgar Hoover had written in the early 1950s. *"Only his goals must remain unwavering."*

It was strange, Joe Butler reflected, but he hadn't thought of Hoover for years. Maybe it was because his own plight was so much on his mind. The Hoover of those earlier years, when Joe had been a new agent, would have been considerate and sympathetic, reacting as Mr. Kelley had. What the unpredictable Hoover of latter days would have said or done was anybody's guess, and Joe was glad he didn't have that to worry about. His problem was already difficult enough.

All the same, it was true that a man had to be malleable, which meant he had the right to change his mind. Which meant that, in spite of his fierce protestations to the contrary, he would visit Joey. Right now.

The sun was beginning to drop behind the skyscrapers to the west as Joe walked the short distance to the federal lockup, maintained for the government by the city of Winthrop as a temporary place of detention for prisoners awaiting trial. He tried to think about the new ITSMV case, but couldn't concentrate, and he couldn't empty his mind, either. But, goddammit to hell, this was no time to be remembering the day Joey had been born, or the way he had looked in his crib that first day at home.

The night warden was a Winthrop police sergeant who wasn't acquainted with the ASAC, but he was quick to recognize the name on his credentials. "I can guess why you're here," he said.

"Yes." Joe was in no mood to exchange the customary pleasantries.

"Do you want me to bring him up here to the office?" The sergeant was trying, in his own way, to be kind.

Joe shook his head. "No special privileges. I'll see him in one of the usual visitors' rooms." He handed the sergeant his .38 before following a policeman down a flight of stairs.

The second-floor room was bare, with whitewashed walls; its only furniture was a plain, heavy table and two solid wooden armchairs, and the window set high in one wall was covered by a steel mesh grill. Joe had interrogated prisoners in scores of such rooms, but had never realized they could be so drab.

Joey came into the room, tieless and beltless, with his shoelaces also removed, a shock of black hair falling over one side of his forehead. The door closed behind him.

Joe instinctively started forward, wanting to take the skinny kid into his arms and hug him, but managed to stop himself. Instead they stared at each other. "Well, Joey," he said at last.

"I never expected you to show up," Joey said, his voice metallic.

"Well, I'm here." Joe gestured toward a chair.

"I'll stand, if you don't mind."

"Suit yourself." Joe sat, not because he wanted to create an issue, but for the simple reason that he was afraid his legs might give way beneath him.

His son still stared at him with the defiance that had been his habitual expression for a long time.

"Your mother is the chief reason I'm here," Joe said. "She came to see you today, and you turned her away. Don't do that again. You came into this world out of her body, and she's looked after you ever since. Hate me all you want, if that will make you happy, but you've hurt your mother enough already. If she comes again, be civil to her. And decent. I won't stand for anybody kicking her around. You hear?"

"I hear."

"So behave yourself when you see her."

"Okay," Joey said.

"I'm not going to ask you why you got mixed up with those

punks, or what you thought you were accomplishing by robbing three banks. You can save your answers for the judge. I'm not going to deliver any lectures, either."

"That's good."

Joe had to curb a desire to slap him across the face.

His son's expression remained unchanged.

All at once the wall Joe had erected for his self-defense began to crumble. "Are they treating you all right?"

"It isn't the Ritz. But I'm not complaining."

"Anything you want?"

Joey thought for a time. "I could stand some cigarettes," he said.

The damn kid had been smoking too much for the past couple of years. "I imagine your mother will bring you a carton tomorrow. What brand?"

"Mom knows."

There was nothing else to say—or too much—and Joe sat in silence. The boy had been too thin for a long time, and he had lost more weight since his incarceration. But it was useless to tell him to eat more, just as it was a waste of breath to tell him anything; Joey had lost the ability to listen.

The youngster betrayed his own nervousness by shifting his weight from one foot to the other.

He needed clean clothes, but Stella would attend to that. Joe pressed a button at one end of the table.

The door opened, and the policeman who had stationed himself outside reappeared.

"I'll be seeing you," Joe said.

"Bye." His son preceded the policeman from the room and disappeared down the corridor.

Joe heaved himself to his feet, went to the office to retrieve his .38, and soon found himself on the street. He walked slowly toward the parking lot.

No matter what the circumstances, the Assistant Special Agent in charge of the Winthrop Field Office could not break down and cry his guts out in broad daylight and in a public place.

The staff on duty during the day had departed and the smaller group that had just reported for work had settled in for the evening by the time Ray Merrill cleaned up his desk. But he was in no hurry to leave, and wandered to the water cooler. Perhaps, if he stuck around for a time, Linda and Benjamin would show up from New York. The assignment had made it impossible for Linda to keep her lunch date with him, but if she had no plans for the evening she might be willing to have dinner with him.

The SAC was just coming out of his office, accompanied by a handsome, trim woman with graying hair, and Dave Daniels presented the supervisor to his wife.

She reminded Ray of an aunt of whom he had always been in awe, and he felt uncomfortable.

Carolyn Daniels tried to put him at his ease. "Consider yourself lucky that you don't have to go with us this evening, Mr. Merrill. We're scheduled to attend so many banquets and dinners that I'm never quite sure which is which."

Ray forced a polite laugh.

"All I know is that every last one is held at the Wellington Room in the Hilton Hotel, and the menu is always the same."

"Hope, as they say, springs eternal." Her husband smiled. "This may be the night they feed us something other than country fried chicken. I'm sure the speeches will be the same, though. Including mine."

"Be glad you're going home to your family, Mr. Merrill," Carolyn said as she shook hands.

Dave winced.

Ray took a deep breath, but by the time he summoned the nerve to tell her he had no family, she was gone. Not that it mattered. Besides, the boss would tell her.

Ray meandered back to his office, pausing to exchange a few words with an Academy classmate who had chosen to remain a street agent. Tommy had a wife and three kids, so he could use the money a promotion would bring, but he was happy in what he was doing, and that was what counted.

The trouble, Ray thought, was that he himself was no longer happy doing anything. Routines were a bore, the daily grind was a bore. Maybe this new ring case would give him something of the zest for life that had been lacking of late. At least his hunch about the cars stolen from the All-American lot at Kennedy Airport had been right, but he took no real sense of satisfaction in the knowledge. If he hadn't smelled out that caper after all the years he had spent in ITSMV, something would have been very wrong with his nose.

Sitting at his desk again, he glanced at the wall clock. If Linda and Benjamin were coming straight back to the office they'd be here by now, even allowing time for a long stop-off for a talk with the president of All-American. He imagined they were having dinner somewhere on the road and felt a strong twinge of jealousy. But he tried to put Linda out of his mind. He was beginning to lean on her, and that was bad. She was too alive, too vibrant —and too young, damn it!—to want an involvement with a man who had hit middle age.

Okay, it was high time to think about doing something tonight. Ray picked up the Winthrop *Herald* and turned to the entertainment pages. There was a new play at the Palace, trying out prior to Broadway, but the reviews had been just fair and he had no desire to see it. None of the movies interested him, either.

It wasn't too late to call the nurse he sometimes dated, but there would be complications. If they followed their usual practice they'd return to her apartment after dinner and go to bed, which was fine when he was in the mood. But he was tired tonight, and as he had been discovering, he was no longer a boy who had only sex on his mind. He and the nurse had little else in common, and he had no idea what they could talk about all evening.

Another possibility was the widow who lived down the hall from his apartment, an attractive woman of his own generation who ran the local adjustment office of a national insurance company. She was good company, and he could chat with her without strain. Unfortunately, however, he had detected a gleam in her eye the last couple of times they had been together, and he had to tread warily. He had no intention of complicating his life by marrying a widow with two children.

There was no point in hanging around any longer, waiting for Linda, but Ray continued to linger, looking again at the beginnings of the file on the new ITSMV ring case before putting it into his safe for the night. He killed an additional quarter of an hour by watching the NCIC teletype, but his mind was wandering, so he finally closed up his office.

Someone else was heading for the elevators at the same time.

The cute redheaded stenographer with the slick figure. What the devil was her name? Ray had to search before he remembered it. Lisa Talbot.

They stood together at the elevator, and he felt compelled to make small talk. "You've been working late tonight."

"Kind of," she said.

She was very pretty when she smiled, he decided.

"You're working late, too, Mr. Merrill," she said, "but I guess you must do it all the time."

"More often than I like," he said, thinking the reply was appropriate for someone of his rank. Merrill, he told himself, you're turning into a middle-aged phony.

"I saw you dashing all over the office today," the girl volunteered.

"Um. It was one of those days." He tried not to stare, but her figure really was spectacular.

Again Lisa Talbot smiled.

Ray wondered whether she was extending an invitation, and as the elevator neared the ground floor he asked suddenly, "Can I give you a lift somewhere?"

"Thanks very much," she said as the door opened, "but I'm not going very far."

He watched her as she left the building and joined two other girls who appeared to have been waiting for her. All three hurried off together.

Serves me right, Ray thought. Almost old enough to be that kid's father, and I'm turning into a dirty old man. Come to think of it, she and Johnny Hedley have been cozy ever since he joined the staff. He's more her speed. In fact, their combined ages roughly equal mine.

With nothing better to occupy his time he wandered over to Pete's Bar & Grill, taking a place at the old mahogany bar and ordering his inevitable Manhattan, which he drank a little too quickly.

Two of the younger agents were eating together in the back room, and Ray waved to them but did not join them. They didn't want a supervisor horning in, and he wasn't eager for their company, either. He'd spent a long day at the office, and enough was enough. After all, he wasn't married to the Bureau.

A Winthrop police lieutenant in civvies paused long enough to clap Ray on the shoulder. "How's it going?"

"Not bad, but I've got to catch up with you guys." Ray ordered a second drink. "What's new with you?"

"Not much." The lieutenant knew the question was rhetorical, it being a basic rule that details of law enforcement were not discussed in a public place. He drifted away.

Ray reached into his breast pocket for a cigar, then changed his mind. He was smoking far too much these days, and it was time to start cutting down. Seriously.

He looked off into space for a time, ignoring the conversation around him, but returned to the present when three couples came in and took bar stools. Two of the women, in their early thirties, weren't at all bad looking. The world, it seemed, was made for couples. Not for middle-aged oddballs who traveled alone.

Ray held a brief debate with himself, then ordered a third drink. One too many to drive, and he was momentarily overcome by every Special Agent's private nightmare, the fear of cracking up a Bureau car while under the influence. Goodbye, job; goodbye, career; goodbye, future.

It was easier to eat here than to go back to the apartment and open a couple of cans. Ray ordered corned beef hash and a salad, which were served to him at the bar. He never minded eating breakfast or lunch alone, but dinner was different, somehow, and he gulped his food.

"A big cup of coffee, black," he said, and when it was served to him he gulped it, too.

He had spent less than an hour in Pete's, and it was time to leave. Unless he wanted to slug down a few bourbons, which didn't appeal to him. He guessed he'd go back to the apartment and see what was on TV. It was easier than reading, especially on a night when he didn't want to use his mind. He belched as he walked out of Pete's, unconsciously falling into a middle-aged slump as he started off toward the parking lot.

The Silver Windmill Restaurant and its adjoining motel were located just off the Connecticut Turnpike, approximately halfway between Winthrop and New Haven. Habitués, among them members of the faculties of both cities' major universities, other professional men, and senior industrial executives, regarded it as the most sophisticated dining spot on Long Island Sound. The menu was ersatz French and the specialties were flaming sword dishes, which, as the chef observed, didn't really scorch the food. Male guests were well groomed, ladies showed the effects of health salons, beauty parlors, and winter vacations in the tropics, so the clientele was chic, even by Eastern Seaboard standards.

The decor was ordinary. The walls were made of pale, knotted pine, the hurricane lamps that provided table illumination had been purchased by the owner at an off-season sale in Maine, and the red cotton tablecloths and napkins, which were stain-resistant, were similar to those found in hundreds of restaurants from coast to coast. But the waiters were white-jacketed, the wine steward wore a gilded chain and key, and no staff member, no customer, was troubled by the fact that the name of the place was not reflected in the interior design.

Sid Benjamin's steak had been cut from prime beef, the bay scallops Linda had ordered for her figure's sake had been tender, and by unspoken consent they settled into a small banquette table in the bar for an after-dinner drink. Sid had to hand it to the girl: she could hold her liquor. She had consumed two Manhattans and a half-bottle of wine, and she was still sober as she sipped a stinger. She seemed relaxed, her invisible guard lowered for the first time, so he decided to indulge his curiosity.

"What impelled you to become an agent?"

"You mean I'm not the type?"

"If there is a type, I don't know it. I've met only two other woman agents."

She smiled, no longer surprised that every male colleague asked the same question. "I imagine we had the same motivation. A good job with the world's most elite agency. A lot of excitement, a solid future, and the opportunity to serve my country."

"I've been put in my place," Sid said, and raised his stinger in a toast.

Linda felt like expanding beyond the limits of what had become a set speech. "I thought of applying for a commission in the Navy or the Air Force after I got out of college. Or joining the Peace Corps. The private business sector never appealed to me.

Then I learned I qualified for agent's training. I applied, I was investigated, and I managed to squeak through the Academy. So here I am." She finished her drink and allowed him to order another. Their accomplishments at Kennedy Airport entitled them to a small celebration.

A couple approached, threading their way through the crowded bar. The man was dark, well dressed, and slender, but no one in the place paid much attention to him. His companion, whose red hair fell almost to her waist in back, wore an open-fronted jumpsuit of red lamé, and everyone in the bar gaped at her.

"Wow!" Linda said, and felt dowdy in the workday outfit she had been wearing since early morning.

Sid paid no attention to the flashy girl, but looked at the man, smiling slightly.

As they came face to face the man's eyes bulged. Then he quickly averted his face and pushed forward.

"I'll give you three to one odds they clear out of here without sitting down," Sid said.

"A friend?"

"We've met, but not socially. He's a *capo* in the Paulo Agnelli mob."

Linda watched the couple beat a hasty retreat and disappear. "I'm glad they're gone."

"You're allergic to people from organized crime?"

"I wouldn't know. I haven't yet worked for an S-A-C who has trusted me with that assignment. This was strictly personal."

"I'll take you," Sid said, "any day I can get you."

She turned and faced him, her smile enigmatic.

He couldn't figure her reaction, and could only hope she was beginning to weaken.

"You need very little encouragement," Linda said, "to become the world's champion male chauvinist pig. Your problem is that you've been spoiled by too many women."

He raised his glass to her. "Deservedly."

"Unfortunately," she said with a sigh, "you're probably right."

His confidence increased, and he placed a hand on her thigh.

She made no attempt to remove it, and addressed him in a

calm, conversational tone. "With almost no effort I can throw you about as far as that wall."

"You wouldn't care to try? I've been told the rooms here are very large, very comfortable."

"I know why you're a first-class agent, Sid. You never give up, not matter how much you're discouraged."

He removed his hand. "Okay, so your beams and my beams don't make laser beams."

"That isn't what I said."

She might be a Special Agent, he thought, but she was as difficult to understand as any other woman. "I don't dig you."

"Obviously, so I'll spell it out. I like you, and I'm enjoying the evening. I'll even make a contribution to your swollen head and tell you I'm attracted to you. But that doesn't mean I'm going to fall into bed with you."

Sid was genuinely puzzled. "Why the hell not?"

"I have two reasons. Number one. As much as I may enjoy horizontal sports, I don't yet know you well enough, and I *am* rather discriminating. Number two. Through no choice of yours or mine, we're working together on a case that you yourself admit is going to be very complex. I think we'd be stupid to snarl it even worse."

"In other words, we're going to have a platonic relationship until we solve this ITSMV case and send the members of the ring to prison."

Linda shook her head. "No, my dear, I didn't say that, either." Linda patted him on the cheek. "One step at a time. The next step is a teensy, weensy stinger for the road. Period. Tomorrow is going to be a hard day, what with the goodies chasing the baddies to hell and gone."

It was late by the time Samson Grant finished establishing contact with his various informants, too late for him to expect his mother, who kept house for him, to serve him a hot meal. His sister and her husband were visiting, but he'd seen eough of his brother-in-law, a Chicago physician, to last him for a while. The family had struggled hard to achieve respectable, middle-class standing, but the trouble was that respectable, middle-class people bored the daylights out of him. He had no desire to listen to the litany: why he should marry, buy a house, and rear a family. No matter what time he got home, his sister and brother-in-law would be waiting for him, ready to deliver the sermon.

Samson thought of going to Pete's, but he knew the menu by heart, so he stopped instead at a small restaurant near the University district, where he ate a steak, baked potato, and salad. Then, still restless and unwilling to face his relatives, he decided to have a nightcap at Powers' Pavillion, one of the few integrated nightspots in town that wasn't a dump. A Special Agent, moseying around on his own time, had to be careful of the watering holes he frequented.

The Pavillion, as always, was jammed with blacks, whites, and yellows, among them exchange students from five continents. The strobe lights were blinding, the five-piece combo was deafening, thanks to electronic amplification, and the dance floor was jammed. But Samson, crowded against the wall at one end of the bar, was totally relaxed as he sipped a beer. A single was not out of place here, no one cared about color, and he felt at home. The noise and confusion made it difficult to think, and that was all to the good, too. Meeting informants was a delicate, painstaking business, and he needed the soothing that only a chaotic mob scene could provide.

Paying little attention to others in the place, he enjoyed himself. A white girl wearing a yellow caftan and little else gave him the eye, but he ignored her; he didn't mind an occasional dance, but pickups in a place like the Pavillion were not his specialty, and could create problems. In the next day or two he'd need a woman, principally so he'd have strength to avoid paying a social call on Claudia, the barmaid-informant. She got to him, and he was beginning to realize it. But the minute he stepped across the line with her she would lose her value as an informant.

A vague irritation on the dance floor gradually took shape, and Samson saw that a girl was trying to resist the persistent advances of her partner. A tall, black man. A slender, redheaded white girl. Who looked familiar. Lisa Talbot. From the office.

Leaving his beer on the bar, Samson walked quickly to the floor and tapped the man on the shoulder. "I'm cutting in."

"Who says?"

"I do." It was no trick for Samson to outstare the man, whose instinct told him he would come out second best in a fight.

"Am I ever glad to see you, Mr. Grant!"

Samson glowered as he started to dance with her. "What are you doing here, Lisa?" His annoyance was real. "You shouldn't come to a joint like this!"

"My friends come here all the time, and they think it's great. So I came with them."

"Girlfriends?"

She nodded.

"Get your bag, and I'll take you home. Your friends, too, if they want to leave." He guided her firmly to the edge of the floor and followed her to an empty table.

"They've found dates, so they're set for the evening," Lisa said, and hesitated.

"You're leaving," Samson told her. "You can settle the tab with them tomorrow."

The girl could not argue, and made her way toward the exit.

The man who had been dancing with her came forward, saw her companion, and turned away again.

Samson took Lisa's elbow and led her down the street toward his car. "The Pavillion is okay if you go there with a date," he said. "Otherwise it isn't for you."

Lisa was recovering from her unpleasant experience. "Lots of singles go there!"

He opened the door of his car for her. "You aren't one of them."

She waited until he sat behind the wheel. "Why aren't I?"

"Because," he said as he started the car, "you work for the Bureau."

Many of the agents seemed to believe their profession set them apart from the rest of the world, and the girl was irritated. "I type reports and letters, and I file papers. That's how I earn my salary. I have a Civil Service rating. Does that mean I've got to live in a convent?"

"Not quite. But you don't happen to have a job in any old government agency. You work for the Bureau." Samson's tone indicated that no further explanation was necessary.

The girl's guilt caused her to react too strongly. "I don't buy that!"

"Then go back to the Pavillion and get yourself mauled," he said. "And first thing tomorrow put in for a transfer to the Department of Agriculture. Their office here is taking on typists."

"Don't be so hateful." Lisa began to sniffle.

"I'm not psychic, so suppose you tell me where you live."

She blew her nose, then gave him her address.

He drove there in silence.

"I'm sorry, Mr. Grant," she said as the car pulled to a halt before a long row of nineteenth-century homes that had been converted into apartments. "I was like upset, and I didn't mean to be nasty. Would you come up for a drink?"

Samson realized she was trying to make amends, and smiled. "Your family might not care for my color."

"For one thing, I room with my girlfriend, and for another, color doesn't come off."

His smile broadened, and he followed her into the building.

She waved him into a tiny, simply furnished living room. "What would you like?"

"Whatever you have."

Lisa vanished into a kitchenette, returning with two glasses, a small bucket of ice, and an unopened bottle of rum. "I got this when I went to the Bahamas on a vacation."

Realizing she knew little about liquor, he took the bottle from her and poured token quantities into both glasses. "Add some cola or tonic or something to these," he said.

She disappeared into the kitchenette again.

He tried in vain to make himself comfortable on the thin cushions of the small maple sofa.

Lisa returned, handed him his drink, and sat down beside him. "Cheers, Mr. Grant. You're okay."

"I've been thinking," Samson said as she clinked glasses with him. "I'm going to make you a private deal. Give me your word you won't go into joints like the Pavillion again, and I'll give you my word I won't mention tonight's fun-and-games to the Ay-sack. Who would have your head on a platter if he knew about it."

"I promise," the girl said, her face solemn. "I didn't much care for it, you know."

She was sitting disturbingly close to him, but he knew she was unaware of the effect of her proximity. She was a kitten, a child-woman, and she had no business being out in the world on her own. He couldn't allow himself to take advantage of her naïveté, no matter how great the temptation.

"What bugs me," she said, "is what somebody who works for the Bureau is supposed to do for fun."

"Most places in Winthrop are okay," he said. "And just about any place in the suburbs. Stay away from the downtown saloons after dark, that's all."

Lisa's sigh was tremulous.

"What you need," he told her, "is a steady boyfriend."

"I'm not interested in anybody," she replied promptly.

"Then find somebody. But not in pickup bars."

"Do you know of any candidates, Mr. Grant?"

He realized she had no idea she had asked a leading question that most men would gladly misinterpret. "I'm sure you don't need me to draw up a list," he said, his voice becoming crisp. "There's been no lack of boys in your life."

"That's for sure," Lisa said, and giggled.

For politeness' sake he bolted his drink, then quickly took his leave, her thanks following him down the stairs.

As Samson walked back to his car he was almost stunned by his own nobility. He could have had the girl with a snap of his fingers, and it wasn't her employment by the Bureau that had deterred him. Nor her color. White or black didn't matter; a man of principle had to have standards.

Besides, an affair with a girl like Lisa Talbot would quickly become complicated, and that was something he didn't need. If he resigned his job and went into private industry he could marry anyone, and color wouldn't mean a thing. If he stayed in the Bureau, however—and it was a big if—he fully intended to remain black all the way.

The day was fast approaching when blacks would become SACs and ASACs, and he fully intended to be one of them. Black all the way, with a black wife and black children, not compromising by creeping halfway into the white world. Provided he stayed in the Bureau.

He wanted to stay, which was something his sister and brother-in-law couldn't understand. Certainly he couldn't answer the logic of their arguments: he'd make far more money in private life, he wouldn't work as hard, and he'd rise higher and faster on the social ladder. What he couldn't explain to them or anyone else was the way he felt when he thought of himself as a Special Agent. There were only 8,600 other men and women in America who had that same feeling. Plus the alumni, of course; they were part of the club, too.

Oh, the Bureau was taking a beating these days for past errors real and imagined, deserved and undeserved, but it was still unique, still the most exclusive, extraordinary organization of its kind on earth. Outsiders could criticize, and the ignorant could look down their noses, but a second-office agent with more than five years of service under his belt knew better. As did 8,600 others. There was just no substitute for being number one.

Stella Butler couldn't sleep, and she could tell from her husband's breathing that he was awake, too. "Joe."

"Mmm?"

"Can we talk?"

"Sure, Stell." Joe Butler snapped on the night-table light.

"I think I'm thirsty," she said.

He left the bedroom, returning with two glasses of milk.

Stella made a face as he handed one to her.

"We've got to go easy on the booze, both of us."

"I know, Joe. It would be so easy to just get drunk and stay that way."

He knew she disliked the odor of smoke in their bedroom, so he refrained from reaching for a cigarette.

"I've been thinking. You said you wouldn't go to see Joey, but you went."

"I had my reasons."

"Such as?"

"If you must know," Joe said, "I was upset by the way he treated you when you visited him, and I wanted to make sure it wouldn't happen again the next time."

Stella pushed back her hair in a weary gesture, then donned a robe over her nightgown and held it closed at the throat. "That was sweet of you, Joe. Thank you. But it wasn't your only reason."

He became defensively strident. "Okay. I went because I

couldn't help myself. I had to go. Does that satisfy you?"

She spoke very quietly. "We've got to get him a lawyer."

Joe's temper flared. "The court will arrange legal representation for him. It's customary in such cases. He's guaranteed a fair trial under our system, and that means a lawyer will stand before the bench on his behalf."

"There's a difference between somebody we hire ourselves and a nobody who depends on court appointments for his fees. I want the very best for Joey. He'll need somebody good."

"Stell, I'm paid my salary by the U.S. Government to perform duties that include the protection of the public from bank robberies. You got that much? Okay. So it makes no sense for that money to be used for the defense of someone who is guilty of bank robbery. Not just one bank, but three. The evidence is conclusive. I've spent the better part of my life dealing with federal prosecutors and federal courts, so you'll have to take my word for it that this is an open-and-shut case, no matter what Joey pleads. My situation is already painful enough, and I don't see going out and deliberately mocking the process of justice I'm under oath to defend!"

"Excuse me a minute," she said and left the bedroom.

Joe pulled on a dressing robe and lighted a cigarette. If there was one thing he couldn't stand in this already intolerable mess it was being bugged by a wife who couldn't think of anything except the protection of her lamb. Who couldn't be saved. Who didn't want to be saved, and was refusing help from the parents he was rejecting.

Stella returned, carrying a stiff bourbon and water.

"You ought to lay off that stuff," her husband said.

"I'll do anything to help me sleep!"

"Stell, you have two other kids. You have a husband. And most of all, you have yourself. Don't follow Joey into the sewer."

"That's easy enough for you to say. You've never really cared about him, anyway. Or me. Or any of us. Nothing has ever mattered to you except your goddamn, precious FBI!"

"That's bullshit, and you know it!"

Stella raised her glass. "I'd rather be blind, cockeyed drunk then the way I am right now. At least I'll be out of my misery."

Joe wanted to knock the glass out of her hand, but was afraid he would be unable to regain control of his temper if he indulged in an act of violence. Instead he watched in despair as she drank the bourbon.

Carolyn Daniels yawned and slipped out of her pumps as soon as she took her place in the car. "You did well tonight, dear. You delivered the speech with more feeling than usual."

Dave Daniels began to ease the vehicle out of the Hilton garage. "I'm surprised you could even listen to it. You must know it by heart."

"Oh, I do. And I don't really listen to anything except your tone of voice. I watch the audience to see how they're responding. I liked the new material defending the Bureau against criticism, and I think it went down nicely, at least with this audience."

"It isn't very difficult to win the applause of people who are already Bureau supporters," Dave said, heading into downtown Winthrop traffic. "As soon as I get things battened down tighter at the office I'm going to write a whole new speech. For the benefit of those who have declared open season on the FBI."

"Are you getting any guidelines from Washington?"

"Certainly not! I've been thinking about it a great deal lately, and I'm going to use my own ideas. I'll send External Affairs a copy for their information, but I don't need anyone's approval. Under today's decentralization they have enough faith in me not to interfere. If I can be trusted with the job of Special Agent in Charge, I can make my own speeches."

Carolyn realized he was touchy, but refrained from comment.

"Something has struck me pretty forcibly for a long time," Dave said. "A democracy is a country that swings to extremes in its thinking. During World War Two and the Korean War most Americans felt the same way, but even during the fifties there were witch hunters who exaggerated the Red scare. Oh, there were valid grounds for searching out paid Russian agents and unpaid sympathizers, even though some people were inclined to go too far."

"You're including all this in your new speech, Dave?"

"You bet! As I see it, the real troubles came in the sixties. The Vietnam War. Racial tensions. The disaffection of the young, the loss of respect for the Establishment, and all the rest. When the

American people aren't united in their beliefs, people of many persuasions push too hard, and their views become warped. Those on the left, those on the right and often those who are left in the middle, too."

"What has all this to do with the FBI?"

"I'm coming to that. We did many things in the Bureau that seemed right at the time. To Presidents of the United States and their Attorneys General. At no time did the Bureau charge off on its own. I'm not going to defend anything we did in those days, Carolyn, and I have no intention of answering specific criticisms. Mr. Hoover is no longer here to speak for himself, and Mr. Tolson isn't here to speak for him. What concerns me is the Bureau of the mid to late Nineteen Seventies. The Bureau today, right now. The victim of that violent swing of the pendulum."

"I'm not sure I understand."

"For many years the FBI could do no wrong. We were the fair-haired boys, the protectors of the United States, and people developed wildly unrealistic ideas about our role in American society. I doubt if any other organization in our history has been admired as much as we were, and a lot of that praise was never earned or deserved."

"You and I knew it, as other Bureau families did, but few people on the outside realized it."

"That's the key to the point I intend to make," Dave said. "Now the pendulum has swung the other way, and we're dirty villains, being blamed for all kinds of things we've never done. We're being lumped with the CIA, an outfit ten to fifteen times our size, with a completely different mission, and being accused of all sorts of dirty tricks. Well, I haven't had much contact with the CIA, and I hold no brief for them, although I do say they're a necessary evil in today's world. But it isn't my place to decide whether they're needed. That's up to the people, acting through Congress and the President."

"You aren't going to mention the CIA in your new speech?"

"No. What I say would be taken out of context and blown up." He drove onto a Turnpike ramp and increased his speed. "I plan to concentrate exclusively on the FBI. We have an agency that's incorruptible and remarkably efficient, that does a tremendous job with a minimum of fuss. The annual crime solution figures we release speak for themselves, and as long as human nature results in the commissions of crimes, we—or somebody like us—are needed. Well, there is nobody like us. By all means, let the Attorney General and a Congressional watchdog committee keep an eye on us. We welcome it. But don't slap handcuffs on us and then expect us to do the job we're responsible for doing under the law!"

"Hear, hear."

"Sorry, Carolyn, but I let myself get worked up."

"Turn off at the next exit," she said, knowing he paid no attention to such mundane matters as roads and destinations when his mind was occupied. "Dave, if the Bureau waived your retirement age at fifty-five so you could become an Assistant Director, would you accept?"

The question surprised him, but he grinned. "It won't happen. I'm just one of fifty-nine S-A-Cs."

"But suppose. You feel so intensely about restoring the Bureau's image and good name that I can't help wondering."

"In a way," Dave said, "I've been looking forward to getting out after I do a job in Winthrop. On the other hand, I—well, I honestly don't know."

Carolyn made no reply, but none was necessary. No matter what his seeming indecision, she knew exactly what he would do if given an opportunity.

Johnny Hedley went straight from work to the Winthrop YMCA, where he joined a pickup basketball team for a quick game, then swam thirty lengths in the pool. He went to the coffee shop at the Hilton for dinner, and when meatloaf, mashed potatoes, green peas, and salad failed to satisfy him he ordered peach pie with a double scoop of butterscotch ice cream, long his favorite, which he washed down with two glasses of milk.

He would have enjoyed going to a movie with a girl tonight, or just driving around, which he wouldn't have dreamed of doing with a date in a Bureau car. One of these days he'd buy a car of his own, but he didn't really need one, so he held off. He could afford it, to be sure, but it would be sinful to waste money, and he hadn't been brought up that way. Certainly, by every standard he had ever known, his salary was terrific. Including obligatory overtime he was making almost $14,000 per year. Dad had brought up a family on less.

Johnny was sending $100 per month to his parents, a gesture that not only pleased him but was a great help to his mother, even though she kept writing that she didn't want or need it. He knew better.

Draining the last of his milk, Johnny faced the problem of how to spend the evening, a frequent dilemma. He knew what he wanted to do: the SAC was delivering a speech in the Wellington Room upstairs, and Johnny was drying to hear what he had to say about the Bureau. It would be easy enough to get in; credentials would see to it, but that wasn't the catch.

He'd exchanged only a few words with the new boss, and he didn't want Mr. Daniels to think he was trying to accumulate brownie points. It would be too embarrassing to explain that he really wanted to hear the speech, that perhaps he'd learn something. The ballroom would be crowded, so maybe he wouldn't be noticed, but he didn't want to take the chance. It would be just his luck that Mr. Daniels would catch his eye, and then he'd be ready to sink into the floor.

If he'd had the courage, he would have asked the redheaded stenographer at the office, Lisa Talbot, to go to dinner and a movie. But John Philip Hedley, FBI Special Agent by the grace of the breaks, the good fortune to qualify, and the ability to pass a rugged course at the Academy, was lacking in guts.

He was willing to face the open muzzle of a loaded rifle; at least he hoped he could do it without flinching. But he didn't have the basic courage to ask a girl of twenty or twenty-one for an innocent date. He could blame only himself, but there were extenuating circumstances. Lisa was pretty. Lisa had been around, and was sophisticated. Lisa had the looks, brains, and personality to attract a slew of admirers, enough to form a line that would stretch all the way down John Winthrop Boulevard. So a nobody, a new agent who hailed from the sticks, who had never been anywhere or done anything glamorous, would be inviting a swift turndown.

He guessed his ego couldn't take it. For whatever the reason, he'd cringe every time he saw Lisa in the bullpen, and his life would be miserable. He had to be a realist, and he told himself not to reach too high. If he had any sense he would put her out of his mind.

That still left tonight, and as Johnny thought about the stacks of newspaper want-ad sections that awaited him at the office, a resolve took shape in his mind, then grew. The sooner he broke the back of that miserable assignment, the sooner Mr. Merrill would give him something other than a clerical task to perform. He would slug away for a few hours tonight, as long as his nerves could stand it.

Johnny walked back to the office, where he had to show his credentials before he was allowed inside the building. The night security system was in effect, so he stood beneath the television cameras inside the entrance on the Field Office floor. Eventually one of the older agents recognized him, a buzzer was pressed, and he was allowed to enter.

"If it isn't our very own eager beaver," someone called as he walked into the bullpen.

Several agents laughed.

Johnny made no reply, knowing they would razz him without mercy if he tried to answer in kind. Instead he simply went to his desk, picked up the top newspaper on the stack, and began to wade through the want-ads.

Occasionally his mind wandered, but he persisted. Once upon a time even Director Kelley had been a new agent, forced to plow through dreary assignments. After about an hour he became sleepy, but persisted. If he kept going he might work his way through the whole stack of today's newspapers.

Thoroughly bored and increasingly disgruntled, he came at last to that evening's edition of the Winthrop *Herald,* and found himself scanning instead of reading. All at once he felt as though an electric current was passing through him. He stared at a small ad, read it a second time, and then hurried to the office of the night supervisor.

The agent listened to his eager explanation, then smiled. "I've never yet known of an ITSMV ring case that wouldn't hold overnight. Why don't you take it up with Merrill tomorrow morning?"

"Yes, sir," Johnny said, but had no intention of obeying.

Instead he looked up Ray Merrill's home number in the registry and called him.

Ray was polite. "Slow down, kid," he said, "and start again from the beginning."

Johnny knew enough not to speak too freely on the telephone when a scrambler wasn't in use. "I believe," he said, speaking with care, "that I've come across a very important lead in the job you gave me today."

"Will it keep until after breakfast?"

"Whatever you say, sir."

There was a pause, and then Ray said, "What the hell. I haven't gone to bed yet. Hang around, and I'll be right over."

Johnny clipped the ad he had seen and pasted it on a blank sheet of paper.

Less than ten minutes later a rumpled Ray Merrill came into the office. "This had better be good," he said. "You made me miss the climax of a great cops and robbers thriller on the tube."

Johnny handed him the want-ad:

> FOR SALE. This year's Mercury Monarch, 2-door sedan. Only 5,000 miles. Mint condition. Many extras, including air condit., tape deck, AM/FM radio, steel radial tires. Owner leaving the country, and willing to make major sacrifice for immediate sale. Hernando Reyes Gomez. 865–9102.

Johnny could scarcely contain his excitement. "That's the name I was told about. Warned against. In the anonymous call I got the other night. Hernando Reyes Gomez."

5

As soon as the day staff assembled the ASAC called a meeting of the team assigned to the ITSMV case. Supervisor Ray Merrill already had been in touch with the telephone company, and had obtained additional data based on the number listed in the classified ad that had appeared in the Winthrop *Herald.*

"The owner of the phone," he said, "is one Juan Garcia. There's no record of Hernando Reyes Gomez. The address is in the Latin section of the city."

"I checked it out on my way to work," Johnny Hedley said. "It's a four-story building. Frame. I don't know how many apartments it contains because I didn't leave my car. I didn't want to alarm anybody by obvious snooping."

"Let's review the situation," the ASAC said. "One. We know for certain that a clever gang has been stealing new cars from All-American at Kennedy. Two. We may or may not learn later today that the same thing has been happening at other All-American lots."

"Particularly in this same general area," Ray added. "The usual pattern is that a gang—a well-organized gang—will concentrate on lots within a radius of fifty to one hundred and fifty miles."

"To continue," Joe Butler said. "We now have a promising lead on what may be a ring stealing Monarchs and Buicks. I want to stress that it might not be the same ring, however. I don't want any of you proceeding on the assumption that the same gang is responsible for both operations."

"It can't be coincidence," Ray said, interrupting again and braving the ASAC's obvious displeasure. "Follow the M.O. statistical patterns."

Joe Butler, like everyone who had spent many years in the Bureau, shared the Supervisor's conviction that individual bands of criminals left their trademarks behind them by observing a *modus operandi* distinctly their own. But Merrill was missing the point he was trying to make, and in so doing was confusing the younger agents who were working on the street. "We don't yet know enough about this case—or these cases—to slap on an M.O. tag!"

Ray had been rebuked, and shrugged. The ASAC could think what he pleased, but would soon discover that the two operations were being conducted by the same network. The trouble with executives was their insistence that they knew best.

"Stay loose until we pick up more details," Joe said. "Our next step, obviously, is to do something about Hernando Reyes Gomez. Any suggestions?"

Samson Grant hitched forward in his chair. "Yes, sir. We have the address. I say we move in and round up everybody we find."

"Impossible," Ray said. "We totally lack evidence that the car listed in the *Herald* ad is a stolen vehicle. We can't make arrests on mere assumption."

"I know we need hard evidence, sir," Samson said, appealing to the ASAC, "but if these people are slippery, they'll disappear as soon as they learn we're interested in them."

"Mr. Merrill is right, unfortunately," the ASAC said, aware of rising tensions that inevitably came to the surface when an investigation moved into high gear. "If we're onto something of consequence, we don't want to do anything that will give a defense attorney a chance to have the case thrown out of court."

"It seems to me," Sid Benjamin said, "that one of us calls up the number listed in the ad, and then goes to see the car. Posing as a customer."

"No." Samson was stubborn. "One of us simply shows up at the apartment without calling first. Why give them warning?"

"We'll be switching on a red light by appearing there. How would an ordinary person happen to find out the address? Put yourself in the position of this fellow Reyes. A guy shows up out of nowhere wanting to see the car that's been advertised. How did he get the address?" Sid was emphatic. "One stupid mistake like that, and we can blow the whole case."

"I think your way is stupid," Samson said. "If we're onto something big, we don't play games."

The ASAC looked at Linda Bartlett, who was remaining discreetly silent. "Where do you stand on this?"

"I can see both sides of the problem," she said, refusing to be caught in the middle.

It was the ASAC's duty to remain conscious of his role as a teacher on every level. "Hedley?"

Johnny was uncomfortable. "I'm the new kid on the block, sir. I just do what I'm told."

The others laughed, but the tensions were not relieved.

"Okay, Merrill," Joe Butler said. "Suppose you make a formal recommendation so we can put this on ice."

"Benjamin and Linda," Ray said, "pose as a married couple. Linda calls the number, and they follow up as soon as possible by going to the apartment. Try to work it so one of you stays at the apartment while the other takes the car out—alone—for a trial run. Check the Vehicle Identification Number, and get the secret number, too, if you can. The immediate objective is to obtain factual proof that the Monarch being sold is a stolen car. As soon as you have validation, make your arrests. Move fast, and don't waste time getting an advance approval from us."

"I'll have to go along with that," the ASAC said.

Damn generous of him, Ray thought as he went back to his own office. Just because he's struggling with personal problems is no reason to denigrate a senior subordinate who knows as much about ITSMV ring cases as anybody in the business.

Samson Grant and Sid Benjamin paused for a moment in the corridor outside the ASAC's office, both of them wanting a final word.

"The Ay-sack would have given the okay to move my way if you hadn't made your little purity speech," he said. "You're going to fall on your butt."

Sid glared at him. "If I do, pal, I won't ask you to pick me up. Okay?"

"From what they tell me," Samson said, "you were a pretty good agent until you let this hero bullshit go to your head. It's fine with me if you want to play it safe now so you can get promotions and wind up a big wheel in Washington. But there are some of us who are into all this because we care about doing a job for the job's sake. So don't screw up this operation, that's all I ask."

"I didn't know you had become a guardian of Bureau morality," Sid replied, his voice becoming metallic. "Thanks for filling me in."

Samson continued to face him, and was equally unyielding. "You're welcome."

Linda was afraid they might come to blows, which would bring a special Inspector to Winthrop from Washington, and certain transfer of both agents to dreary Resident spots in the sticks. She suspected that the cause of their friction was their similarity: both were highly ambitious men of action, and smelling blood, they wanted to get cracking. If she were the ASAC she would think twice before assigning two such prima donnas to the same team. But she wasn't wearing Joe Butler's shoes, so she'd have to restore peace in her own way. "I've got to make that call," she said, "and I'd like both of you covering me on extension lines. So come along."

They fell in on either side of her, both still spoiling for a fight, with their feud only temporarily suspended.

Linda made her call from Ray Merrill's office, where the clicking of typewriters in the bullpen couldn't be heard on the line.

A woman answered the telephone, and there was a long pause after Linda said she and her husband wanted to see the car that had been advertised. Finally the woman replied in Spanish. "Could you speak more slow? I don't understand English very good."

Linda pretended not to have understood, and repeated her request, but spoke much more slowly.

Again there was a silence.

Then a deep man's voice came on the line, "Yeah?"

For the third time Linda stated her business.

The man mumbled an address, then rang off.

Sid Benjamin and Samson Grant came into the Supervisor's office. "I don't like this," the former said.

Samson nodded. "For once we agree."

Ray took charge. "Sid, you and Linda get out there. Now. Samson, give them backup. If they get hold of the car, feed the statistics to NCIC, and be prepared to join in a bust."

Johnny Hedley wanted a role in the enterprise, too, but no one thought of including him, and he continued to sit at his desk, looking wistful, as the others left. He noticed that the little red-headed stenographer favored Samson with a special smile, warm and personal, as he walked past her desk, and that bothered him, too. He hadn't known her to be friendly with anyone in the office.

Sid drove, with Linda beside him, and he made a wry face when he looked in the rear-view mirror and saw Samson close behind him. "I'm glad old gangbuster didn't get the primary assignment. He'd shoot his way in."

"That isn't fair," Linda said. "Both of you had legitimate points of view, and you needn't be smug because the brass decided to play along with your approach."

"Grant doesn't need any help, but I'm happy to learn you're his defender."

She was annoyed. "I'm defending no one. I'm being objective."

"I can tell." Sid lighted a cigarette and let it dangle from a corner of his mouth. "It might be a lot easier just to smash down doors, but the Bureau has to be careful to observe every legality. More than we've ever done. I have no idea whether the criticisms of what we did years ago are justified or not. I wasn't around in those days. What I do know is that the public is keeping watch on us these days. Through a microscope. So we can't afford any goofs."

Linda studied him. "I can't argue with your conclusions, but I don't see why they should be a matter of life or death to you."

Sid's laugh was harsh. "Did you ever go to bed hungry as a kid? I did, and for a lot of years the idea of making money was first on my list. Well, I could have become a professional athlete, but here I am, earning a fraction as much. I'll skip the flag-waving, and just say it's enough that I expect to spend the rest of my life in the Bureau. I had ancestors killed in pogroms over in Europe, so I'm saying thanks to a country where things like that don't happen. I'm doing my part to make damn good and sure they don't happen, and if that makes me an Eagle Scout in your opinion, to hell with you."

"I had a few other careers open to me, too," she said, "and maybe I ought to switch to one of them, seeing that you need no help protecting the land of the free and home of the brave."

"If you weren't a woman, I'd tell you what you could do to yourself."

"But you're a man, so you'd rather do it to me."

They made the rest of the short drive in a mutually hostile silence.

Sid found a parking place directly opposite the frame apartment building, and a glance in the rear-view mirror told him that Samson Grant had moved into a spot farther down the street.

Linda took care to lock the door on her side. In spite of strenuous efforts made by federal, state, and local governments, the district remained a hopeless slum. Most of the buildings were dilapidated, badly in need of repair, and even the high-rise apartment houses that dotted the neighborhood were in obvious need of repair. Garbage littered the street, most of the residents not bothering to use trash cans, and even though it was still early spring, most of the area's life was lived out of doors. Elderly men and women in shabby attire huddled on stoops and creaking front porches, groups of youths and girls were congregated outside a chili parlor and a cheap bar directly across from it, and several small boys were throwing a baseball in an empty lot strewn with broken beer bottles and rusting tin cans.

Linda slipped into her role of a loving wife, and took Sid's arm. "Not exactly the kind of neighborhood to buy a high-priced Monarch," she murmured.

He made no reply, and after looking in vain up and down the block for the advertised car, he headed into the building.

Linda was glad Samson was parked a short distance away, ready to provide reinforcement. It was not surprising that members of the Winthrop Police Department patrolled the district in threes.

Sid led the way up a creaking flight of wooden stairs, pausing occasionally to nudge a rotting apple and other debris out of his way.

When they reached the third-floor landing Linda unzipped the special compartment of her shoulder bag in which she carried her .38.

Sid tapped at the door.

A girl in her late teens, heavily made up, her henna-dyed hair tousled, answered the knock. She was braless beneath a soiled white T-shirt, and her ragged jeans slopped over her bare feet. Ignoring the woman, she eyed the husky male visitor. "Si, Señor?"

"We've come about the car that was advertised."

The girl appeared not to understand, but waved them into the apartment as she shouted, "Ramon."

The only furniture in what appeared to be a living room, Linda noted, was an old couch with broken springs, several crates that served as tables and chairs, and, in a corner, an incongruously expensive color television set. She wondered if the set had been stolen.

A slender, dark young man in his early twenties came into the room, consciously or otherwise carrying unisex dressing to its ultimate limit by wearing a T-shirt and jeans identical to those of the girl. He stared insolently at Linda, making it plain he was mentally removing her clothes.

"We've come to see Hernando Reyes Gomez," she said.

The youth shrugged, then spoke in a deep voice. "He ain't here."

"He advertised a car in last night's *Herald*—"

"I don't know nothin' about that. He ain't here no more." The young man was sullen.

His companion asked him in Spanish why the visitors had come.

Linda and Sid remained blank, giving no indication they were familiar with the language.

"They want to see Reyes," the young man explained. "They have an interest in the automobile."

"Do you know where we can locate him?" Sid was polite. "The car sounded like a great bargain."

"He just rented here," the young man said, "and now he's gone. He didn't tell us where he was headin'."

"Oh, dear." Linda looked sad. "We really could use that car, if the price is right."

"We don't have nothin' to do with that," the youth said.

Linda seemed even more disappointed. "Perhaps he sold it to someone else?"

The youth's bored expression indicated his indifference.

Sid took charge. "This apartment is rented by someone named Juan Garcia. Is that you?"

"I am Ramon Garcia. His brother."

"Where is Juan?" Sid persisted.

"He went with Reyes."

The conversation was leading nowhere, and after the visitors exchanged swift glances they produced their credentials.

"We're FBI," Sid said.

The girl gasped.

A switchblade appeared in the young man's hand, seemingly produced out of nowhere, but in the same instant he changed his mind about resistance and dropped it to the floor. "We ain't done nothin' wrong," he said.

Sid kicked the knife into a corner. "You and I," he said, "are going to have a little chat. Anyone else here?"

The girl betrayed her knowledge of English by shaking her head.

"Suppose," Linda said, "you and I go off for a private talk of our own." She allowed the girl to lead her into a tiny, barren kitchen that smelled of stale onions, its sink piled with dirty, cheap dishes.

"We pay for our grass," the girl said. "It belong us."

"Cooperate with me, and you can keep your marijuana," Linda said. "We want to find Reyes, that's all."

The frightened girl's eyes looked enormous. "He go. Juan go, too. In car."

"In the Monarch that was advertised in the newspaper?"

The girl nodded.

"When did they leave?"

The girl appeared not to understand.

Linda repeated the question in Spanish.

The heavily made up eyes grew still larger.

"If I must," Linda said, "I'll turn you over to the Winthrop police for possession of marijuana. Stop evading, tell me what you know about Hernando Reyes Gomez, and you'll have no troubles. Now, who are you, what are you doing here, and what information can you give me?" She hoped Sid was enjoying better luck in his interrogation of the young man in the adjoining room.

"I am called Carlotta, and I live with Ramon."

"How do you and Ramon earn a living?"

The girl thought the question was astonishing. "We live on relief."

"Here?"

"For two years. The telephone belongs to Juan, and he permits us to use it. When he comes here he pays us for it."

"How often is that?"

"Perhaps he comes two times in a year. Sometimes three."

"And Reyes comes with him?"

"Only one other time." The girl grew a trifle calmer. "That one I don't like. He is a pig."

Linda looked sympathetic.

"All women exist for one purpose, Reyes's purpose, and he makes love like a beast."

"Then why did you—"

"Ramon is afraid of him. I, also."

"But he has no right to force you—"

"That Reyes, he is very quick with a knife, and when he becomes angry he uses it. One does as he wishes if one does not want to be scarred."

Linda sat on a rickety, straight-backed chair at the kitchen table. "Perhaps we could arrange it so that Reyes never bothers you again. Tell me everything you can about him."

The plump shoulders rose and fell. "He is very rich. He comes here with Juan for a few days, then he leaves."

"Juan works for him?"

"We think so. Ramon and I do not ask. When they come we are required to leave while they use the telephone. Reyes brings his own whisky." She pointed to an empty Scotch bottle standing in a corner.

Linda retrieved it, handling it gently with tissues to preserve possible fingerprints. "You think, perhaps, that Reyes disobeys the laws?"

The girl shrank into a shell again. "Ramon and I do not know, and we do not wish to know. Reyes comes here, he gives me one hundred dollars after he takes me to bed, and for treating me like a prostitute I can never forgive him."

It was impossible to determine whether she was telling the truth or whether fear was silencing her. Linda temporarily took another approach, leading Carlotta into describing both Reyes and Juan Garcia in detail.

By this time the girl was sufficiently at ease to speak freely, but she became blank when Linda tried to draw her out. Last night, she said, Reyes and Ramon's brother had returned very late. They had conferred for a time, with Reyes drinking the last of his Scotch, and then had departed together before dawn. "Juan gave us fifty dollars for the telephone, and two hundred because they slept in our bed for a week. So that money belongs to us."

"Of course it does, Carlotta." Linda was soothing. "Spend it on clothes, food, anything you like."

The girl giggled. "I would like to spend some on good grass."

The couple's way of life was self-explanatory, and Linda wasted no breath on lectures. "Do you happen to know which glasses Reyes and Juan Garcia used?"

Carlotta smiled. "In this place, we don't have many glasses, so we just grab from the sink."

"I'll come to see you again," Linda said. "If Reyes comes back, it would be wise not to tell him we were here—"

"I am not that insane!" The girl pulled back again. "I tell him nothing!"

"Good. Perhaps I can help you. Perhaps I can make it possible that he won't molest you again."

"I would like that very much." Carlotta's eyes were solemn.

Linda rose and went back to the living room, where conversation obviously had been exhausted.

Ramon Garcia was slumped in a corner of the couch, looking miserable, while a grim-faced Sid loomed over him.

"We'll be back," Sid said as they left.

"Don't come here no more!" Ramon said. "We don't want no troubles! With nobody! We're little people."

Linda carried the empty Scotch bottle with care. "If we're lucky," she said, "we may get prints from this. She gave me descriptions of both Reyes and Garcia, plus some tidbits, but that's about all. How did you make out?"

"The kid was scared silly. All he'd say is that his brother and Reyes left very suddenly, early this morning. The only time he even smiled was when I asked whether they were driving the Mercury Monarch that was advertised in the paper. Ramon was emphatic. 'No, Señor, Reyes drives only the biggest, finest car,' he said. But he didn't know the make, what Reyes and brother Juan do for a living, or anything else."

"It could be they know more than they're telling us, and are too frightened to talk. I did find out that Reyes forces the girl to go to bed with him, and then hands her one hundred dollars. Also, she said they did use the Monarch."

"Well, we've picked up enough for a starter, anyway." Sid saw in the rear-view mirror that Samson Grant was following them back to the Field Office.

When they arrived they learned of new developments elsewhere. Three new Granadas had been stolen from the All-American lot at Bradley Field, which served the Hartford-Springfield, Massachusetts, area, and two others had vanished from the All-American fold at Tweed New Haven Airport. Meanwhile two Monarchs had been taken from the showroom of a dealer in New London, which strengthened Ray Merrill's contention that the two ring cases were connected in some manner that was not yet clear.

Linda and Sid dictated their 302 raw interview reports, with the former concentrating heavily on the physical descriptions she had been given by Carlotta:

REYES GOMEZ, HERNANDO
Male, Latin extraction
Approx. 40 yrs.
Pale café au lait coloring
170 lbs.

Approx. 5'10"
Gray eyes
Dark brown hair, balding
Short, jagged scar on left shoulder

GARCIA, JUAN
Male, Puerto Rican
34 yrs.
Medium-dark
140 lbs.
5'6"
Black eyes
Black hair
No distinguishing marks

Meanwhile Samson Grant went off to the small laboratory at the rear of the Field Office, with Johnny Hedley assigned to assist him in a search for latent fingerprints on the empty Scotch bottle. Here, perhaps, they might find a solid clue that would tell the Bureau more about the identity of the elusive Reyes.

All Special Agents were required to understand the process of fingerprint lifting, and an arduous course was given in the subject at the Academy. Some agents became more adept at the delicate art than others, and Samson was the master of the art at Winthrop.

The Identification Division had more than 160 million sets of individual fingerprints on file. All of them classified according to types under a system that made it possible to check on any single set within a matter of minutes. Experts were at work on an ambitious plan that envisioned the full automation of fingerprint identification, which would make it possible to obtain data instantly, but that still lay in the future. Until that day arrived, the work still had to be done by highly trained specialists whose contribution to the extraordinary results obtained in the world's largest fingerprint repository were incalculable.

Since the beginnings of recorded history man has realized that no two individuals have identical diversified ridges on the tips of their fingers, and in ancient Babylon, China, and other civilizations, business agreements were legalized by placing the fingertip impressions of the various participants on clay tablets. But it was not until 1686 that the actual science of identifying individuals by their fingerprints had its formal beginnings. In that year a professor of anatomy at the University of Bologna, Marcello Malpighi, examined prints under a new instrument, the microscope, and discovered differing patterns of loops and spirals.

The first to classify these patterns by types was Johannes E. Purkinje, a professor at the University of Breslau, who published a thesis on the subject in 1823. But another thirty-five years passed before Sir William J. Herschel, a British administrator in colonial India, began the official use of fingerprints on a large scale. His efforts, initiated in 1858, made it mandatory for fingerprints as well as signatures to be affixed to all contracts. Nineteen years later he tried to extend the practice to include the fingerprinting of all prisoners held by the state.

Dr. Henry Faulds, a British scientist working in Japan, is generally regarded as the founder of modern fingerprinting. In a treatise published in 1880 he established the first detailed classification of prints of types, recommended the use of a thin film of ink to obtain prints, and observed that latent prints could be taken from drinking glasses and other smooth, hard objects.

In 1882 fingerprinting was introduced in the United States when Gilbert Thompson, an official of the Geological Survey, placed his own prints on various documents in order to prevent their forgery. Mark Twain, one of the most popular authors in the country, became interested in the subject, writing about it at length in several of his books.

In 1891 Juan Vucetich, an Argentinian police official, first installed fingerprint files as an official means of criminal identification. His system of classification is still used in most Spanish-speaking countries and a number of other nations.

A decade later fingerprinting for criminal identification was introduced in Great Britain, and in the following year Dr. Henry P. DeForest developed a system that was introduced in the United States. Thereafter the use of fingerprinting spread rapidly in America, and was adopted by federal penitentiaries and various police departments, the first in St. Louis. In 1905 the U.S. Army adopted a fingerprinting system.

An act of Congress established the Identification Division of the FBI in 1924, and less than ten years later citizens by the millions were voluntarily submitting prints to the rapidly growing files. Fingerprints continue to offer an infallible means of personal identification. For this reason they have supplanted other methods of establishing the identities of criminals reluctant to admit previous arrests. Other personal characteristics change; fingerprints do not.

The FBI files continue to grow at a pace that taxes the ingenuity of the Identification Division. More than 33,000 sets of prints are sent in each day of the year by over 7,200 contributing agencies. These prints are immediately classified and filed. Under a system developed soon after the turn of the twentieth century by Sir Edward Henry, Commissioner of London's Scotland Yard, there are eight basic classification groups. Numerous subdivisions have been added as identification has become increasingly sophisticated, and as a result the expert FBI technician can establish an identity within minutes by examining only a few of the millions of individual cards on file. In order to conserve space as the vast records continue to multiply, all fingerprints are being reduced to microfilm.

Placing the tissue-wrapped whisky bottle on the clean surface of a bare table, Samson Grant first donned a pair of rubber gloves. In spite of the potential importance of the task he was about to perform, he could not allow himself to forget that he had a secondary duty as an instructor.

"Suppose we were trying to develop latent prints on a piece of paper," he said. "Like a bank check. How would we go about it?"

What Johnny had learned at the Academy was no longer just theoretical. "We'd spray it," he said, "with a chemical solution. Ninhydrin, I believe."

"Correct." Samson examined the bottle under a magnifying glass. "We may be in luck. There are several latent prints here, and a couple don't look too badly smudged."

He made the prints more clearly visible by brushing them lightly with a special powder that contrasted in color with the background of the prints. This powder was used exclusively on glass; others were available for use on metals, smooth woods, and other surfaces.

The powder adhered to the almost imperceptible oily residue

left by the contact of the skin ridges with the bottle, and thus traced the pattern of the ridge formations.

Meanwhile Johnny loaded a special camera with film, and when Samson was done he took several photographs. "Two of these prints really look pretty good. Do you know which fingers they are?"

"I'm not that expert, but I don't have to be. A single print can be enough for Washington to make a positive identification." Samson waited until the photographing was done, then lifted the powder tracing from the bottle by the application of a special, flexible tape having an adhesive surface to which the powder particles stuck. This powder pattern was sealed onto the tape by the application of a protective, transparent cover of cellophane.

Johnny examined the older agent's handiwork. "That's great."

"What's the next step?"

"We transmit these tapes to Washington on the facsimile machine."

"No," Samson said. "You've left out something vital. We label the bottle, we label the tape card, and as soon as the photographs are developed, we also label them. We say what they are, we date them, and we initial the label. We don't know whether we'll want to use the bottle, the tape, and the photos in court, but we do know they won't be admissible as evidence unless we follow the steps that every federal judge will demand."

Johnny was embarrassed. The principle of labeling all evidence had been drilled into him at the Academy.

Samson prepared and attached the necessary labels, then went to the communications center, where a clerk slid the cellophane-protected tape into a facsimile machine that transmitted a picture of the latent fingerprints to the Identification Division, together with a request for immediate action. Depending on the backlog of urgent orders from other Bureau offices around the country, a reply would be received within hours. Under no circumstances would it come in later than the end of the same day.

Meanwhile Johnny went to the photo lab, where he developed his film. His photographs had been intended to provide security in case the latent fingerprints themselves had been damaged or obliterated in the process of transferring them to tape. That had not happened, but the photos would still be useful, and would be forwarded to the Identification Division for permanent filing.

Nothing more could be done in Winthrop. Now everything depended upon the ability of the experts in Washington to match two individual prints with a set already on file.

Shortly before noon Ray Merrill called a progress meeting in his office, passing around several airtels that had come in during the course of the morning. "One aspect of the case is developing rapidly," he said. "We now know for certain that thirty-seven Ford Granadas have been stolen from All-American rental lots in Connecticut and the greater New York City area. Every last one at an airport."

"In other words," Samson said, "this has got to be a large-scale operation conducted by a ring."

"Right. The Ay-sack has given the okay for a formal designation of an ITSMV ring case."

"But we've established no connection with the stolen Monarchs and Buicks," Sid Benjamin said.

Ray wondered if he was being needled. He wouldn't put it past the smartass. "Other aspects will fall into place in due time," he said. "The next step depends on what we learn from the Identification Division. That will help us evaluate the question of whether the two young people Linda and Benjamin interviewed this morning were as blank as they seemed or were afraid to talk more openly."

"I think I can develop the girl as a potential source of information," Linda said. "She hates Reyes because he's used her sexually and has humiliated her, so it shouldn't take too much effort to win her confidence."

"Fine," Ray said, "but hold off until we find out where the fingerprints will lead. If anywhere. The big development so far is the extent of the thefts from All-American. And this raises a fundamental question. Can you take a stab at it, Hedley?"

Johnny thought hard, but didn't know the answer, so he decided to keep his mouth shut. A first-office agent didn't stick his neck out unless he was sure of his facts.

"Thirty-seven stolen cars is a great number of vehicles," Ray said. "They can't be disposed of one by one because the risks would be too great."

"The ring," Sid said, "could operate in several ways. The most obvious is to utilize several crooked agencies or second-hand lots as outlets."

"You're jumping too fast," Ray said. "As long as the papers for each car are in order, the ring could sell them to perfectly legitimate agencies. Or to an agency that's okay but has one salesman who is in on the take. For a cut of a hundred dollars or so—per car—there are a great many salesmen who'd be willing to cooperate. We're on very tricky ground in working up this case."

Samson stretched his long legs, resting on the base of his spine. "The easiest way to get rid of a large number of stolen cars is to send them somewhere else. By freighter to one of the Gulf states, or by way of the Panama Canal to the West Coast."

"It would be even easier," Sid interjected, "to ship them to one of the Latin American countries, where they would command a far higher price than they'd get anywhere in the United States."

"I was just coming to that angle," Samson said, and glowered at him.

"So was I." Ray was annoyed when subordinates tried to usurp his expertise. "We've got to keep watch on exports by freighter, and I don't know of anything tougher. U.S. Customs has no control of outgoing ships, and hundreds of freighters sail every day of the week from scores of ports on the Eastern Seaboard. The Bureau simply doesn't have enough personnel to do monitoring and patrolling that extensive."

Again Sid cut in. "In other words, we'll need informants who will tip us off when there's going to be a large automobile shipment from some Eastern port."

Samson looked at him, making no attempt to conceal his pleasure over scoring at the expense of a colleague he obviously disliked. "I've already alerted my informants, and they're keeping a lookout for freighters that are shipping cars."

Sid's smile was bloodless. "Good for you."

Ray was afraid their rivalry might lead to blows, in which case he'd find himself cheering for Samson. He was uncertain why Sid irritated him, but he knew it was wrong to show partiality to one subordinate at the expense of another, so he decided to end the meeting before he became more involved. "That's it for now. If you have anything that takes you out of the office, try to get back here late in the afternoon for a roundup with Mr. Butler. Miss Bartlett, stick around for a minute, will you?"

The male agents filed out.

Linda guessed why she had been asked to stay behind.

"Your trip down to Kennedy Airport knocked out our lunch date yesterday," Ray said. "Let's go today instead."

Her fears were confirmed. "I'm sorry, Ray, but I can't. Sid and I want to double-check our findings on our separate talks with that young couple this morning, and we'll have to do it at lunch if we're going to talk while the interviews are still fresh in our minds."

"By all means," Ray said, "do it then. You and I can always go to lunch some other day."

"I'd rather relax with you for an hour," Linda said, and hoped she sounded sincere.

He watched her as she returned to the bullpen, and he knew why his opinion of Sid Benjamin was worsening. His own interest in Linda was greater than he had admitted to himself, and his instinct told him Sid—many years his junior, with a promising career ahead—could become a serious rival for her affections.

Less than three hours after the two latent fingerprints were sent to Washington the Identification Division produced positive results, and the Assistant Director who headed the unit made a personal telephone call to the SAC in Winthrop. "Dave," he said, "it looks as though we've dug up a live one for you. We've made a positive identification of the right thumbprint of the man known to you as Hernando Reyes Gomez. The print of the middle finger, same hand, is incomplete, but we picked up a partial."

"What have you found, Chuck?"

"I'm sending you a copy of the entire file," the Assistant Director said. "We know him as Hernando Romero, a citizen of the Central American Republic of Dorado. He's forty-six, with a scar that matches the description your people picked up, so there's no doubt whatever that he's the same man."

"What's his record?" Dave Daniels wanted to know.

"Skimpy. But interesting. We arrested him in Galveston three years ago in an ITSMV ring case, but we couldn't scrape up enough evidence to sting him, and the charges against him were dismissed. According to a woman he jilted—and he seems to be a great skirt chaser—he was the mastermind of the ring, but we couldn't find anyone who would testify against him. That ring operated in the Southwest, and not one of the seventeen members we were able to convict could be persuaded to say a word against Romero."

"Afraid of reprisals?"

"Apparently, although your guess is as good as ours. There's nothing positive in the records."

"What happened to the woman who gave us the tip and then backed off?"

"Now your new case gets interesting. She lives in Fairlawn, Connecticut."

Dave laughed. "That's where Carolyn and I are living. As respectable a shoreline community as you'll find in the state."

"Her name is Louise Elizabeth Poole." The Assistant Director went on to give him her address.

"Any criminal record?"

"No, she's completely clean, as nearly as we know. Blond, in her late twenties by now, and that's all we have on her."

"It's our first lead, Chuck, so I'm grateful to you."

"Good hunting. I'll slap everything we have on the teletype to you, and I'll send you stats of Romero's record, such as it is."

Dave immediately summoned the ASAC and Supervisor Merrill. "See what the Fairlawn P.D. knows about the Poole woman, and then send somebody to have a chat with her."

"Right away," Joe Butler said. "I'll call Galveston, too, and ask them for a copy of their ITSMV case of three years ago that this Romero or Reyes was involved in."

"Washington will send us a complete file as a matter of routine," Ray Merrill said, "but your way is better, Mr. Butler."

All three veterans exchanged tight smiles, but none needed an explanation. The Bureau in Washington was marvelously efficient when it chose to move quickly, but agents who had spent their careers in the field had their own, private opinions of the bureaucrats who lived their professional lives in the J. Edgar Hoover Building. The red tape could hold up receipt of a copy of the case in question for many days, and it was far simpler to go to the source. Galveston would respond within twenty-four hours, as was customary when one Field Office extended a hand to another.

The Winthrop Field Office had something substantial on which to work now, and the brass wasted no time. Samson Grant, a skilled interrogator, was sent to see Louise Elizabeth Poole, and at the same time Sid Benjamin was dispatched to the Fairlawn police, with orders to visit the woman's neighbors, too, in order to glean what he could about her. Meanwhile Linda Bartlett was sent back to see the young couple to whom she had spoken that morning. "You're strictly on a fishing expedition," Ray told her, "but now you've got some bait to put on the hook."

Sid was the first to leave the office, and drove straight to the red brick headquarters of the Fairlawn Police Department located just off the Boston Post Road.

Chief Howard, himself an alumnus of the National Police School at the Academy, received him without delay. "I don't blame you for being interested in Louise Poole, Mr. Benjamin," he said. "I'd like to do a bit of moseying around her myself. What's she done?"

Sid's shrug was noncommittal.

The Chief knew better than to ask questions when the FBI chose to be uncommunicative. "There's been a lot of speculation in town about her, mostly because she's so good-looking, and because nobody hereabouts can get close to her. She bought her house two and a half years ago. A couple of bedrooms. Three-quarters of an acre site, about a block or so from the water. Paid fifty-two thousand for it. In cash, with no mortgage."

"How do you know that without looking it up?"

"Well, my brother-in-law was the real estate agent who sold it to her." The Chief smiled, then sobered. "She does her marketing at the Stop and Shop, and buys her liquor at the same place I go, in the shopping center. I see her there every once in a while, getting wine. Never hard stuff, to my knowledge. Some people in town have made social overtures to her, but she sidesteps them. Very polite and all that, but she don't mix much with the locals."

"Her friends come in from the outside, then?"

"Don't know that she's ever had a party there. She goes out of town a lot, and always asks us to keep an eye on her house when she's gone. Sometimes for a day or two, sometimes for as long as three weeks."

"Where does she go?"

"Lots of folks wonder about that, but she don't say. There's a rumor that she goes off to Florida or the Caribbean a lot in the winter because she's always tanned. And in the warm weather she spends most of her days on a deck out back of her house, working on her tan. I like to help out the FBI when I can, Mr. Benjamin, but I can't tell you much of anything about Miss Poole. She minds her own business, lives quiet, and don't even have a traffic violation on her record."

"What kind of a car does she drive?"

"Plenty damn fancy. She had a Mercedes sports coupe, the expensive one, and a couple of months ago she traded it in on a new Porsche. She has several fur coats worth a fortune, too, and I saw her in the liquor store one day wearing a diamond ring that near knocked my eye out."

"Where does she get her money?"

"She don't say."

"Does she do her banking locally?"

"No, now you mention it. Always pays in cash."

"Does she have a boyfriend who drops around?"

"Now you've hit the situation in the gut. There must be a hundred fellows in town who'd like nothing better than to lay her, but she won't as much as go out for a beer with any of them. If she's got some guy bankrolling her, nobody in Fairlawn has ever set eyes on him. There's speculation about her at every cocktail party and church social in town, I can tell you. You hear it said she's an heiress. Or the secret mistress of the Shah of Iran. Or a call girl who does business out of town. Or a rich widow. You name it, and that's what you hear."

Sid checked all three of the Fairlawn banks, which confirmed that Louise Elizabeth Poole had no accounts in town. Then, after obtaining a record of her automobile registration from the state Motor Vehicle Bureau, he paid calls on several of the woman's neighbors.

They were able to tell him little he hadn't already gleaned from the Chief of Police. Two neighboring ladies said she wore expensive, stylish clothes, slightly flashy but always in good taste, that she necessarily purchased elsewhere. "No store in Fairlawn carries anything like her wardrobe," one of the women said. "She has to do her buying in boutiques in New York and Miami Beach, places like that."

The most curious aspect of the young woman's life in Fairlawn was her isolation. Consistently turning down invitations to lunch, dinner, and even informal drinks, she seemed content to live alone, although it was true that she spent about two-thirds of her time elsewhere. She replied cordially when the neighbors on either side saw her sunning on her deck while they worked in their gardens, but she had never asked anyone to drop in for as much as a cup of coffee.

To the best of her neighbors' knowledge she did not drink to excess, and had no other bad habits worthy of note. They had no idea whether she received books or periodicals in the mail, but none could recall seeing her read when on her deck. Lights in a second-floor bedroom at night indicated that she spent her evenings watching television there, and by midnight the house invariably was dark.

Slowing to a crawl as he approached the place, Sid saw that it was small but substantial, made of gray fieldstone native to Connecticut. Then he saw Samson Grant's Bureau car parked in the driveway, and quietly cursed Ray Merrill for not giving him that assignment, too. He was far more subtle than Grant, who was accustomed to dealing with waterfront whores, and could have done an infinitely better job talking to her.

Linda Bartlett knew Merrill better than anyone else in the office, and seemed to get along well with him, so he'd have to ask her why the Supervisor disliked him. There was a rumor that Linda was having a romance with Merrill, but he refused to believe it. She was a lively chick, ripe for a romp, and he couldn't believe she saw anything attractive in that dried prune.

The young woman who came to the door when Samson Grant rang the bell wore a tight white jumpsuit, its zipper open to the waist. Her hair cascaded down her back, and the polish on her long fingernails was the same shade of green as her eyes. Wary, alert eyes, very much on guard when she looked at his FBI credentials.

"May I come in?" he asked politely.

"I suppose." She led him into a sunken living room that overlooked her backyard.

High fence. No flower gardens. The furniture, like the young woman herself, was somewhat flashy but appeared expensive. She was a high-class model, maybe, or a hooker whose fees were astronomical. The way she waggled her tail slightly when she walked on her high platform sandals was a giveaway. Samson was neither fooled nor impressed.

"You're Louise Elizabeth Poole," he said, sitting opposite her in an armchair with a floral-patterned slipcover.

"How did you guess?" Pouring herself a glass of white wine and not bothering to offer him any.

"Two and a half years ago you moved in here."

"That's what I call putting the facts together." She sipped her wine, then lighted a long cigarette with a red filter tip.

Samson remained unruffled. "Six months before that, down in Galveston, you told agents of the FBI that a man named Hernando Romero was head of a gang of car thieves."

"I did?"

"You let it be understood that he'd been your lover, but had walked out on you."

"News from all over."

"Then," Samson persisted, "just before he was scheduled to go on trial you changed your mind and refused to testify against him."

"Now you know the story of my life," Louise Elizabeth Poole said. "Only you left out something important. You bastards claimed I said certain things about Hernando Romero. But I never signed anything and I never made a sworn statement, so you couldn't prove it. You had no way you could hang me."

"We didn't want to hang you then, and we don't now."

With studied insolence she blew a thin stream of smoke at him. Under other circumstances the gesture might have been regarded as provocative, but her eyes were hard. This man was the enemy.

"We hope," Samson said, "that you'll prove willing to cooperate with us now."

"Why should I?" she demanded.

"You're a citizen of the United States, Miss Poole, and—"

"I don't owe the government anything. What have they ever done for me? Nothing!"

His manner became almost imperceptibly firmer. "Many people find it pays in the long run to stand with us rather than oppose us."

"Buster," Louise Elizabeth Poole said, "I haven't broken one goddamn law, not one, and I dare you and the whole FBI to prove I have. If I don't want to play ball with you, that's up to me. And if you don't like it, you can stuff it."

"I urge you to reconsider. You don't even know why I'm here."

"I'm just holding my breath waiting to hear," she said.

"How long since you've seen Hernando Romero?"

She raised a thin, plucked eyebrow. "Who?"

A laugh welled up in Samson and exploded. "Lady, you're too much. Would you like to know the real reason I've come here?"

"No," she said, draining her glass and putting it aside.

He was getting nowhere and decided to try a different approach. "I just can't believe a girl as gorgeous as you can be so unpleasant. It doesn't fit."

Louise Elizabeth Poole's expression remained unchanged. "You think I'm gorgeous."

"Naturally."

"And you're the great big hunk of man who is going to turn on the sex power and persuade me to change my mind."

"No, FBI agents don't go around making passes at women they interrogate, not even beautiful ones like you. More's the pity."

She stubbed out her cigarette. "Buster, I'm going to make a little suggestion, and I hope you take it to heart. Go fuck yourself."

Samson sighed as he hauled himself to his feet. "Miss Poole, you're making a big mistake."

"Don't send flowers to my funeral, okay? I'm allergic to them. And you won't mind letting yourself out."

He could feel her steady, hostile scrutiny as he left the room and the house. She was tough, no question about it, and if the ASAC wanted to pick up leads on Hernando Reyes Gomez, or

Romero, or whatever he might be calling himself these days, she would have to be placed under surveillance. He didn't envy the agents who got that assignment.

Although it was midafternoon the rumpled bed wasn't yet made, the kitchen sink was still filled with dirty dishes, and a thick layer of dust covered the furniture and floor. Linda Bartlett tried to ignore the surroundings and devote her full attention to the lethargic girl who slumped on the tattered couch.

"Carlotta," she said, speaking in Spanish, "I've come back because I've been thinking about you, and I believe I can help you. Ramon, too. Where is he?"

"He went out," the girl replied vaguely. "Later, when he comes home again, he will bring food."

"You haven't eaten today?"

Carlotta shook her head.

"I'll buy you a meal right now. Come along."

"No. Ramon will be very unhappy if I am not here when he returns. I am not hungry."

Linda noted that her eyes were clear, so it was unlikely that she had either been smoking pot or drinking, but she was as indifferent to her basic needs as she was to her surroundings. "Where has Ramon gone?"

"To New Haven, on an errand for his brother. I don't know what it was, and he didn't tell me."

Linda's manner became offhand. "Oh, you have a car?"

"It is Juan's, I think. He left it for Ramon to use."

Ramon Garcia was of greater interest to the Bureau than anyone at the Field Office had realized. Before the day ended someone would check the car he was driving, but enough had been said on the subject for the moment. "You would like it, I think, if you never saw Hernando Reyes Gomez again."

Carlotta nodded. "Very much."

"Ramon, too."

"Ramon is loyal to his brother."

Linda wondered whether it might be possible to separate Carlotta from her lover and make a deal with her alone. The thought was premature, but was worth remembering. "We believe," she said, "that you and Ramon know more about Reyes than you have told us."

The girl glanced at her for a moment, then looked away again, making no reply.

"We think he has done things that would send him to prison. For a long time." Linda tried to present a complicated situation in simple terms. "Help us to send him there, and we'll protect you. We'll make sure you never see him again."

"He would follow," Carlotta said, and there was fear in her voice.

Linda knew she was on to something. "The FBI has helped many people who cooperate with us," she said. "We would send you to a new city, where you could make a new life for yourself. Under a new name."

"Reyes would follow," the girl said again.

"We would make very certain that he couldn't."

Carlotta was silent.

The agent wondered what tack to take now.

Suddenly the girl spoke. "For myself, I would like it. But Ramon would never desert his brother, and I would not leave without Ramon."

The development had to be exploited. "Perhaps it could be arranged that you could go first and Ramon could follow."

For the first time Carlotta stirred. "No!" she cried, her voice rising. "If I leave him, even for a little time, he will find another woman."

It was difficult to understand a girl whose hold on her lover was so tenuous, but Linda had to present her offer in the best possible light. "We would make it attractive for Ramon to go, too."

"You do not know Ramon." Carlotta fell back onto the couch again, her energies dissipated. "His brother is the friend and helper of Reyes. If harm comes to Reyes, it comes also to Juan Garcia. And Ramon would die before he would betray Juan."

Linda realized she had to consult with higher authority before going any farther. She appeared to be stymied, at least for the moment, but she wanted to keep every approach open. "Think about what I've said, Carlotta. If you'll help us you'll have a new home, a good job, a real future for yourself. For Ramon, too," she added, although she thought it likely that it wouldn't be long, no matter what the circumstances, before Ramon drifted on to another girl.

"I will think," Carlotta said, and sat listlessly, staring off into space.

Linda let herself out of the filthy apartment, the girl scarcely aware of her departure.

Less than a half-hour later an emergency meeting was held in the office of the ASAC.

"Is there any chance of prying this broad away from Ramon Garcia and making a separate deal with her?" Ray Merrill asked.

"None, in my opinion," Linda said. "She's one of those ferociously devoted Latin women. Ramon is her man, and Ramon comes first."

Joe Butler reached a rapid, firm decision. "Merrill," he said, "send two agents over to the Puerto Rican neighborhood to keep watch for Ramon Garcia. You'll go with them, Bartlett, so you can identify him when he appears. I want a fast check made on the car he's driving. Put it through NCIC immediately, and if it's a stolen vehicle, take Ramon Garcia into custody."

"Yes, sir." Ray knew what he had in mind.

But Linda was confused. "The girl will go into a complete panic if her boyfriend is thrown into jail, Mr. Butler."

The ASAC was crisp. "I'm not concerned about her at the moment. I want to get a handle on Ramon Garcia, who won't talk. He may find his voice if he faces a prison sentence, even if it means spilling some information about his brother. When we find a crack of daylight in a case like this we've got to exploit it. Fast."

After they left his office Joe pondered for a time, then went through the secretary's suite to the inner sanctum of the SAC. "Got a minute?"

"Sure," Dave Daniels said, waving him to a chair.

"Our new ITSMV ring case is beginning to open up, even though a great many of the pieces are still missing. Right now our crying need is for information on this guy Reyes, who seems to be the kingpin. I've been talking to Washington this afternoon, and Matt O'Brien down at the Bureau rode herd on the previous

Reyes case in Texas three years ago. Somebody ought to fly to Washington tomorrow for a chat with Matt. By morning, of course, we'll have a copy of the full Two-Sixty-Three," he added, referring to the file on the Galveston case that was retained by the FBI. "Matt thinks he might be able to fill in some details that aren't necessarily on paper, so it would be useful."

"Make your reservation right now and catch the early-morning flight. Naturally."

"That's what I wanted to hash over with you," the ASAC said. "I know that ordinarily I'm the logical one to go down to the Bureau. But it will probably entail an overnight stay, and I'd rather not be away from Stella that long." He was reluctant to admit he was afraid his wife would drink herself insensible if he left her alone overnight.

Dave needed no explanation. "Send Merrill," he said. "Shoot him down there tonight so he can talk to O'Brien first thing in the morning."

"Thanks, boss." Joe paused, then recovered. "I want to send several teams through the Spanish section tonight to learn what they can. The few signs we've had so far point in that direction, so I intend to saturate the neighborhood."

6

Most street agents welcomed an occasional undercover assignment because it offered a break in routines as well as a novelty. But tonight's job was different. Samson Grant and Sid Benjamin were tired, having reported for work at 7:30 A.M., and neither enjoyed being teamed with the other. But here they were at the San Juan, their third crummy bar of the night, wearing old clothes and windbreakers, smoking black cigarettes as strong as cigars, and drinking bitter Colombian beer, with no progress to show for their efforts.

Samson was still out of sorts after his total failure with Louise Elizabeth Poole. He was proud of his ability to cajole, persuade, and nudge even the most recalcitrant into saying more than they intended in an interview, but he had achieved literally nothing in his talk with the blond bitch. She was tough. Not only had she made him look like the hind end of a horse, but if she had any connections with Reyes and his gang currently, she would be in a position to pass along an alert to the effect that the FBI was snooping into their business.

What galled Samson more than anything else was that he had displayed no finesse. He could have handled the interview in any one of a hundred ways, but his self-confidence had blinded him, and he had committed errors that even a new agent would have the sense not to make. He shouldn't have mentioned Reyes, and he had known it the second he had opened his blabbermouth, but by then it had been too late. He should have made up some story to explain his visit, then used his charm to win the woman's confidence. She had been as conscious of him as a man as he'd been aware of her as a woman, and that kind of chemistry could have led to one hell of a good interview.

Instead he had blown it. The ASAC hadn't bawled him out, but that hadn't been necessary. He had a far lower opinion of himself than Joe Butler could hold. Maybe he was right to think about quitting the Bureau. A few lousy successes over the years had given him an inflated opinion of himself, and he was thoroughly disgusted with Special Agent Samson Grant.

An extra burr under the saddle, which he sure didn't need, was the knowledge that Sid Benjamin knew of his failure. So far the smartass hadn't mentioned the interview with the Poole woman, which was fortunate. It would be a pleasure to relieve his frustrations by poking some of Benjamin's pretty teeth down his throat. On second thought, transfer to Butte wasn't worth that momentary joy.

"You want another beer?" Samson was careful to address his partner in flawless Spanish.

Sid shrugged. "Why not?"

Tonight's exercise was a bore, but Sid didn't mind. Experience had taught him that a Special Agent had to endure countless hours of ennui for each minute of satisfaction he obtained from his work. Even Mel Purvis and the other Bureau heroes of the thirties had spent the better part of their lives slugging through routine assignments, and their moments of triumph had been fleeting. By definition investigative work was plodding and dull, but that was okay; all an agent really needed to overcome the drudgery was that instant when some crooked bastard was nailed to the wall.

Sid could admit he found his job glamorous, that he romanticized it, and was proud of what he liked to regard as his contribution to an orderly society that respected the law. Guys like Mel Purvis must have felt the same way. And old Mr. Hoover. And Mr. Kelley. And all the hard-working, anonymous slobs—a good percentage of the Bureau's 8,600 agents—who could earn more money in the civilian sector, live in one place instead of being transferred every few years, and even have evenings and weekends for their private pursuits.

Some people stayed in the Bureau just long enough to grab juicy jobs in private industry, but Sid felt contempt for opportunists. The Bureau was more than a job, more than a career. It was a way of life he had chosen to follow, and he felt no regrets.

Feeling as he did, he didn't know why a familiar restlessness was bugging him. He realized he was jealous of his temporary partner, annoyed because Grant had been given a plum and had fallen, while he himself had not erred in carrying out a subsidiary, supporting assignment. Sometimes he had goofed, too, so he could feel sorry for Grant. Almost. The role of a junior partner wasn't conducive to the development of charitable sentiments.

Maybe Linda Bartlett was responsible for Sid's dissatisfaction, and the mere idea made him even more upset. He tried to review the facts dispassionately, as an agent should. She had turned down a dinner date with him tonight, saying she had to go out with Ray Merrill. Okay, so Merrill was hightailing it to Washington, Linda had an assignment somewhere in the Puerto Rican neighborhood, and he himself was tied up by work. Game postponed, with the score tied, and a sudden-death overtime would be played at a later date.

What did he care if Linda went out with Merrill? If she preferred a granny to someone with zing, she'd get what she deserved. What really troubled Sid, however, was the realization that he didn't quite know what he wanted to achieve in a relationship with Linda Bartlett.

He wanted her, of course, but that much was obvious. She inspired such desires in any man, and Sid had become sufficiently adult—he hoped—not to want another notch on his .38 for its own sake. He wasn't Wyatt Earp.

On the other hand, certain catastrophe lay ahead if he was allowing himself to think seriously about Linda. Her dedication to the Bureau matched his, and he admired her for it. But he'd be crazy if he allowed himself to forget that a religious barrier separated them.

To be sure, Bureau work made a hash of race and religion. The fact that Samson Grant was black didn't bother him, and he hoped Grant didn't care that he was white. That, however, was the essence of a Bureau partnership, in which two lives depended on mutual trust.

Marriage was something else. He was a Jew, even though he didn't work at his faith, and Linda was a *shiksa,* regardless of whether she attended church. He knew how his parents would react if they as much as guessed the thoughts going through his mind. But that was nonsense. Ma and Pa operated on another wavelength.

What he had to do was haul himself into line. He might be drawn to Linda, but he didn't want her as a wife, any more than she wanted him as a husband. A night or two in bed with her, and he'd be better able to put her out of his mind.

The bartender approached, and Samson, slouching on his stool, ordered two more Colombian beers.

Sid flipped his black cigarette butt into a cuspidor, picked his teeth, and made a point of studying an unattractive woman in her thirties who was drinking with a middle-aged man. He and Grant blended perfectly into their undercover assignment, for all the good it did. They had been on the prowl for hours, but hadn't picked up one useful crumb.

The bartender placed their glasses before them, and Samson went into action. "Hey, Pedro," he said. "How are jobs in this town?"

"What kind of jobs?"

"Anything, just so we earn some bread. Winthrop has to be better than Bridgeport."

"Bridgeport is bad," Sid said. "You need a union card there, or the bosses spit at you."

The bartender scrutinized the husky pair. "Where else have you been?"

"Many towns," Samson said, "and every place is the same. No union card, no Social Security number, and they throw you out of the hiring hall."

Sid looked morose as he sipped his beer. "Pretty soon, Chico," he said, "we'll have to go back to Puerto Rico."

Samson could match anyone in an ad lib session. "I wouldn't mind going home if I had a girl like Maria waiting for me. But I'm staying here."

"I want to stay, too," Sid said, "but if we run out of money we can't live on air."

The bartender mopped his face with his apron. "I have a friend who comes here two-three times a week," he said. "Sometimes he has jobs."

This was the type of lead the agents were seeking, but Samson remained calm. "What kind of work?"

"Not too hard. With good money."

Sid drank another swallow of the raw beer and belched. "How good?"

"Plenty," the bartender said. "If you're interested, come back tomorrow night, maybe the next night, and maybe he'll talk to you."

"Thanks," Samson said, paying for the beers and turning to his companion. "We'll see how it goes, Chico. Maybe we hang around Winthrop for a day or two and give it a chance."

"Could be," Sid replied. It was surprising how often drifters were offered work, honest and illegitimate jobs alike. So the lead might be vague, but it was worth following, particularly if the ITSMV ring was still active in the area. The technique he and Grant were using was simple, but it often paid off.

The two agents left the bar together and sauntered off down the street, only their athletic builds making them conspicuous.

"All we got out of tonight was heartburn," Samson said, tugging at the visor of his cloth cap.

Sid couldn't resist the opportunity to needle him. "I had so much fun I can't wait until we do it again."

They had reached the corner where they had previously agreed to separate for the night. Samson looked hard at his partner, again resisting the urge to deck him, and stalked off in the direction of his car, which was parked beyond the fringe of the Latin neighborhood.

As Sid headed in the opposite direction he knew he had behaved badly, needlessly antagonizing a colleague who was hypersensitive because of his failure earlier in the day. They would continue to see a great deal of each other while working on the ring case, like it or not, so professional courtesy would require him to offer apologies in the morning. There was no telling what problems might lie ahead, and he needed a partner who would be reliable in the crunch.

Ramon Garcia failed to reappear, so Linda and the two agents with whom she shared her assignment were relieved by another pair at midnight.

The following morning, after insufficient sleep, she showed up for work at her usual 7:30 A.M. arrival time, and a few minutes later she was summoned by the ASAC.

"Go back to the barrio," Joe Butler told her, "and keep waiting for young Garcia. We're short-handed today, so I'll have to give you Johnny Hedley as a partner. Keep him under control, and don't let him use his gun."

Linda started out at once in her Bureau car, with Johnny beside her, and as they approached the Spanish-speaking district she pulled on a beret to conceal her blond hair. "I'll explain the assignment to you after we get there," she said.

She reduced her speed to a crawl as they approached the now-familiar tenement. The agents who had been maintaining a vigil since midnight pulled out, and Linda eased her car into the space they vacated. There were no signs of life in the tenement, and she felt a twinge of sympathy for Carlotta. The girl undoubtedly was still waiting for her man to show up, and Linda hoped there was food in the apartment. If not, Carlotta would be very hungry.

"Change places with me."

Johnny Hedley walked around the car and settled behind the wheel.

"That's better," Linda said. "In these parts we'd be too conspicuous with me in the driver's seat." She locked her door, directed him to do the same, and then leaned against him. "Put your arm around me," she said.

Johnny was startled, but obeyed.

"Hold me as though you mean it! That's better." Linda laughed. "A man and a woman sitting in a car call attention to themselves. But nobody will look twice at a couple who are necking."

He tried to display more sophistication than he felt, and drew her closer.

"There are some things you don't learn at the Academy," Linda said. "Now. If and when Ramon Garcia shows up, leave him to me. While I keep him occupied, I'll want you to take his license number and VIN, and call them in on the radio for immediate transmittal to NCIC. Have you got it?"

"Yes, ma'am," he said.

The combination of their clinch and his politeness made her giggle. "Mr. Butler told me not to let you use your gun," she said. "He didn't mean it quite literally, but almost." She saw no need to humiliate him by explaining that all new agents were assumed to be trigger-happy. "However, no fireworks unless I give you the order. Okay?"

"Sure." Johnny forced a laugh. "When I applied for training as an agent it never crossed my mind I'd be taking orders from a girl."

"Does that bother you?" She made herself more comfortable, in the process snuggling still closer to him.

Johnny's embarrassment deepened. "I'll tell you the truth, ma'am. I don't know what to think."

"Don't even try to sort it out until later," Linda said. "And relax. There's no telling how long we may be here."

A heavyset woman came out of a tenement, scarcely glanced at the couple in the car, and walked down the block to a bakery.

Soon men began to emerge from various buildings and walked to a corner bus stop.

"This is crazy, but they act as though we're invisible," Johnny said.

"We are. As long as we melt into their background." She snapped on the two-way radio, reported to the Field Office communications center, and told Johnny to smoke if he wished.

Soon a Winthrop police cruiser moved slowly down the block. Neither of the uniformed men in the front seat appeared to notice the pair in the parked car.

"The city P.D. was tuned in to our wavelength, obviously," Linda said. "So they sent a patrol car around to check on us. Very friendly of them."

Johnny didn't want to tell her he felt relieved. In principle he had no objection to women agents, but he doubted if a girl who weighed less than 115 pounds would be of much help if real trouble developed, and he was secretly pleased that the local police were prepared to send reinforcements to the scene.

An hour passed slowly, and gradually the neighborhood came to life. Two small boys went into the empty lot, one of them clutching a greasy tennis ball, and several older children carrying schoolbooks walked down the street. Men went off to work, as did a number of women, and housewives went in increasing numbers to a grocery store down the block.

At 9:30 A.M. a large Buick began to maneuver into the parking space two cars in front of the parked Bureau vehicle.

Linda stiffened and reached for the microphone. "This is WFO Eighty-four," she said. "Our friend has just shown up in a shiny new Buick. Stand by, please."

The dark young man in a dirty T-shirt who was parking the Buick was unaware of the agents' existence.

"Get his license number now," Linda said, "so you can concentrate later on the VIN."

Johnny called in the six-digit number.

Linda waited until Ramon Garcia finished parking the car, turned off the ignition, and opened his door. By the time he reached the sidewalk she blocked his path. "Well," she said, "what a surprise seeing you again."

Ramon stared at her for a moment, recognized her, and tried to brush past her.

"I need to have a little talk with you," she said.

"I ain't talkin' to you. Get to hell out of my way." Ramon tried to move around her, but she stayed in front of him, and he reached out, intending to shove her away.

Linda caught hold of his wrist, and two fingers pressed into a nerve.

He gasped and seemed unable to move.

"If you'll change your mind, we'll have a brief chat. Can I persuade you?"

"Okay, okay. Just lemme go!"

Linda remained calm and smiling as she released him. "Just show me your driver's license and car registration," she said, "and then you can go upstairs to Carlotta. I'm sure she's waiting for you."

As Ramon led the way to the Buick she saw that Johnny

Hedley had taken the Vehicle Identification Number from the left door post and was calling it in on the two-way radio. In less than sixty seconds there would be a reply from the NCIC master computer in Washington, which the Winthrop Field Office communications center would relay.

Ramon unlocked the right-hand car door, fumbled with the keys, and finally unlocked the glove compartment. "I got all the papers in here," he said.

Linda realized, as he opened the glove compartment, that he blocked her view.

Suddenly Ramon turned, a six-inch knife with a double blade in his hand. "Now get to hell out of my way and leave me alone," he said.

She braced herself, waiting for him to make the first move.

Without warning he slashed at her, the blade aimed at her face.

Linda moved swiftly, seemingly without exerting herself. She caught Ramon's wrist with one hand, twisting it, and the knife dropped into her other hand. At almost the same instant her knee caught him in the groin, and he doubled over, falling back against the Buick.

It was difficult for Linda to conceal a smile as the worried Johnny Hedley raced toward her.

At almost the same instant a police cruiser pulled up, its brakes screeching, and a patrolman leaped out.

"Book Ramon Garcia here on charges of assaulting a federal law-enforcement officer with a deadly weapon," Linda said.

"You can also charge him with possession of a stolen motor vehicle," Johnny Hedley said. "NCIC says this car was taken in Fairlawn night before last. But the State Motor Vehicle Bureau reports there is no such license number."

Handcuffs were snapped on Ramon, and he was taken into the cruiser quickly, before a crowd could gather.

"We'll send somebody over to the cooler for a talk with him," Linda told the policeman. "And we'll bring the car into your garage. Thanks for your help."

Ramon sat with a drooping head as the cruiser started off down the street.

"Are you all right?" Johnny demanded. "By the time I saw

that knife in his hand, you took it away from him."

"If you must know," Linda said with a slightly breathless laugh, "my insides have turned to pure jelly. I don't think I've ever been so scared."

"You sure didn't look it or act it."

"That, as they used to tell us at the Academy, is half the battle. You took care of your part just fine, Johnny."

"I don't understand about the license. How can the state say there is no such number?" He pointed at the white-on-blue Connecticut license, which had six digits: LL8240.

"I think I know." This was Linda's first experience in giving instruction to a new agent, and she leaned over the license. "The thieves who took this car also stole two separate license plates. Each with six digits. They cut both in half, then put together the left side of one and the right side of the other. Look closely, and you can see, under the new paint job, where the two parts have been welded together."

Johnny examined the license, and understood. LL8 had been the starting sequence of one number, and 240 had been the closing sequence of another. Together they made a new number which was not registered at the Motor Vehicle Bureau.

There would be an opportunity later, Linda thought, to explain in detail that the job appeared to have been done by professional thieves. They had not changed the VIN, however, perhaps because they had been confident they wouldn't be caught, perhaps because they had intended to attach a substitute number later.

She picked the keys up from the floor of the Buick, where Ramon had dropped them. "Here," she said. "Take this car into the P.D. garage."

Johnny wondered how long new agents had to serve before they no longer were given mop-up assignments.

"But first," Linda said, "call in to the office on my radio, and with Ray Merrill away from his desk today, speak direct to the Ay-sack. I'm sure he'll want to send somebody straight to the cooler to interrogate Garcia. I'll join our agent there. Just lock up my car when you're through with it. I have my keys."

"Wait a second," Johnny said. "Where are you going?"

"Tell the Ay-sack I'm going to have another bash at Ramon

Garcia's girl," Linda said. "She wouldn't talk yesterday for fear of incriminating him, but now that he's under arrest—with two major felony charges against him—she may decide to share a few secrets with us."

Johnny returned to the Bureau car to make the report to the Field Office.

Linda went into the tenement, its odors even more pronounced than they had been the previous day. As she climbed the stairs she thought her legs would collapse beneath her, and she knew that her brief, violent encounter with Ramon Garcia had exhausted her. She had presented a cool facade to the Winthrop police and had made an effort to speak calmly to Johnny, even though she had admitted the truth to him. Well, part of the truth: the rest of it was that she felt drained, and the memory of the double-edged knife made her skin crawl. She had known ever since she had joined the Bureau that Special Agents weren't supermen, and now she had learned that she was no superwoman, either.

Women agents had to take the same risks the men faced, but this was the first time she had ever been in such physical peril. She didn't relish the experience, although she knew she'd be obliged to take similar chances in the future. For the present, certainly, whatever sympathy she had felt for Ramon Garcia had evaporated.

She knocked on the peeling door of the apartment, noting with wry amusement that her hand was still trembling.

There was no response, no sound inside.

Linda knocked again, more loudly.

After another long wait shuffling footsteps sounded on the bare floor, and the door was opened a few inches. Carlotta, her eyes puffy with sleep, her hair matted and snarled, peered out.

"I've got to talk to you again," Linda said. "Ramon has been arrested for driving a stolen car—"

The girl's wail cut her short, the sound that emanated from her developing into a protracted, high-pitched scream.

"Please," Linda said. "I want to help—"

"Get out! It's you who brought this evil on us!" Carlotta cursed hysterically, then slammed the door.

For the present, at least, the girl could not be reached, and Linda turned away.

Large government edifices lined both sides of Washington's broad Pennsylvania Avenue, some of them graceful and many utilitarian. All were dominated by the massive bulk of the new J. Edgar Hoover Building, where the entire national headquarters of the Federal Bureau of Investigation was gathered under one vast roof. Only the Washington Field Office was housed elsewhere.

Long a subject of aesthetic controversy, the building was almost universally condemned as an architectural eyesore, and the most that its few Justice Department defenders could say in its favor was that it admirably suited the purposes for which it had been constructed. The Bureau was blamed for its ugliness, even though its officials had played no major role in its design, planning, or construction. Their two basic requests had been met: they had wanted a headquarters easy to make secure against attacks by terrorists or other extremists, and they wanted enough space to hold the many tens of thousands of files that provided the Bureau with its core.

Many who had known the man for whom the building had been named said he would have hated it. He had spent his career maintaining a low Bureau profile, and the new home was flamboyantly gargantuan. It was a self-contained city, the working home of 17,000 agents, clerks, and stenographers, and from the outside it looked much like a fortress, a touch the designers had not intended.

Ray Merrill ate an early breakfast in the coffee shop of his hotel, then walked the short distance to the J. Edgar Hoover Building. Field agents were supposed to be pleased by any opportunity to visit the fountainhead of all Bureau power and promotions, but this was just the fourth time Ray had come to Washington in fifteen years, and he discovered he was ill at ease.

On his first two trips he had paid a courtesy call on old Mr. Hoover, and last time he had been received by Mr. Kelley, who had surprised him by asking his candid opinion of liaison between the Bureau and the field and had urged him to suggest possible improvements. He anticipated a similar session today, provided Mr. Kelley was in town, and this time he was better prepared to express his views.

The headquarters loomed up ahead, and Ray felt a strong surge of resentment. This was the home of the padded chair brigade and the pencil pushers, the men with fancy offices, fancy titles, and impractical ideas about the workings of Field Offices. Many officials settled into headquarters early in their careers and left it only for token periods. When they rose to the rank of Inspector they spent six to eight weeks at a time traveling to Field Offices and Resident Agencies, but Washington remained their base.

The Bureau mentality was essentially tied up in red tape, and officials here were immersed in the Washington gossip that was the staple of the town. It was their job to know what was happening in Congress, what the White House thought, what the Supreme Court was ruling, but Ray—like thousands of his colleagues in the field—felt contempt for men he regarded as far removed from the day-to-day, real-life problems of the FBI.

He knew, too, that officialdom looked down its collective nose at the yokels who gave the Field Offices and Resident Agencies their muscle. In their eyes he lacked sophistication, and was incapable of viewing any problem at long range. Fair enough, but he'd like to see them move in a hurry when a bank robbery occurred. They were chained to their desks, and only because it was mandatory were some of the busier officials able to make the time to go out to Quantico once each year to qualify with firearms. They were welcome to the life they were leading.

Several uniformed policemen, armed Justice Department guards in gray uniforms, and a few unobtrusive Special Agents in mufti were gathered at the main entrance, and Ray's credentials were subjected to a thorough scrutiny.

"I'm from the sticks," he said. "I'm here for a meeting with Matt O'Brien of the Investigations Division."

A young first-office agent in a blue blazer with the Bureau shield over the breast pocket led him to the check-in office.

"How do you like this place?"

"It's just great, sir!"

Ray thought of the training that Johnny Hedley was getting, and made no comment.

A somewhat older Special Agent, also wearing the identifying blazer of the welcoming corps, make a telephone call, and Ray signed in, filling out a complicated form.

Then the young guide conducted him down a maze of corridors to an elevator the size of a small living room, and they rode up to the eighth floor, where the executive offices were located. Ray matched his stride to that of his escort as they walked down miles of broad corridors, painted white.

"This place," he said, "makes me think of a hospital."

The young agent grinned. "Everybody from the field says the same thing, sir."

Ray noted that the doors of private offices and suites were closed, and wondered why.

"Regulations, sir," the escort explained. "All doors are kept closed—and locked—at all times."

"Suppose I had to go down the hall to see somebody. Do I phone ahead of time so he'll let me in?"

The young agent laughed. "It isn't that complicated, sir. You just knock, and somebody lets you in."

The damn place was like a prison, Ray told himself, and thought that the door of his own cubicle in Winthrop stayed open at all times. Hell, the SAC and ASAC rarely closed their doors, even when holding meetings and engaging in conferences. Some people around here had been reading too many books of fiction about clever spies sneaking in and stealing FBI secrets. The headquarters mentality was not for him.

They passed through a huge open area, about as long as a city block and half as wide, that was filled with filing cabinets, with clerks' desks placed at regular intervals in each aisle. Here, Ray knew, was the heart of the Bureau. There were miles and miles of such areas in the J. Edgar Hoover Building, and it was these marvelous files, with their automated cross-reference systems making data available within minutes, that enabled the Bureau to wage war against crime. No miracles were performed here, just as none were performed in the field. The never-ending paperwork provided the system with its fuel.

Ray estimated they had walked the equivalent of three or four blocks by the time they came to a door, painted a dark gray like all the rest, with a number at eye level.

A secretary answered the summons. "Come in, Mr. Merrill," she said, and the escort vanished.

Ray followed her through a miniature bullpen, crowded and informally subdivided by file cabinets, where a dozen Special Agents and about twenty-five clerks and stenographers worked. Beyond stood several tiny private cubbyholes, and at the end of the suite was an office overlooking the inner courtyard, its one double window letting in so little daylight that, even on sunny days, it was necessary to use electric lighting. Matthew O'Brien held a rank equivalent to that of a SAC, but at Bureau headquarters he was only one of many, and his office was about half the size of that of the Winthrop ASAC. Symbols were more important in Washington than they were in the field, but here there were many generals and few privates.

"Mr. O'Brien had to go to a meeting with the Assistant Director," the secretary said, "so he thought you'd like to look through the records of the Galveston case."

Ray saw two bound folders, each more than a foot thick, awaiting him on a glass-topped table. This, he knew, had to be the 263 file of the Texas ITSMV case, which contained the Bureau's copies of all raw interviews as well as summaries, conclusions, and dispositions. "I'll have enough to keep me busy if he's delayed."

The irony appeared lost on the secretary, who withdrew.

Ray began to read, and soon lost consciousness of his surroundings. An amateur might have spent a full day wading through the voluminous report, but he felt at home and made swift progress. He read the summaries with care, making mental notes of salient points, and dipped into the 302 raw interview reports only when they seemed pertinent.

In less than a half-hour a number of basics began to emerge:

A major car theft ring had succeeded in stealing eighty-one Chevrolets, all less than a year old, as well as about fifteen much larger, more expensive vehicles.

Only forty-three of the stolen cars had been traced and recovered. The rest had disappeared permanently.

A total of twenty-three persons were arrested and placed on trial. Of these seventeen were convicted and sent to prison for terms ranging from one year to five years. These persons were small fry, and it was apparent to Ray that none of the leaders of the ring had been jailed.

The mastermind of the operation, or so it seemed, had been one Hernando Romero. But not one of those placed on trial with him had been able to offer evidence against him sufficiently concrete to obtain a conviction, and the charges against him had been dismissed.

The ring had specialized in obtaining title and registration papers that looked legitimate. All had been issued on the motor vehicle forms provided by the so-called nontitle states. Thanks to the apparent authenticity of these documents, no attempts had been made to alter the Vehicle Identification Numbers of the stolen Chevrolets. But counterfeit plates, expertly fashioned, had been substituted for the VINs on eleven of the fifteen larger cars.

Ray drew up a comparison table. The Galveston case seemed to bear out his contention that the thefts of the Ford Granadas taken from the All-American lots and those of the larger Monarchs and Buicks had been perpetrated by the same ring, but he still had no idea why they operated on a two-tier level.

Suspicion pointed at Hernando Romero, also known as Hernando Reyes Gomez, as the head of the operation.

The *modus operandi* was identical, as nearly as he could judge on the basis of what he had read so far, and this was of critical importance. Unfortunately, those persons who had been convicted and imprisoned had been punks, youngsters in their late teens, and early twenties who had been paid $50 to $100 for each car they had stolen, and who had known literally nothing about higher-echelon operations.

It was significant, however, that nine of the seventeen sent to prison were of Latin American extraction or had Spanish names. This was not surprising, thanks to the growing participation of Latins in ITSMV ring cases.

Matthew O'Brien came into the office, interrupting Ray's reading, and stashed away a manila folder in his safe before shaking hands. In his late forties, with dark, wavy hair, he had a deceptively pudgy face, but at worst was only a few pounds overweight. Not even a desk-bound Special Agent in Washington allowed himself to get out of physical condition, and O'Brien did daily calisthenics as well as keep watch on his diet. There was less talk about overweight in the Bureau now than there had been in the day of J. Edgar Hoover, who had been almost fanatical on the subject, but even Assistant Directors knew that excess weight would force their immediate retirement.

"Have you sent your name in to the Director, Merrill?"

"Yes, sir, and I hope he can give me a couple of minutes."

"You'll get much more than that. Mr. Kelley is never satisfied with efficiency levels, and he'll pick your brains as long as you have something to contribute. While you're here you ought to have a look at the ground-floor laboratories behind glass that tour groups by the thousands are shown."

"I saw them last time I was here," Ray said. "The Ballistics Lab. The Explosives Unit. Neutron Activation Analysis Unit. Instrumental Analysis, Serology, Chemistry-Toxology, Mineralogy, Microscopic Analysis, Metallurgy, and all the rest."

"You do all right, just remembering that many."

"In the field," Ray said, a hint of acerbity in his voice, "we depend on the labs to help us solve a great many cases."

"So I've been told." O'Brien was well aware of the hostility of street agents for the Bureau, and concealed a smile.

Ray knew better than to waste the time of a busy executive. "I've been going over the Galveston file, Mr. O'Brien, and I have some questions. I haven't yet established a definite connection in our new case between the thefts of Granadas and those of a smaller number of more expensive cars, but I'm sure there is one. I haven't run across it in your Galveston file yet—"

"Because it isn't there. I was sure there was a tie-in, too, but I couldn't prove it. And I still don't know the motive for it. None of the people we sent to prison knew, including those who were willing to tell us anything and everything in return for a touch of clemency."

"To my way of thinking," Ray said, "the two-tier thefts offer a key to the M.O. of the entire operation. But I don't know why, and I can't even guess."

"When you find out, please let me know, just to satisfy my personal curiosity," O'Brien said. "The problem bugged me for a long time, and I wouldn't be surprised if only Hernando Romero knows the answer. But he isn't talking. By the way, we sent his vital statistics, fingerprints, and photograph up to the Winthrop Field Office last night."

"Thanks. What can you tell me about him, sir?"

"He's as slippery as they come. He uses the names of Romero and Reyes interchangeably, by the way. I thought we'd heard the last of him when he was exonerated three years ago, but he appears to have been lying low, and is just surfacing again in your case. If you can nail him. Which is going to be very, very tough."

"He's that slick?"

"Top drawer. Before the Galveston case came along we tried to connect him with a ring that specialized in stealing heavy equipment. Tractors, bulldozers, and the like. But we couldn't touch him."

"Can you give me a rundown on him, sir?"

"To an extent. He has U.S. citizenship. He was born here of an American mother, and he speaks an accentless American English. Doesn't even look Latin. But he had a Doradan father, and he maintains a big home down in Ciudad Dorado. He seems to go there when the heat here becomes uncomfortable for him. A very convenient arrangement, and he seems to have friends in Central America who don't ask too many embarrassing questions."

"Can he be extradited from Dorado, Mr. O'Brien?"

"Sure, if we come up with evidence, but it has to be solid."

"What are his weaknesses?"

"I wish I knew," O'Brien said, and sighed.

"I thought, on the basis of what little we've put together so far, that he might have a soft spot for women."

"He controls them. They don't run him."

"Does that include someone named Louise Elizabeth Poole, who has been living in a Winthrop suburb for the past two and a half years?"

"Good Lord!" O'Brien was startled. "Don't tell me she's involved!"

"We don't yet know, sir."

O'Brien reached for his pipe. "Her involvement was one of the strangest features of the Galveston case. As nearly as we could learn, she had no direct connection with the ITSMV ring that we broke up, but she traveled with him."

Ray made a mental note to have Louise Elizabeth Poole placed under full surveillance as soon as he returned to Winthrop.

"When a subordinate did a particularly good job," O'Brien continued, "Romero-Reyes rewarded him by loaning the blonde to him for a night."

Ray was so startled he didn't know what to say.

"That's the way I felt," O'Brien said. "He gave her to three or four different men, but we couldn't plaster her with any charges that would stick. Not one of the men paid her a penny, so we couldn't even nab her for prostitution. If Romero-Reyes paid her for her extracurricular services to his faithful boys, we couldn't prove it."

"Wow!"

"Now we come to the tricky part. They had a fight, and apparently he got somebody else to take her place. So the Poole woman got hold of one of our agents, made a date with him in a Galveston bar, and told him that Romero-Reyes was the head of the ring. Not in so many words, but she hinted it. Strongly."

"We gathered that much, sir."

"Well," O'Brien said, "she must have told Romero-Reyes what she had done, and that was enough to cause him to make up with her. Within twenty-four hours she claimed we had misunderstood her. It was her word against the agent's, and when she held firm our whole case collapsed."

"She appears to have been living in total isolation on the Connecticut shore," Ray said, "although she spends only a fraction of her time there. I find it hard to believe it coincidental that an ITSMV ring case is developing in the area. Particularly when two of our agents learned just yesterday that Reyes was in Winthrop earlier this week."

"All you've got to do now is pin him down. Good luck." O'Brien gestured toward the bulky file. "I'll give you an empty office so you can go through the rest of the Galveston case this morning, and you'll be on tap whenever Mr. Kelley can fit you in for a talk. Then you and I can lunch in the cafeteria and review any other angles that may come to mind before you leave this afternoon."

Ray was taken to an unused room, and was glad to settle down to the familiar grind of combing a case file. His feeling of depression was intense, and he was willing to admit to himself that he missed Linda Bartlett. When he returned to Winthrop he'd have to make it clear to her that his interest in her was greater than either of them had realized.

But it was more than his separation from Linda that was responsible for his feeling. If he hoped to spend another fifteen years in the Bureau and rise higher than his present rank, he'd need a tour of duty here under his belt. And the mere thought of coming to work daily in this enormous mausoleum was unbearable.

Youngsters like Johnny Hedley had stars in their eyes when they contemplated their Bureau careers, but Ray knew better. Nit-picking solved cases. Reading reams of papers solved cases. Common sense solved cases. There was no glamor in this business, and he wondered why he didn't have the brains to get out. Probably for one reason: his long years of training and experience made him unsuitable for any career other than that of an FBI investigator.

The ASAC decided to interrogate Ramon Garcia himself, and with Linda Bartlett accompanying him at her own request, he went to the federal lockup. The presence of a subordinate was a help, making it more difficult for him to give in to the temptation to see Joey again.

That didn't make him any less eager to have another visit with his son. Even though he knew another confrontation that led nowhere would be frustrating.

To make matters worse, he and Bartlett were shown into the same room where he had seen Joey.

Joe put his son out of his mind when a guard led a stone-faced Ramon Garcia into the room.

Ramon glared at the woman agent. "You come to laugh at me, huh? I could kick myself for letting a chick do what you done!"

"I'm not laughing," Linda said.

"I'm sure you know your rights, Garcia," Joe Butler said, throwing a pack of cigarettes onto the bare table as a gesture. "We have no intention of trying to force or trap you into incriminating yourself. But if you're sensible, I'm sure the prosecutor and the court will be sensible. I can make you no promises—and I stress this—but if you'll cooperate and tell us about the higher-ups in the syndicate that's been employing you, I believe the court may let you off with a minimum sentence."

Ramon helped himself to a cigarette, and the ASAC lighted it for him.

"Who hired you?"

"Nobody."

"We know that Hernando Reyes Gomez and Juan Garcia spent at least one night in your apartment."

"So what's with that?" Ramon demanded, flaring. "Juan is my brother."

"Did Reyes or your brother hire you to steal that Buick you were driving this morning?"

"No."

"Did they hire you or persuade you as a favor to drive it back to your house?"

"No."

"Where did you pick it up?"

"I don't remember."

Joe Butler's patience was monumental. "Did you know you were driving a stolen car?"

"No."

"How do you account for the altered license plate?"

"I dunno." Ramon appeared blank.

"You're on relief, but you had three hundred dollars in your pocket at the time of your arrest. Where did you get it?"

"Here and there."

Linda looked at her superior, and his almost imperceptible nod gave her permission to take part in the questioning. "Maybe Carlotta gave it to you. She told me Reyes paid her well for going to bed with him."

Ramon spat on the stone floor, but his expression remained unchanged.

"You're in bad trouble, Garcia," the ASAC said. "But half of it could disappear in no time. Miss Bartlett here might be willing to withdraw the charge that you attacked an FBI agent with a switchblade."

"Don't do me no favors," Ramon muttered.

Linda decided to try a different approach. "Carlotta is badly upset by your arrest."

"She'll get over it."

"I think not," Linda said. "She needs you."

"She ain't gonna have me." Ramon's voice became strident. "So she'll have to find somebody else." He scooped up the pack of cigarettes and jammed it into a pocket of his jeans.

A policeman escorted him back to his cell.

The two agents continued to sit at the table. "I think the best approach to him, ultimately, lies in the girl," Linda said. "I don't want to predict that she'll tell us what she knows, if anything. That might be asking too much. But I suggest we let her visit him as often as she wants, after she recovers from the initial shock of his arrest. Let her come daily. We'll drill it into her that he may get a lighter sentence if he cooperates. And she's so crazy about him I'm pretty sure she'll use her influence to persuade him to talk."

Joe Butler drew a pattern on the table with his forefinger. "You may be right, Bartlett."

"But you don't think so, sir?"

Joe found his mind turning again to his son. "I've spent a quarter of a century dealing with criminals, Bartlett, and I've seen all kinds. They fall into types, as all people do. And there's one type that is unrepentant, stubborn, and indifferent to any suggestion of leniency. The type that can't be moved by either threats or favors, and dares you to do your worst." He felt weary as he hauled himself to his feet. "Let's get back to the office."

If Carter L. Franklin had lived in New York he would have worn tailor-made suits, shirts, and shoes, and his hair would have been trimmed weekly by a stylist who specialized in razor cuts. In Manhattan such niceties would have been expected of the president of the National Motor Vehicle Insurance Corporation, the largest company of its kind in the world. Instead, because he lived in Hartford, where his headquarters were located, he bought his suits off the rack, wore shirts that were beginning to fray at the cuffs, and had his hair cut every other week by a barber who used clippers with more enthusiasm than judgment.

As a consequence Carter L. Franklin looked more like a salesman on commission than a top-ranking executive who earned $150,000 per year. But in Hartford such things didn't matter, perhaps because everyone in town knew him, was aware of his position, and accorded him the respect his post deserved.

The receptionist at the FBI Field Office in Winthrop recognized his name, too, and lost no time notifying the SAC that a distinguished visitor had come to see him.

Dave Daniels went to the reception room and escorted the visitor to his office. "This is great, Mr. Franklin," he said. "You've saved me a trip to Hartford to see you."

"I had to be in Winthrop this afternoon anyway, and I'm as anxious to have a little talk with you as you've been to get together with me."

"I'm going to be blunt, and I hope you don't mind," Dave said. "But I'm disturbed, and so are some of my colleagues in Washington, by the attitude that All-American Car Rentals has been displaying. Thirty-seven of their new Ford Granadas have been stolen, and the toll may go much higher. So far only four have been recovered, but they literally don't care."

"For good reason," Franklin said. "This is costing my company close to one hundred and fifty thousand dollars. All-American's insurance rate will go up, of course, but they pass that cost along to the consumer. We suffer. The man who rents a car suffers. But All-American isn't hurt."

"The situation may be even more unpleasant than you realize," Dave said. "There's an underground criminal network, and word gets around pretty quickly. Every All-American lot in the country is going to be fair game from now on. So far nothing has appeared in print about the thefts, and we hope we can keep the story quiet until we move closer to a solution of the case. Once the press picks this thing up, though, All-American is going to have its hands full."

The president of the insurance company frowned. "Which means that we'll be shelling out cash again."

"Unless you take positive steps, immediately, to force All-American into line. The FBI," Dave said, "believes in the prescription of preventive medication in obvious instances. You don't wave a diamond necklace under the nose of a jewel thief and then give him a key to your house."

"I begin to see what you mean, Mr. Daniels."

"There's nothing the FBI can do to persuade All-American to take a more responsible attitude. There's nothing we want to do, actually, because that isn't our function. All I can do is advise you, in a friendly gesture to a major insurer, that we anticipate further, substantial losses at All-American in the near future unless they mend their ways without delay."

"I'm very grateful to you." Franklin was grim.

"Not at all. Our personnel is limited, and we prefer to see the barn door locked before the horses, tractors, and the load of hay have disappeared. I'm trying to make it unnecessary for a great many of our agents all over the country to become tied up in wave after wave of cases like the present headache."

Carter Franklin sat back in his chair and pressed his fingertips together. "If National cancels All-American's contract, no other insurer will want to touch them. I'm sure we have the leverage to persuade them to adopt tighter procedures on automobile pickups and returns."

"Everyone concerned will benefit."

"I'd like to go to All-American with a specific procedural plan that we can urge them to adopt. Is the FBI willing to give us the benefit of your technical experience?"

"If you'll make a formal request, Mr. Franklin."

"You'll have a letter on your desk first thing tomorrow morning, Mr. Daniels. I can assure you I want that barn door bolted, and every day is important. Where do we go from here?"

"Ordinarily I'd send someone from our Hartford office to consult with your people. As it happens, our best expert on car thefts is a Supervisor here, and this present case has him running around in circles. But if you can have someone here at eight tomorrow morning, he can work with them to devise new procedures for All-American. Nothing is foolproof when dealing with criminals, of course."

"Between your specialists and ours," the insurance executive said, "I'm certain we can make it far harder to steal cars from the All-American lots."

Members of the day staff were putting the finishing touches on their interview reports, classified documents were being locked in safes over night, and several of the stenographers, after glancing at the bullpen clock, began to apply their lipstick so they could leave promptly. The usual routines were being followed, and the atmosphere was relaxed.

Only Johnny Hedley was nervous, although no one else realized it. He was a real turkey, he told himself. He was willing to put his life on the line for the Bureau and his country, but he was a gutless wonder. So he was a nobody from nowhere. So a girl attractive enough to be dated for weeks ahead wouldn't be interested in him, even though she was pleasant to him in the office. The worst she could do would be to turn him down; she couldn't force him to face a firing squad.

Johnny straightened his necktie, buttoned his jacket, and crossed the bullpen to Lisa Talbot's desk. "Have you got a minute?"

Lisa knew he was shy, and encouraged him with a smile. "Sure."

"I expect you know this town pretty well, being a native and all."

"I come from upstate," she said. "About a two-hour drive from Winthrop."

His strategy was spoiled, and he was nonplussed.

"But I've lived here for almost a year, ever since I got this job with the Bureau."

He returned to his original plan. "I've been eating at the Hilton coffee shop most nights, but lately I've been wanting to gorge myself on pizza. You wouldn't happen to know of a good pizza restaurant, would you?"

An alarm bell began to sound on one of the teletype machines in the communications center, but neither heard it.

"Well," she said, "there's Mario and Maria's."

A clerk raced to the SAC's office with a strip of paper from a teletype machine.

"Where is it?"

Lisa told him the address.

"I'm not sure I know where that is," Johnny said. "I don't know my way around Winthrop all that well yet."

Samson Grant was summoned to the front office, along with several other agents.

"I've only been there once, but it's pretty easy to find, I think."

"Not with my sense of direction," Johnny said, and took a deep breath. "Maybe I could talk you into going with me."

At last! "I'd love it," Lisa said.

Linda Bartlett and Sid Benjamin were called to the ASAC's office.

"You wouldn't be free this evening, would you?" Johnny began to gain confidence.

"It just happens that I am," Lisa said.

The SAC's voice came over the intercom. "All agents stand by, please."

Johnny's laugh was shaky. "It looks as though the front office has other ideas."

The girl made no attempt to conceal her disappointment. "I guess so."

He quailed at the thought of going through the routine again.

Lisa had no intention of waiting until he summoned the courage. "I happen to be free tomorrow night, too."

A grin spread across Johnny's face. "It's a date," he said.

Samson Grant walked rapidly through the bullpen, leading a group of three other agents who were carrying cameras, fingerprinting kits, and other technical equipment.

"Come along, kid," Samson called, not slowing his pace. "Tonight you get a real education."

Lisa had just enough time to return Johnny's smile before he fell in with the group.

"Here," Samson said, and thrust a copy of the teletype into Johnny's hand. It read:

> 4TH PRECINCT, WINTHROP P.D. INDICATES APPARENT HOMICIDE: CARLOTTA RUIZ, 19, 4721 GRAND STREET, APT

3F. PATROLMAN SUMMONED BY NEIGHBORS INDICATES STABBING. INVESTIGATION INITIATED. NMD

"What's NMD?" Johnny asked as they headed out the door.

"No motive discerned. You're in for a real session."

As the group departed, others in the office were equally busy. A supervisor reached the head of the Winthrop Police Department detective bureau on the telephone and asked that as few people as possible be admitted to the apartment. The FBI was moving into the case.

Meanwhile another supervisor reached the State Police captain in command of the Criminal Investigation Division, who immediately dispatched a squad to assist the FBI in any way possible.

Linda Bartlett and Sid Benjamin composed messages dispatched immediately by teletype to all FBI Field Offices and Resident Agencies, requesting information on the whereabouts of Hernando Reyes Gomez and Juan Garcia. Similar messages were disseminated to all major police departments throughout the United States, and contained descriptions of both men.

No photographs of the pair were as yet available in Winthrop, so the SAC himself telephoned Bureau headquarters in Washington, and within minutes the country was being flooded with photos.

Linda and Sid were summoned to the SAC's office, where Dave Daniels and Joe Butler awaited them.

"The Ay-sack and I aren't going over to Grand Street," Dave said. "The newspapers have picked up the bulletin by now, and we want to avoid the press. When you two get there, Benjamin will act as spokesman. The reporters will hound you, wanting to know why the Bureau has an interest in this murder. You'll give a two-word reply."

"No comment?" Sid asked with a smile.

"No comment."

"It won't be long," Dave said, "before they also learn we've put out a national query on the whereabouts of Reyes and Juan Garcia. You've got to be particularly careful in the way you field that one. Remember, the FBI doesn't make arrests based on suspicion. We take such action only on the basis of hard evidence.

So don't connect Reyes and Garcia with this case in any way. We're simply trying to establish whether the two men were in Winthrop today."

"Which isn't likely," Joe Butler added. "For one thing, I doubt if Reyes engages in much strong-arm stuff himself. He can hire people to do that kind of dirty work for him. But we can't afford to miss any angles."

"The obvious conclusion, although we can't allow ourselves to jump to it," the SAC said, "is that the girl was killed to shut her up. Make sure of each step as you go along."

"Yes sir," Sid said.

Linda didn't yet know any details of what had happened at the tenement, much less why, yet she felt certain Carlotta had been murdered because she knew too much about the operations of the ITSMV ring. She refrained from expressing her opinion, however; the Bureau developed cases on facts, not on a woman's intuitions.

"For the sake of argument," Joe Butler said, "let's assume the girl was killed because of what she knew. If that's the case, there's more at stake here than the stealing of thirty-seven low-priced cars and a half-dozen medium-priced cars. We're into something big, and it's pointless at this stage to speculate. Let's find out."

Linda was silent on the better part of the drive to the tenement, and Sid respected her mood. Finally she roused herself.

"I offered Carlotta protection," she said. "I should have followed through."

"She turned you down, didn't she? Don't start blaming yourself for something you couldn't control."

"If you and I hadn't gone to Grand Street in the first place, this might not have happened."

Sid lost his patience with her. "If there hadn't been good cause, we wouldn't have gone to Grand Street!"

Linda made no reply.

When they reached their destination they saw that the area had been transformed. Several hundred residents of the area stood behind police barricades, most of them silent, and Sid had to show his credentials before he was allowed to park in the middle of the street.

Other Winthrop policemen blocked the entrance to the building, and when the two agents again displayed their credentials they were immediately surrounded by newspaper, television, and radio reporters. Linda's presence particularly aroused their interest.

Sid took Linda's elbow as he threaded a path through the throng, raising his free hand to halt the barrage of questions. "We just got here, fellows," he said. "You know more than we do."

Someone responded with the inevitable. "Why is the FBI interested in this case?"

"No comment," Sid said as they ducked into the building.

Frightened residents of ground-floor apartments peered out at the couple through doors that were opened no more than an inch or two.

Two uniformed Winthrop policemen stationed at the entrance to the apartment of Carlotta and Ramon allowed the pair to pass.

Samson Grant had the immediate situation under control. His three agents, aided by a State Police trooper from the Criminal Investigation Division, were testing every object, every surface in the apartment for fingerprints. Scores of photographs had been taken. Bits of dirt, lint, and other materials had been scooped into envelopes, which had been carefully labeled. Nothing that might provide a clue had been overlooked.

Linda felt ill when she looked at the body of Carlotta Ruiz slumped on the dilapidated sofa.

The girl's throat had been cut, and a stiletto still protruded from her back, the blade surrounded by a ragged circle of brown, dried blood that stained her dirty T-shirt. Her eyes were still open, and her expression was placid.

Linda turned away.

Samson Grant took his colleagues into the empty bedroom, which had already been tested for fingerprints and other clues. He and Sid Benjamin were professionals, so by unspoken consent they laid aside their mutual animosities.

"We waited until you got here before moving the body," Samson said. "The coroner has already been here, and so has the chairman of the Pathology Department of the University Medical School, who has volunteered to perform the autopsy as soon as we release the body. The S-A-C has accepted."

"What have you found out so far?" Sid wanted to know.

"The apartment door was open, and two little kids—eight-year-olds, who live on the next-higher floor—wandered in. They saw the body and went screaming to the mother of one, who came down, took one look, and notified the police."

Linda found her voice. "What time was that?"

Samson consulted his notebook. "The lady upstairs is too rattled to remember. The Winthrop P.D. desk log says four forty-three. Let's start at the beginning. The coroner and the pathologist agree on a preliminary finding that the girl was killed when her throat was cut. The knife was thrust into her back for good measure. There are no fire escapes, and the windows are too small for the killer to have gone out through one of them. Besides, all of them were open only a few inches."

Sid clasped his hands behind his back and rocked on the balls of his feet. "She knew the killer."

"That's the way I figure it," Samson said. "There are no signs of a struggle in the apartment. She let the murderer in, they went into the living room, and she sat on the couch. That's where she died. There are blood stains only on the couch, so she wasn't dragged there after the killing. Her throat was slashed, she was stabbed, and the murderer walked out."

"Forgetting to close the front door behind him, apparently," Sid said.

Samson nodded.

Linda was afraid she would become sick to her stomach unless she took a more active role. "Were there any witnesses?"

"Everyone in the building has been interrogated, and so have people next door and across the street. All of them will be questioned again, of course, as a double-check. So far nobody—literally nobody—saw anyone either strange or familiar come in or out of this apartment. Which is par for the course."

"Why do you call it normal?" Linda asked.

"People who are cooped up in tenements live ugly lives," the black agent said, "so they become adept at insulating themselves from the ugliness of others. They see nothing, they hear nothing, they know nothing. Their own situations are desperate, and they don't want to borrow the troubles of others."

Sid was in rare agreement with him. "I'll be very much surprised if the interrogation of the neighbors turns up anything positive. I suppose you found a lot of latent fingerprints?"

"A few hundred of them. We'll have the Identification Division working overtime tomorrow, I can tell you."

While they spoke the body of Carlotta Ruiz was removed from the apartment.

Linda saw two members of the State Police C.I.D. cover the girl with a sheet, and averted her gaze.

Both of her colleagues were aware of her discomfort. "I'll carry on here until we have the place scoured and scrubbed," Samson said. "What's next on your agenda?"

"I think we're due for a session at the federal lockup," Sid said.

Linda roused herself. "I want to talk to Ramon Garcia alone," she said. "You antagonize him, Sid, so it's best if you listen outside the door. There's always the chance he'll open up when I shock him with the news."

They ran the gauntlet of the reporters as they departed, with Sid repeating, "No comment," as they hurried to his car. A flurry of interest in the case was natural, particularly with the FBI and State Police involved, but Carlotta had been a nobody, and with luck the press and television reporters would turn their attentions elsewhere in the next day or two.

They parked in the basement garage of the lockup, and Linda questioned the Winthrop police sergeant in charge. "Does Ramon Garcia know what happened to his girl?"

"No. Somebody from the FBI called us, and we took away the prisoners' radios for the evening without giving them an explanation. They beefed, of course, but Garcia doesn't know a thing."

"I want to talk to him," Linda said.

"Alone, lady? That's dangerous!"

Linda saw no need to tell the sergeant she had disarmed Ramon at the time of his arrest. "Mr. Benjamin will be outside the door, and we'll leave it open," she said sweetly, giving the policeman her gun.

She was sitting at the bare table in the visiting room when Ramon was brought in, the guard who accompanied him quietly withdrawing.

"Why the hell don't you quit buggin' me?" he demanded. "I got a right to be left alone."

"I came here this evening," Linda said, "to tell you about Carlotta. I thought you'd want to know."

"If you're goin' to hand me some bull about her talkin', save your breath. She wouldn't talk to cops!"

"She can't," Linda said. "She's dead."

Ramon smiled. "You got to be kiddin'."

"She was murdered in your living room this afternoon. By someone who cut her throat and stabbed her." She watched him closely.

For an instant Ramon's eyes narrowed, but he remained composed and showed no other sign of surprise. "Who done it to her?" he asked, his voice calm.

"I'm hoping you can tell me."

"It wasn't me," he said, and laughed harshly. "I've had me the perfect alibi since you and them cops grabbed me this morning!"

"Who might have done it, Ramon?"

His shrug was scornful. "Beats me."

Linda shifted gears. "You don't seem very badly upset."

"Cryin' don't do no good. She was an A-okay chick, but there's others. Not that I'll be ballin' with anybody for a while, the way it looks. Unless you want to come back to my cell with me."

His indifference to Carlotta was even greater than Linda had imagined, and she felt a surge of anger on behalf of the dead girl. She couldn't allow her own emotions to show, however, and quickly regained command of herself. "Carlotta was your woman, and she's gone. If you had any feeling at all for her, you'll tell us who might have killed her. An old boyfriend, maybe—"

"I'm the only one she had."

"Except when Reyes made her go to bed with him."

"That didn't count!" For the first time he showed emotion.

"Maybe there were others."

"She didn't know hardly anybody in the States except me. Her family is in Puerto Rico someplace. Carlotta didn't know where, and didn't care. If she's dead, let her rest! And get off my back, lady. There's no law says I got to see you fifty times a day!"

He was returned to his cell, and the two agents didn't speak until they reached Sid's car.

Linda was subdued and reflective. "What do you think?"

"Garcia is tough. I'll have a bash at him tomorrow, and then Grant will have his innings, but it doesn't look as though either of us will get anything positive out of him."

"Do you think he knows, Sid?"

"I'm just a Special Agent. I don't read people's minds or crystal balls."

"I—I can't get that pathetic girl out of my mind. She was so defenseless. In spite of her bravado. And so badly abused by people who didn't care what they did to her!"

Sid covered her hand with his for a moment. "Don't let it get you down, baby. The old man may be right when he says we're onto something big."

"How can you be calm when that girl was killed this very day in cold blood?"

Sid knew better than to argue with her.

By the time they reached the Field Office the vast resources of the Bureau had been mobilized. Latent fingerprints were being transmitted to Washington as rapidly as facilities would permit, and the many photographs were being sent on to the Crime Laboratory, too, as quickly as they were developed. The samples of dirt, lint, and other debris found in the dead girl's apartment were sent on in a special pouch, along with carefully culled flecks of dried blood. It was possible that the killer had been injured during the murder, and laboratory tests would reveal whether the blood of one or more persons had been found at the scene of the crime.

A dozen agents were using telephones, and more than fifty people were at work on various aspects of the case. Linda thought it ironic that Carlotta Ruiz was attracting more attention in death than had been given her in the nineteen years of her life.

The office was quiet, as it always was when everyone was bearing down, but Sid became aware of an undercurrent of tension.

Linda sat down to dictate a raw interview report of her latest talk with Ramon Garcia.

Sid saw a red-faced agent hurrying out of the ASAC's office. Something very much out of the ordinary was happening, and he decided to make a check before he submitted his own verbal report. Johnny Hedley was emerging from the lab, and Sid went to him.

"Everybody around here is uptight tonight, kid. How come?"

Johnny spoke in a low tone. "Nobody has said anything to me, but I heard Mr. Grant telling a couple of the others in the lab just now. Mr. Butler pulled a big boner tonight, and he's mad at himself. I guess he's taking it out on everybody."

"What kind of a goof?"

"Well. There's a woman in Fairlawn who has some kind of an association with this fellow Reyes—"

"Louise Elizabeth Poole."

"That's the name. Well, Mr. Butler intended to put her under full surveillance tonight, but he was so busy he forgot all about it. And by the time an agent got out to her house the woman had gone off in her car. One of her neighbors said she was carrying a suitcase."

"Oh-oh." Sid made an immediate decision to avoid the ASAC.

"All the airports have been notified to keep watch for the woman, but we have no grounds to arrest her, and it would be easy for her to give us the slip. All she'd need would be a dark wig, or—"

"I know." Sid patted him on the shoulder. "Thanks, kid." He wandered away, checked with a Supervisor, who told him staff members were free to leave as they finished their immediate assignments.

Sid made a point of giving the ASAC's office a wide berth and went instead to Dave Daniels, who was cleaning up his own desk prior to going home.

"What do you think, Benjamin?" the SAC asked as soon as his subordinate appeared on his threshold.

"Not much of anything, sir. The murder and the ITSMV ring case have to be connected, but the pattern isn't clear yet. Maybe the tests they'll make down at the Crime Lab will turn up something."

"Maybe. I'm borrowing a half-dozen men from Boston to help out on this new wrinkle. I don't suppose you'd like to be an Acting Supervisor."

"I'll do what I'm told, Mr. Daniels."

Dave's smile was weary. "I didn't think you'd want it. Neither does Grant. Well, never mind. Before you leave for the night, do me a favor and get a clerk to wire Washington this copy of a cable I sent tonight to the Legat in Dorado."

As Sid obeyed it occurred to him that the scope of the case was growing. In various key United States embassies around the world the Legal Attachés—known in slang as Legats—were in actuality Special Agents who performed liaison duties for the Bureau. He was tempted to read the cable, but refrained. He was already up to his ears in the case, now complicated by the murder, and would be told anything else he needed to know.

Linda had just finished dictating her report, and he joined her.

"I was hoping you hadn't gone," she said. "You're taking me to Pete's for a nightcap I need more than I've ever needed a drink in my life."

A few minutes later they entered the bar and made their way to a table at the rear.

Neither of them saw Ray Merrill, who had stopped in for a quick drink on his way back from Washington. Unaware of the new crisis that had erupted at the Field Office, he was following regular procedures by waiting until morning to submit a report on what he had learned from Matt O'Brien and what he had read about the Galveston case.

Washington had depressed him, and he had been thinking about Linda, wondering how she would react if he called just to tell her he had returned. Now, damn it, here she was with Benjamin. At least he hadn't made a complete jackass out of himself by phoning her.

Ray quickly paid his bill, retrieved his suitcase from a corner, and went off to hail a taxi. Life was even drearier than he had thought it could be.

Linda removed her jacket and placed it on the banquette beside her shoulder bag. "I want a double Manhattan," she announced.

"You mean a bourbon on the rocks, don't you? Or bourbon and water? A Manhattan is a before-dinner drink."

"A double Manhattan," she insisted.

Sid placed the order.

"For the rest of the evening," she said, "we're not going to mention Carlotta. Or the ring case."

"Fine." He'd had no intention of bringing up the subject of the murder. She was already at the point of explosion.

Linda slugged down her drink, demanded another, and said, "Now I'll have a cigarette, if you'll be a gentleman and give me one."

"I thought you don't smoke." He offered her a cigarette.

"I do tonight because all rules are off. Tonight is different." She took a large swallow of her second double Manhattan.

He remembered a hostage-extortion case in which he had become emotionally involved, and knew how she felt.

Linda drained her glass before Sid finished his first drink.

He refused to order another for her. "We'd better grab a sandwich," he said. "We missed dinner tonight."

"I'll fix us something at my place," she said.

He agreed only because he wanted to deposit her safely at home. She was becoming unpredictable, and as the liquor took hold she might be more difficult to handle.

As they drove to her apartment she demanded and was given another cigarette. "I suppose," she said, "you think I'm being soft and falling apart just because I'm a woman."

"You're wrong," Sid said. "I've seen a lot of agents get upset when certain cases reach out and hit them across the back of the head. I've had it happen to me." He saw no reason to mention that she was in turmoil because she identified with Carlotta Ruiz and felt she had been at least partly responsible for the girl's death.

"You want to know something, Benjamin? You're okay." Linda giggled and leaned against him.

When they reached her apartment building he held her arm to steady her as they walked to the elevator, and silently took the door key from her when she fumbled with the lock.

Linda disappeared into the kitchen.

The living room was furnished in good taste, although he

couldn't have described the decor in other than a professional investigator's terms. He noted, however, that she was a plant nut; at least a score of house plants were either hanging from ceiling containers or resting on tables in front of a row of windows. She might be a Special Agent, but she had a feminine talent for creating an attractive atmosphere.

She reappeared, a stiff bourbon on the rocks in each hand, and had already consumed a portion of her drink.

"What about those sandwiches?" Sid asked, placing his unwanted drink on a coffee table.

"Later," she said. "There's lots of time to eat. We've got other things to do first." She staggered slightly as she crossed the room.

"I think," Sid said, "you should get to bed."

"Right on! We'll make a real night of it!"

"Not tonight," Sid said. "You aren't going to use sex as a cathartic, at least with me. You're going to sleep with me, baby, but you'll be sober, and you'll do it because you want me." He guided her into her bedroom, then left quickly, before he weakened and changed his mind.

7

The FBI Laboratory worked at top speed, but discovered no conclusive evidence that would solve the murder of Carlotta Ruiz. The hundreds of latent fingerprints found in her apartment were those of the girl herself and of Ramon Garcia. There were no prints left by Hernando Reyes Gomez other than on the empty Scotch bottle previously identified, nor were there prints left by anyone else.

The Soil Analysis Unit came up with fragmentary information that had to await further developments before it could be used. A few flecks of dirt found on the floor of the living room came from a type of soil not found in Connecticut or other states of the Northeastern United States. But it was not yet possible to pinpoint the locale from which these samples had come.

The Firearms and Toolmarks Unit reported that the knife used to kill the girl was not of American manufacture. Further research revealed that it had been made by a factory in São Paulo, Brazil, and was three to five years old. It had been wiped clean of fingerprints. But the Chemistry-Toxicology Unit found microscopic, dried beads of perspiration on the handle, and a preliminary analysis of the salt and other chemicals contained in the beads showed they were those of a male. The Serology Unit reported finding no blood other than that of the dead girl.

The most startling evidence in the case came from the autopsy performed by the head of the Pathology Department at the University, who was assisted by the Winthrop coroner. They discovered quantities of cocaine in the girl's system, a portion of it in her bloodstream and a minute quantity still in her stomach. They speculated, in an analysis with which scientists at the FBI Laboratory concurred, that Carlotta had been given cocaine, probably in its refined, white crystalline form, and that her throat had been cut within seconds of the time she had swallowed the drug.

It was also confirmed that her throat had been slashed before she had been stabbed. But the physicians were unable to determine whether she had still been alive at the time she had received the second blow.

Armed with the various findings, ASAC Joe Butler conferred at length with Supervisor Ray Merrill. "There's no way of knowing," he said, "whether the Ruiz girl was a habitual user of cocaine, whether she took it infrequently, or whether this was the first time."

"I think we can conclude, sir," Ray said, "that she was given the cocaine to lull any suspicions about her visitor that she may have entertained. The pathology report indicates she took it voluntarily, by mouth, and that it wasn't forced on her."

"Let's reconstruct the crime, Ray. The killer was a man, and the girl knew him sufficiently well to admit him to the apartment. In fact, she went into the living room with him and sat on the couch. He may have sat beside her, or perhaps stood over her. He gave her the cocaine, presumably pocketing the customary paper packet in which we assume it was wrapped. Are we agreed so far?"

"I think so, Joe. We know the girl was upset by the arrest of Ramon Garcia. Perhaps for that reason she didn't wait until she was alone again to take the dose of cocaine. She swallowed it immediately. Are we sure, by the way, that she didn't sniff it or take it in a hypodermic?"

"The pathology report is clear on that point. There were no needle marks anywhere on her body, and no residual remains of the drug in her nostrils or any other part of the nasal passages. So she must have swallowed it."

"As soon as she took it, then, the cocaine took effect. We know it's one of the fastest-moving drugs, and that the user feels the effects instantly. The girl's first reaction was that of having received a pleasant electric shock. While she was in the first stage of euphoria, even before the last of the cocaine went from her stomach into her bloodstream, which is something that takes place within seconds, the killer slashed her throat." Ray studied a set of photographs of the girl's body on the couch. "These pictures indicate she showed no fear, and didn't even raise a hand to protect herself. I'd say her throat was slashed before she realized she was about to be attacked. He worked fast."

The ASAC nodded. "Then, as she slumped forward, he drove the knife into her back. It was buried up to the hilt, which indicates that he was a man of physical strength. Someone weak would find it difficult to drive a knife into a body that deeply. As a final step, he had the presence of mind to wipe his fingerprints from the hilt before he left. But he wasn't all that calm. He forgot to close the front door of the apartment behind him."

"He could have had a different motive," Ray said. "Maybe he was afraid of leaving fingerprints on the door knob. Suppose, for instance, there was blood on a handkerchief he used to wipe the hilt of the knife. He may not have wanted to leave smears on the door knobs, inside or out. So it was simpler just to walk out, leaving the door wide open."

"That's a detail we may never learn," Joe said. "Now, we have no idea whether the cocaine was a gift, or whether the girl paid fifty dollars or more for it. It may be significant that she was given a shot of the pure stuff, which is very expensive on today's market. It wasn't cut or adulterated in any way."

"From what the Federal Drug Enforcement Agency tells me," Ray said, "there hasn't been much cocaine coming into Winthrop lately, which may or may not be meaningful. We also know that the principal source is South America, where the coca plant grows on high hillsides in the Andes. A lesser source is the mountains of Central America, particularly Dorado."

"I know what you're thinking," the ASAC said, "and I'm trying to resist the same temptation. Reyes has a Doradan background and maintains a home there. Cocaine is easy to buy in Ciudad Dorado. But we're wrong if we jump to a conclusion too fast. It would be very neat to connect him with the murder, but let's wait for a few more facts before we start believing he ordered her killed. Or did the job himself."

"One big fact stands out right now," Ray said. "I find it hard to believe the girl was killed simply because of what she may have known about the operations of the ITSMV ring. There's some other angle involved in all this."

"Could be, and again there's an obvious temptation. Drugs. The market for cocaine is extensive, and is growing rapidly as heroin becomes more difficult to obtain. We'll wait to see what the Legat down there tells us before we start building a new house of cards."

Bob Roberts had been the Legal Attaché at the United States Embassy in Ciudad Dorado for two and a half years, and he expected to stay for an additional two years until his retirement. There were far worse jobs in the Bureau, and he was content. He held the rank and received the pay of an SAC, and although his staff consisted only of one assistant and a stenographer, his duties were seldom arduous. He and Helen had become acclimated to the tropics, and day-to-day living could be fun.

To be sure, the pace sometimes galled him. Bob sat at a table in the old sidewalk café on the corner of the Avenida Presidente Beloman and the Calle de Santa Elena, trying to curb his impatience as he sipped a glass of tonic. The man he was meeting was late, but no one in Ciudad Dorado was ever on time. Things just didn't work that way.

Tourists from the cruise ship riding at anchor in the harbor were swarming all over the Avenida Presidente Beloman, taking advantage of free-port facilities to buy watches and cameras, jewelry and glassware and china. Soon, however, they would pile into buses for the customary ride to see the ancient Mayan temples high in the mountains. The shops would empty, and the streets would belong to the natives again.

Bob ordered another small bottle of chilled tonic, carefully instructing the apron-clad waiter not to bring any ice. Even after thirty-one months of living in Dorado he was afraid to trust the local water. The waiter, who knew him as a Yanqui by the cut of his seersucker suit, shrugged as he wandered off to the mahogany bar that stood inside the open doors of the main room. Other North Americans screamed if ice was lacking in their drinks.

Eventually a heavyset man in a rumpled, dark business suit climbed out of a chauffeur-driven limousine, adjusted his dark glasses on the bridge of his broad nose, and sauntered toward the waiting Legat. Luis Alvaro de Silvera was the Captain-General of Doradan police, the man directly responsible for the country's security, and his compatriots often were uncomfortable in his presence. According to vague stories never discussed at length, Alvaro employed unorthodox methods with great success when he found it necessary to interrogate prisoners.

A broad smile creased his dark face when he saw the waiting Yanqui, and his pleasure was genuine. Each year Alvaro returned to Quantico for a refresher course at the National Police School conducted by the FBI, and he liked to think of himself as a member of the Bureau. The Legat, who had to work with and through him, did nothing to discourage that opinion.

The two men embraced, shook hands, and then went through the ritual a second time before they seated themselves. Alvaro ordered coffee, with a shot of white rum in it, and then he and the Legat observed the Doradan amenities. Although they had seen each other only a few days earlier and had already conferred twice on the telephone earlier in the morning, each carefully inquired after the other's health, the welfare of wives and children, and the states of mind enjoyed by Presidente Beloman, the Ministers of Defense and Justice, and the recent head cold suffered by the U.S. Ambassador. They talked about the prospects of the various semi-finalists in the tennis matches being played at the country club, their respective golf scores, and a barracuda scare that had emptied the resort beaches the previous afternoon. They discussed coffee prices, the work being done by an archaeological expedition in some recently discovered Mayan ruins, and the fishing dispute between Guatemala and Nicaragua, in which Dorado was striving to remain neutral.

After a half-hour of chat Alvaro removed his sunglasses and placed them on the table, a sign that he was ready for business. "Very soon now," he said, "you'll see why I asked you to meet me here instead of the Café Toledo."

Bob had waited long enough for the information he was seeking, and wanted to play no games. "What did you find out from your Immigration Department?"

Alvaro unzipped a portfolio of hand-tooled crocodile and removed a sheet of paper. "Five days ago," he said. "Hernando

Reyes Gomez landed at Beloman Airport on flight three-sixty-eight of National Aero Dorado. Two days ago Louise Elizabeth Poole and Juan Garcia arrived at Beloman Airport on flight four-zero-one of Pan American Airways. I have had the flight manifests of the airlines checked also, as I have learned to do at the FBI Academy, and the results tally. Okay?"

"Fair enough. So far." The Legat knew now that Reyes had been in Dorado when the Ruiz girl had been killed, but was less certain that Garcia and the Poole woman were in the clear.

The Captain-General of Doradan police slid the sheet of paper into his leather portfolio and withdrew another. "You asked whether Señora Reyes is still here. She is not. Three days ago she flew to Peru to visit a sister." He chuckled like a man enjoying a smutty joke. "As you suggested, Roberto, I had the past records checked for one and one-half years. Señora Reyes has sisters also in Argentina, Uruguay, and Ecuador, as well as cousins in Venezuela and Colombia. A large family, scattered in many lands. Always she goes off for a visit just before the Señorita Poole arrives from the States for a visit. Always she returns a day or two after the Señorita Poole departs. How I wish my wife were that tolerant and understanding. Oh, no! Mine complains if I stop at the country club pool to inquire after the health of some young lady. Ah!" He broke off, put on his dark glasses again, and gestured toward the curb.

A chauffeur-driven Cadillac Seville had pulled up in front of the sidewalk café, and three persons alighted. Bob Roberts recognized all of them from photos the Bureau had sent him.

Hernando Reyes Gomez looked urbane and well groomed in a handsome suit of white gabardine, white suede shoes, and, in spite of the late-morning heat, a black silk ascot. Juan Garcia, squat in a short-sleeved sports shirt and plaid slacks, was a hairy man with powerful arms, and the Legat studied him with interest. It was difficult to determine whether he was a strong-arm bodyguard or something more. He would bear further observation.

The full attention of everyone in the crowded establishment was riveted on Louise Elizabeth Poole, who showed off her figure in hip-hugger pants of lilac silk and a matching, bare midriff top with a low-cut neckline and billowing sleeves. Conscious of the stir she was creating, she preceded her companions to a reserved table under an awning at the far side of the café.

"How did you know they'd be coming here, Luis?" Bob asked.

Alvaro's laugh was proud. "I have had Reyes's telephones tapped, of course. At the Academy I learned all the new techniques."

No court order authorizing the establishment of a wiretap was necessary in a country that paid only lip service to liberty and the principle of personal freedoms. But Bob knew the FBI could do nothing to halt abuses of the technical expertise it taught in its National Police courses. The State Department asked that places be held for representatives of various friendly nations, so these openings were made. The safeguards that protected the privacy of U.S. citizens were ignored in these lands, and the Bureau was helpless, unable to intervene. The system would improve only when the State Department became more discriminating in its choice of countries entitled to benefit from the advantages enjoyed by the graduates of the FBI schools.

Bob had no intention of delivering a lecture to someone incapable of understanding the need for controls. Instead he sipped his tonic and watched the trio.

Reyes smoked a long, black cigar of the kind that came from Cuba, sipped a weak Scotch and water, and looked at the pedestrians, particularly the girls who copied New York fashions. Juan Garcia gulped a dark Doradan rum, then ordered another. The Poole woman, oblivious to her surroundings, drank tiny quantities of white wine from a glass she had filled with ice. The trio neither conversed nor communicated without words; for all practical purposes each was alone.

Alvaro's eyes glistened behind his sunglasses. "If I have good luck and the saints guide me," he said, "I'll have an opportunity to arrest that woman and question her. I'll conduct the interrogation myself, in private, and it will last all night."

Bob realized the Captain-General of Doradan police was not speaking idly, but meant precisely what he said.

The Poole woman glanced at each table in turn, found no one

who interested her, and, taking a container of polish from her shoulder bag, painted her fingernails.

Juan Garcia stared into his glass as he drank. A bodyguard would have sized up everyone in the establishment, but Garcia was lost in his thoughts, indicating he was a lieutenant rather than a mere hired hand. He appeared well able to look after himself in a fight, and Bob's lifetime of experience as a Special Agent told him the man was dangerous. That estimate would be sent to the Bureau in code before the day ended.

Reyes himself was alert to everything happening around him. He might amuse himself by gazing at the swaying hips of female pedestrians, but he missed nothing in the café or on the street. Certainly he was aware of Bob's scrutiny, and suddenly he issued a silent challenge, staring across the café.

Reyes was indulging in machismo, which offered a key to his character, but Bob refused to be the first to look away. Not that he really cared, but he wanted to see how the man reacted. "I think," he told the Captain-General of Doradan police, "that our friend knows both of us."

Before Alvaro could reply, Reyes rose and sauntered across the café.

Bob elected to insult the man by remaining seated, and Alvaro followed his colleague's lead.

"What have I done, gentlemen, that arouses your interest in me?" Reyes's voice was quiet, his unaccented English that of the Middle West.

Alvaro grinned up at him. "I keep an eye on everyone, especially Doradans, and you hold dual citizenship."

"And you, sir?"

Bob Roberts shrugged.

"You followed me here!" Reyes said.

"You flatter yourself," Bob said. "We were here long before you showed up. If you have problems you want to discuss, I'll be glad to see you at the Embassy."

A hint of doubt appeared in Reyes's eyes, and he hesitated for an instant, then turned away.

Bull's-eye, Bob thought, and waited until the man moved out

of range. "Luis, how does he earn his living? According to your official records, I mean."

"The claim on his personnel file says he's retired. Which may or may not be true. If I could afford to hire a woman like that blonde, I'd lock the two of us in my bedroom and never come out from one year to the next."

"Reyes doesn't know she exists."

"I beg to differ with you, Roberto. Their knees touch under the table."

"So they do. I stand corrected," Bob said. "Luis, the Bureau has reason to believe that Reyes is the sparkplug of a rather big ITSMV ring, and you can help us pin him down."

"I am always happy to help my Bureau brothers!"

"Good. Just tell your people at the docks to keep watch for shipments of second-hand automobiles in good condition. Get me the VINs of those cars, and their secret identification numbers. If and when an illegal shipment arrives, watch Reyes to see whether he takes a rakeoff, and if he does, how much."

"At least two loads of automobiles arrive every week," Alvaro said. "The most recent was several American Motors Ambassadors, which were put ashore yesterday. I'll have every car searched, as you wish, Roberto. But those that may carry false identifications will be very difficult to trace back to their original sources. Today's criminal is both wise and shrewd, so even the secret numbers could be changed by the time it takes for a car to travel all the way from the States to Ciudad Dorado."

Bob understood the situation, and was annoyed when Alvaro parroted basics he had picked up at the Academy. "I know we're scraping the barrel, Luis, but our best chance of finding evidence against Reyes that will stick is here, not in the States. A Ford worth four thousand dollars at home will sell for eight thousand here, so Reyes is willing to take risks. Every logical sign points to his guilt, and I'm relying on you to nail him for us."

The ITSMV ring case continued to gather momentum. Reports from Field Offices all over the United States piled up in Winthrop, until Joe Butler indicated that more than a hundred Ford Granadas had disappeared from All-American lots. Only a very few were recovered, however, and the investigation appeared to be stymied.

No additional Mercury Monarchs or large Buicks were taken in Connecticut or elsewhere, and even Supervisor Ray Merrill began to doubt his thesis that the thefts were related. Efforts to locate the missing vehicles were intensified, but no solid evidence was found.

The murder of Carlotta Ruiz also remained unsolved.

"We're not going to quit," SAC Dave Daniels told his agents. "Double your pressures, and let's see what kind of results we can get."

The one advantage enjoyed by the Bureau was that its national dragnet remained in effect. The younger agents, now spending the bulk of their time in other work, doubted the ITSMV ring case and the murder of Carlotta Ruiz would be solved. But Joe Butler didn't share their pessimism. "Sooner or later," he told Ray Merrill, "shoes will start dropping on the floor. With more than a hundred cars stolen in the same way from the same source, the ring that's responsible stands to make a huge profit. This is big business, so a lot of people are involved, and sooner or later the breaks will start falling our way."

"I hate having to depend on luck," Ray said. "I know the Bureau covers the whole country, but this time we seem to be up against a gang that's too smart for us."

"Have patience," Joe said. "And faith."

His personal crisis required increasing quantities of both. A date had been set for his son's trial in Federal District Court, but Joey remained intransigent, unwilling to cooperate with the authorities or even with the lawyer appointed by the court to represent him. His mother was drinking heavily, and Joe, finding it difficult to concentrate on his work, was tempted to ask for a leave of absence. He refrained, however, afraid he would lose his sanity if he had nothing to occupy his mind other than the problems Joey had created.

Linda Bartlett made the solution of Carlotta Ruiz's murder a personal crusade, but achieved nothing. She paid repeated visits to the federal lockup, but Ramon Garcia was still silent, withdrawn, and totally unwilling to talk. Threats of a longer prison sentence failed to move him.

Ray Merrill felt that the failure to solve the ITSMV ring case was a reflection on his personal talents, and one evening after work, when Linda went with him to Pete's Bar & Grill, he spoke his mind freely to her. "We've hit a dead end," he said, "and I'm strictly to blame."

"No one is to blame!"

"I know better. I'll wait another couple of months to see what develops, and then I'll get out."

"Where do you want to transfer, Ray?" Linda realized she would miss him, and felt sorry for him.

"No transfer. I'll resign."

She was shocked. "You can't!"

"I've let down the Bureau," he said. "Mr. Daniels and Joe Butler have been depending on me, and I've fallen on my face. I'm supposed to be an expert on ITSMV ring cases, and I know there's something in this case that would give us the lead we need. I'm sure of it. For all the good it does me. I've thought myself stupid, and I can't put my finger on it."

"What would you do?" Linda asked.

"Oh, there are a lot of plants that would take me to do security work, either running the department or being number two man. I think that candy factory up in Plymouth would hire me."

"But that would be so dreary, Ray!"

"Not necessarily. I might not earn much, but I could get along. I'm not really too old to marry again, so I might even settle down for keeps in a place like Plymouth."

She wondered if she could improve his mood. "I didn't know you were thinking about marriage, Ray. Do you have anybody in particular in mind?"

He raised his glass to her. "One girl, but she seems to prefer younger men." He took care not to mention that he knew she had dated Sid Benjamin twice within the past week.

Linda realized what he was saying, and knew of no graceful exit. "A person's age is strictly a state of mind."

"You think so?"

"I know it. You're just discouraged because this case has come to a standstill. For the moment. You've told me yourself that eventually we'll start picking up leads."

"I'm not sure I really believe that. I've been whistling in the dark to keep up the morale of you younger people."

Linda smiled, then whistled. "How is that?"

"Nice."

"You'll feel all the difference in the world when you're promoted to Ay-sack and get moved to a new assignment."

"It won't happen. And even if it did, I wouldn't welcome it."

"I can't believe that, Ray."

"But it's true. For a good reason, and you may as well know it." Ray sucked in his breath. "You're the reason."

She had forced the confrontation, and now she had to run. "Don't talk like that, Ray. Please."

"You don't feel the way I do."

"No, and I don't think you do, either. You've been lonely after your divorce. And this case has frustrated you. I've been someone from the Bureau you can talk to, that's all."

"Say it." Ray became bitter. "I'm too old for you."

"That's drivel, and you know it," Linda said. "You're just feeling sorry for yourself, and you don't know me well enough to be in love with me. There's nothing in the world wrong with you, Ray Merrill, that a solution of the ITSMV ring case and the murder of poor little Carlotta won't cure."

The first break took place in Taos, New Mexico, when a Ford Granada driven by a retired businessman living in the city was struck in the rear by another car. The policeman who wrote the routine report submitted the Vehicle Identification Number of the Granada to NCIC as a matter of course, and the desk sergeant was not surprised by the computer's reply to the effect that the car was one of those stolen from All-American Rentals.

Less than an hour later a Special Agent from the local FBI Resident Agency called on the owner at his home.

The man had no hesitation in showing his papers, which appeared to be in order.

"Where did you buy this car?" the agent asked.

"Vera Cruz, Mexico. Just last month. My wife and I were driving, and my old car suddenly fell apart. The porter at our hotel said he knew somebody who might have a bargain for us, and it sure was. I paid only three thousand for it."

"Can you describe the person who sold it to you?"

The businessman was becoming troubled. "As a matter of fact, I only spoke to him on the telephone. He delivered the car to our hotel, and left the keys for me. I tried it out, liked it, and left the money in an envelope for him. In traveler's checks. That night I found the title, properly transferred to me. Do you mind telling me what's wrong?"

"I'm sorry to tell you that the title is phony. You bought a stolen car."

"My God! But I paid cash for it!"

"Your Granada belongs to All-American Car Rentals, and will be claimed by the insurance company."

The elderly man was badly upset. "My income is limited, and I can't dig up another three thousand. I'm out the money, and I'm out of a car, too! What recourse do I have?"

"I'm afraid," the agent said, "you'd have to find the man who sold you the car, bring charges against him, and hope you could collect from him."

The man buried his face in his hands. "I have no way of getting back down to Vera Cruz. He probably gave me a phony name. The hotel porter even made a point of saying he wasn't personally acquainted with the guy."

Virtually every agent who had worked on stolen car cases had seen similar situations.

"No wonder I got such a bargain," the old man said. "I was fleeced. I should have had the sense to know there was a catch in the deal!"

Less than forty-eight hours later an even more significant incident took place on a highway outside Laredo, Texas, where State Police found a Mercury Monarch sedan abandoned at the side of the road. It was in mint condition except for the back seat, which had been ripped out with a knife.

An NCIC check showed that the car had been stolen in Winthrop, Connecticut, six and one-half weeks earlier.

Then a local investigation revealed that the car had been driven across the Mexican border from the city of Nuevo Laredo less than an hour earlier. The two occupants had been a middle-aged American couple, who had shown drivers' licenses and credit cards as identification. The brief notation made by Immigration authorities indicated they had crossed the border into

Mexico only for lunch. U.S. Customs records indicated that the couple had made no purchases, and had been subjected only to a cursory inspection on their return.

The FBI entered the case, two Special Agents from the Laredo Resident Agency receiving the assignment. Within minutes they discovered that the Mercury was using forged Texas license plates. A routine check of the drivers' license numbers quickly revealed that they, too, were false.

An alert was issued to all law-enforcement agencies within a radius of five hundred miles, but the call was hampered by the inability of either Customs or Immigration officials to provide a clear description of the pair. Many hundreds of persons traveled between Laredo and Nuevo Laredo each day, and there had been no reason to pay particular attention to the couple.

The vehicle was scoured for latent fingerprints and other clues that might lead to the identification of the pair. Several prints were found, but did not match any on file at the Bureau in Washington. Nothing else in the car proved to be of value, so —for all practical purposes—the couple had vanished.

Further investigation revealed that something had been concealed under the cover of the back seat, where a portion of the stuffing had been removed to make a space for it. Presumably the package had been placed there to hide it from Customs authorities. Samples of the stuffing and of the cloth cover itself were sent without delay to the FBI Laboratory for analysis.

Less than a week later a third incident took place in the Panama Canal Zone, when a Ford Granada driven by a Panamanian was rammed by a truck. The Canal Zone police sent the Vehicle Identification Number through NCIC as a matter of routine, and it was quickly learned that the car was another that had been stolen from All-American Rentals.

The Panamanian, a respectable businessman in his thirties, had impeccable credentials and was able to prove that he had paid for the car with a check drawn on an American bank in the Canal Zone. He had paid $4,500, and had made out the check to one José Anasto, who was not known in either the Canal Zone or the Republic of Panama. It was apparent that he, too, had been the victim of a swindler using an alias.

Joe Butler had a session with Ray Merrill, the overall case still coming within the jurisdiction of the Winthrop Field Office, where it had originated. "We're finally getting some movement," the ASAC said, "and all the signs point to activity in Central America."

"They sure do," Ray said. "Vera Cruz, Nuevo Laredo, and then the Canal Zone. It doesn't take a genius to realize that suspicion points hardest at our friend Reyes, in Dorado."

"You think he shipped a batch of cars down to that part of the world by freighter?"

"That's the natural assumption. If he's using a network of dealers he can drop off a dozen or so Granadas in various countries and make a real killing. What gets me is his audacity in not even changing the VINs."

"He had no need to change them."

"I know," Ray said. "The reason his operation is so successful is because he keeps it simple."

"Your theory about the Mercury and Buick thefts being tied into the ring's operations is becoming more logical. Have you seen the laboratory reports on the Mercury?"

"Yes, sir, and they're negative. The seat cover was slashed with a blunt knife, otherwise unidentifiable. Nothing was found to indicate the contents of the package or bundle hidden in the stuffing other than that it didn't weigh very much. The stuffing was barely squashed in a few spots. So we don't have much to go on."

"Except for a few basics," the ASAC said. "The Granadas are very definitely being sold. Out of the country. But the Mercury was being used as a delivery vehicle."

"And that doesn't make much sense," Ray said, "because there's a good market for Mercuries in Latin America, and one of them will bring a much higher price than a Ford."

"I've sent a request to all Customs and Immigration officials on the Mexican border to keep watch for Mercuries and Buicks. Field Offices in the area have been notified, and they'll check out these cars for us. We're into another long-haul situation where the breaks come slowly, little by little."

"I hope the Legat in Dorado is keeping a close watch on Reyes and his friends."

"He has the local police there sitting on Reyes's neck."

"Are they reliable?"

"Well, the head of the police has come up to the Academy for refresher courses the past five or six years in a row. So I'd guess he's fairly solid. As to the people who work under him, who knows?"

"I'd guess a lot of them can be had," Ray said. "Graft is pretty common down in that part of the world."

"As it is in most places," Joe said. "They're more open about corruption in some Latin American countries. That's the only real difference." Suddenly he became grim. "There's one other development that may or may not be significant. Reyes's lady friend, Louise Elizabeth Poole, arrived at Kennedy this morning via Pan Am on the night flight from Ciudad Dorado. The New York Field Office put a tail on her at our request, and she's now returned to Fairlawn. I've ordered a round-the-clock surveillance. I made a real hash of it when she went away, and I don't intend to repeat that mistake. God knows whether we'll pick up anything from her, and a full surveillance uses a lot of manpower, but it can't be helped. Eventually we'll land something in the net."

Ray sighed. He constantly preached patience to youngsters like Johnny Hedley, but it wasn't easy to exercise all that much himself. Even though he knew that virtually every investigation was painstaking, and that results rarely were achieved within a brief period.

"I know how you feel," the ASAC said, surprising him.

"There's one angle of this case that puzzles me more and more," Ray said, "If I can find the answers to a couple of questions in my mind, I'm sure we'll be much closer to busting the ring wide open."

Joe leaned back in his swivel chair and waited.

"We learned of Reyes's existence in two ways. Hedley got an anonymous telephone call one night. A few days later he spotted a want-ad in the Winthrop *Herald,* offering a Mercury for sale. With Reyes's name on the ad. Does that strike you as peculiar?"

"Not particularly."

"It does me," Ray said. "Let's assume for the purpose of discussion that Reyes is the kingpin of the ring that has stolen more than one hundred Granadas. He'll sell them—especially if he concentrates on the Latin American market—for a half-million dollars or more. His shipping, the costs of preparing false papers, and the payoffs to the punks who stole the cars for him are low. Even with payoffs to other key people in his organization, he's certain to make a whopping profit."

"I'd guess he'd profit at least a quarter of a million for himself. A good take on one operation."

"Right, sir. So why would a big wheel in that position expose himself to us by putting his own name on a want-ad for the sale of one car? It doesn't make sense."

Joe leaned forward and slapped his desk. "You're right. An obvious fact that's been staring us in the face since this case first started to shape up. As I recall it, neither Reyes nor the car was still around when we sent some agents over to the apartment the very next morning."

"That's correct, Joe. Young Garcia and the girl who was murdered didn't know anything about a car for sale. Or pretended not to know."

The ASAC was more animated than he had been at any time since the arrest of his son. "What you're getting at," he said, "is that the ad ostensibly offering a Mercury Monarch for sale wasn't intended for that purpose at all."

"It could have been a message to someone," Ray said.

Joe shook his head. "As simple and basic as that. Put a watch on all the major newspapers in the state again, and let's see if a similar ad turns up one of these days."

"Yes, sir."

"Let Hedley supervise it, but use a couple of stenographers to do the actual checking of the ads. We're spreading ourselves pretty thin, and we can't spare an agent full-time for the job."

Johnny was getting very chummy with the young Talbot girl, and would love having her working for him. The arrangement was going to be satisfactory for everyone concerned.

"Let's double back to what we were talking about earlier," the ASAC said, "the use of the Mercury abandoned outside Laredo as a delivery vehicle. Did the lab report indicate the approximate size of the package or bundle hidden in the back seat?"

"Yes, sir. About eighteen inches long, maybe twelve inches wide, and eight to twelve inches deep."

"Small," Joe said. "And so valuable that the people who brought the bundle across the border didn't mind abandoning an automobile with a sale value of five thousand dollars in this country. Eight or nine thousand in Latin America."

Ray felt excitement stir. "Brazilian emeralds, perhaps. Or Andean diamonds. You could get a lot of jewels into a bundle that size."

The ASAC picked up a pen and began to write on a sheet of scrap paper. "It could be," he said, "that Reyes's ITSMV operation is only a minor part of his overall work."

"Gold bars are a possibility," Ray said, "but I doubt it. Gold is so heavy it would have pressed down the seat stuffing quite hard, and the lab would have picked up that fact."

"The most obvious answer," Joe said, "is drugs."

Ray snapped his fingers. "Of course. A pack of pure, number four heroin that size would weigh only a few ounces, but it would be worth a fortune. I can check that out with the Drug Enforcement Agency crowd, although I hesitate to call them in on the case until we have more facts."

"Hold off," Joe said. "We'll wait until we have more than surmises."

Ray didn't need to be told that no Bureau executive liked to call in other government agencies and bureaus until it became necessary. The FBI did its best work when it developed a case "inside the house," and utilized the assistance of others only when the outlines of an investigation became clear.

Over the years an investigator developed an intuition that shed light in dark corners. FBI agents had been known to say, "Dig here," when searching for bodies in a large lake, and had seen their judgment vindicated. The process, grounded in accumulated experience based on the knowledge that most criminals followed similar behavior patterns, was instinctive rather than consciously cerebral. A senior agent relied on his inner radar, and his subordinates scoffed at their peril.

FBI agents were not alone in acquiring these hunches. Scotland Yard representatives who visited Bureau installations reported that some of their older men sometimes peered with success into the same crystal ball, and several top members of the Sûreté in Paris had enjoyed phenomenal success in the same manner. A few detectives had achieved international reputations based on their uncanny ability to ferret out criminals in difficult cases, and two, a sergeant in San Francisco and an inspector in Singapore, were believed by their colleagues to possess occult powers, which they themselves denied.

Many bits and pieces fell into place in Joe Butler's mind, and he spoke with a calm certainty that defied logic. "Cocaine," he said. "The ITSMV ring has a side venture more profitable than selling stolen cars. They're smuggling cocaine into the United States."

Ray didn't see how he had reached that conclusion, but was in no position to argue with him.

"In the present market," the ASAC said, "cocaine is worth three times the price of heroin, ounce for ounce. The coca plant grows in the highlands of Dorado, so it should be easily available to someone who has Reyes's money and connections. And I'm not forgetting the Ruiz girl died right after somebody fed her a jolt of cocaine."

Ray was thoughtful. "Are you suggesting the want-ad in the *Herald* was a notice to some dealer to pick up a shipment of cocaine?"

"That's possible and reasonable," Joe said, "although we don't yet know how their M.O. works. Cocaine is one of the most difficult drugs to unearth, unfortunately, because the addict can swallow or sniff it. They don't need pipes or hypodermics or any other paraphernalia. All I have right now is a gut feeling, but I'm prepared to back it up. I'll ask the Legat in Dorado to look into the possibility. And I'll request the Federal Court to issue a warrant so we can make a thorough search of the Poole woman's house."

The Winthrop Field Office was placed on an extended overtime schedule, so Friday evening was like any other night of the week. With the exception of those who had drawn weekend duty, however, most of the staff looked forward to Saturday noon. Johnny Hedley made a tennis date with Lisa Talbot, both of them keeping silent about the engagement so no one from the office would be in a position to tease them.

Carolyn Daniels persuaded her husband to take the afternoon

off, arguing that he had spent every Saturday at his desk since coming to Winthrop. He agreed only because it was essential that he look after his spring planting if he hoped to have a flower garden that summer.

Joe Butler went to the federal lockup for another brief visit with his taciturn son, who rebuffed him again. Then he went home to find that Stella, who had been drinking steadily since midmorning, was in an advanced state of intoxication. They quarreled before he put her to bed, and with little else to occupy his time he tried to watch a baseball game on television. Unable to concentrate, he, too, had a few drinks too many.

Ray Merrill asked Linda Bartlett to drive to a country inn for lunch, but she excused herself on the grounds that she badly needed to spend a few hours doing some overdue shopping. So he ate alone at Pete's. Then, with time heavy on his hands, he wandered back to the office, hating himself because he was sick of the place.

Samson Grant and Sid Benjamin had an assignment. Armed with a search warrant issued by the Federal District Court, they drove out to Fairlawn, laying aside their mutual antagonisms sufficiently to ride together in the former's car.

Before approaching the house of Louise Elizabeth Poole they made a stop at the corner, where other agents had staked out an observation post in a storeroom on the top floor of a small, private secondary school. There they received a report from one of the pair on duty.

"For the past couple of hours," the agent said, "our friend has been sunning herself on her deck. She's wearing a skimpy one-piece bathing suit that's an invitation to rape, and I wish the Ay-sack had given me your assignment."

"If we need any help from you fellows," Samson said, "we'll signal."

He and Sid went on to the house, where they parked across the driveway to prevent the departure of the young woman's Porsche. Then they rang the door chimes repeatedly.

Many minutes passed before Louise Elizabeth Poole came to the door in an outfit which concealed neither her tan nor her figure. She recognized Samson and tried to close the door.

He inserted a foot in the opening. "Sorry, ma'am, but you'll have to let us in." He handed her the warrant.

Her green eyes became icy as she read it. "Why don't you turkeys go chase some Red spies and leave me alone?" she demanded.

Sid eyed her with lazy insolence as she admitted them to the house. "You turn my partner and me on," he said, "so we keep inventing excuses to come out here."

Louise Elizabeth Poole was not flattered. "Well, you goons don't turn me on. What do you want?"

Samson adopted the tactic of allowing Sid to flirt with her while he took the firm approach. "Do you have any firearms here?"

"Me?" Her laugh was brittle. "I couldn't even shoot a bow and arrow, although you inspire me to take lessons on a blowpipe."

Sid laughed.

But Samson remained stern. "Any imported liquor that didn't come through Customs?"

"You're wasting your time. I have a few gallon jugs of California white wine, and that's all."

"How about drugs?"

"You've got to be kidding," Louise Elizabeth Poole said. "I'm allergic to grass, and only a nut would go for the strong stuff. I dare you bastards to find one law I've broken, just one."

"We'll have a look around," Sid said, "and you're so adorable we hope you'll keep us company."

They spent several hours searching the house from cellar to attic, looking for contraband in all of the obvious places and in scores of others where Special Agents were trained to hunt. Both men realized they were wasting their time; the young woman obviously knew she was under FBI scrutiny and was giving the Bureau no excuse to place her under arrest.

"How is our chum?" Samson asked as they examined the contents of the cosmetic jars and pots that sat in long rows on her dressing table.

"I didn't know you had any friends."

"I'm speaking of Hernando." Samson knew that sometimes

the shock of a sudden declaration had an effect.

Louise Elizabeth Poole didn't blink. "I'm afraid I don't know the gentleman."

"You were seen with him, very recently, in Ciudad Dorado."

"Oh, *that* Hernando," she said, and fell silent.

They worked their way upstairs, then back down again, searching everywhere.

"I'd reward you for not messing up my lingerie drawers," the young woman said, "but I don't want to encourage you to come back."

"We're hard to discourage, honey," Sid told her. "We keep turning up like counterfeit money."

She poured herself a goblet of white wine before escorting them to the door. "I don't know if you were just fishing or were looking for something specific," she said, "but whatever it was, you won't find it here. The FBI may have a long memory, but mine is even longer, and you aren't going to catch me in your buzz saw."

"Thanks for giving us your cooperation," Sid said.

"I didn't." An innocent smile lighted her lovely face. "The only thing I'd give you would be a dose of syphilis." The door closed.

"Well, that killed an afternoon," Sid said as they started to drive back to Winthrop.

"It may not have been as much of a waste of time as you think," Samson said.

"Come off it, Grant! No firearms. No drugs. She knows we'd like to nab her, so she's keeping herself very clean."

"I'm speaking of the psychological effect. The woman knows we're doing more than casual snooping. Soon Reyes will know it, too. You can bet she'll write or phone him that we combed her house."

"What of it?" Sid demanded. "We've come away empty-handed, so they enjoy the last laugh."

"I disagree. Assuming that Reyes is engaging in shady enterprises—which we must assume—the fact that the Bureau is keeping close tabs on him has got to have an effect."

Sid's laugh was derisive. "Sure. He'll take greater care not to get caught."

"Admitted," Samson said. "But a close watch will still bug him. Not even the most accomplished crook is all that super-cool, and he may become rattled or panic. Sooner or later he'll make a mistake. All of them do."

"Now you sound like the Ay-sack or Grandma Merrill. I could break this case open. My own way."

"Unfortunately," Samson said, "your methods are illegal."

"I'm not going to get into another hassle with you," Sid said, "any more than I'm going to have another debate with Linda. I've forbidden her to even mention the Bureau tonight."

Samson knew Benjamin and Bartlett were dating frequently, and he wondered whether they were becoming serious. But their private lives were strictly their own business. Personally, he would never be able to marry a woman agent. He threw everything he had into his work, but if he didn't get away from it at night he'd go crazy.

"Ever been to Seaside, Grant?"

"The amusement park? Ferris wheels aren't my bag. Or riding around in little electric cars that smack into each other."

"You don't know what you're missing," Sid said. "Go with the right girl, and Seaside can be a tremendous experience!"

The prisoners in the federal lockup were fed their last meal of the day promptly at 4:30 P.M. They were required to stand at the doors of their cells at 4:25, and one by one they were admitted to the corridor, where they moved into line. No conversation was permitted, and the Winthrop police who were in charge escorted any talker back to his cell, causing him to miss the meal.

Twenty-three men were in the line, and they shuffled in silence to the refectory, a gloomy room that smelled of grease. Three women were being held in the lockup, too, but they were given their meals elsewhere, and had no contact with the men. An armed guard stood at each of the four corners of the refectory, and assistant U.S. Marshals were stationed at the front door and the entrance to the kitchen.

At a signal from the Marshal in charge the prisoners sat, and thereafter were permitted to talk. Joey Butler accepted a plate of meatloaf, boiled potatoes, and coarsely chopped spinach from an extortionist who had the kitchen duty that night. Looking at his meal in disgust, he began to eat listlessly with a thick wooden spoon. Knives and forks were unknown in the refectory.

"Meatloaf again," he said. "I don't think the cook knows how to fix anything else. And to think I used to like it." He refrained from adding, "At home." Joey couldn't allow himself to think about home. Or his mother. Or his Bureau martinet of a father. Sometimes, when they sneaked into his mind and caught him unawares, he became shaken and confused, and he hated the feeling.

Ramon Garcia didn't bother to look across the table. "What the hell," he said. "Food is food." He shoveled in his meal, gulping it with amazing speed.

"If you want the rest of mine," Joey said, "you're welcome to it."

"Yeah?" Ramon looked at him with suspicion. "I ain't got enough cigarettes to pay you."

"I don't want any pay," Joey said. "If you can eat this slop, more power to you. It's better than letting it go to waste." Now, he thought, he sounded like his mother.

"Thanks." Ramon reached for the plate and began to devour the other prisoner's meal. "How soon you going on trial?"

"In a few weeks," Joey said. "The lawyer the court appointed to represent me says they can't hold me any longer than that without trial. How about you?"

"I dunno," Ramon said, "and I don't give a shit. They're gonna send me up for five to ten, no matter what. So it don't matter."

Joey realized that if he thought about his forthcoming trial and the prison term that would follow it he'd have another of his tortured, sleepless nights. So he changed the subject with an effort. "Saturday night," he said.

"Yeah. We'll get us some joints. The good stuff. And a couple of chicks. Then we'll be all set for the night." Ramon's laugh was bitter.

Joey smiled wryly. "They've got a movie for us tonight."

"Like what?"

"You won't believe it. Mickey Mouse and Bugs Bunny shorts. That's all, folks."

Ramon cursed at length.

Joey lighted a cigarette, offered the other prisoner one, and sipped his muddy coffee. "In jail," he said, "you get nutty ideas. You try not to think about girls, so all kinds of things come into your head. You know what I'd like to do? Play a game of chess."

"You're on," Ramon said. "Seein' as this is Saturday, they give us two hours in the recreation room."

"You play chess?" Joey couldn't hide his astonishment.

"My brother taught me when I was a kid." Ramon was proud. "He knows everythin', my brother."

Joey didn't want to say he had been taught by his father, and consequently was almost a master in his own right. Feeling dubious about the other prisoner's talents, he didn't want to hurt Garcia's feelings. "I'm pretty good at chess," he said.

Ramon's quick smile was cocky. "Two cigarettes a game," he said. "Take it or leave it."

Joey had no choice. Besides, he really wanted a game of chess. "You're on," he said.

At precisely 4:50 P.M. the prisoners shuffled out of the refectory, and those who wished were permitted to adjourn to the recreation room for two hours.

The drive into the mountains behind Ciudad Dorado ordinarily took the better part of a half-day. But Luis Alvaro de Silvera, behind the wheel of his own car, negotiated the narrow, rutted roads with the expertise of a racing driver and the daring of a madman. He negotiated hairpin turns at high speed, oblivious to drops of several thousand feet to the lush pineapple plantations and jungles below. Leaning on his horn when roaring through villages, he sent peasants, small children, and assorted fowl scattering in all directions. When he approached a car coming in the opposite direction he played his own version of Russian roulette, forcing the driver of the other vehicle to back up to a siding and crowd onto it so Luis could pass.

Legat Bob Roberts thought of himself as a reasonably courageous man. As a street agent he had emerged the victor in a shootout with a band of kidnappers, and subsequently had won additional honors when he had killed a saboteur in a gun battle. Now, perhaps, advancing age was making him cautious. He couldn't look ahead, and he averted his gaze from the abyss that loomed below every time Luis spun around a curve. The car was air-conditioned, but he was sweating.

They swept past a banana plantation that occupied both sides of a pass between two peaks of more than eleven thousand feet, and Luis announced in triumph, "The backside. I made it in only two hours!"

"Going back," Bob said, "let's take it a bit slower so I can enjoy the scenery."

Luis chuckled but did not reduce his breakneck speed until they came to a steep, ascending section of the road. Then, taking the stub of his cigar from his mouth, he pointed toward a field that lay behind a steel fence topped with barbed wire.

Bob followed his gaze, and saw row after row of plants under cultivation. Many were six to eight feet high, with straight stems and thin, narrow leaves, oval-shaped and opaque. Yellow flowers grew in clusters on some of the plants, and on others had been succeeded by red berries.

Luis reached a steel gate, where he drew to a halt for a muttered exchange with three soldiers wearing the baggy gray uniforms of the Doradan army, all armed with submachine guns. One of the guards, who appeared to be in charge, raised a hand in a sloppy half-salute, and Luis put the car into gear again.

There were similar plants on both sides of the road, and Luis stopped when they reached a clearing.

They climbed out, and a searing blast of heat struck Bob, but a moment later a fluttering of a cooler breeze from the mountain heights made it possible for him to breathe.

He followed the Captain-General of Doradan police a distance of fifteen or twenty feet into the field, and even that slight exertion caused his shirt to cling to his back.

"Not even in the western Andes," Luis said, "are there finer coca plants. I am told there are miles and miles of them down there, but here growing conditions are right for only a few thousand acres."

The coca plant, Bob thought, looked innocent and even attractive.

"The biggest advantage to the grower," Luis said, "is that it requires so little attention. Keep the weeds cleared from the base, and nature does the rest. The coca seeds itself, and requires no care." He searched several plants until he found a large, partly dried leaf, which he plucked and broke in half.

Bob accepted one section from him.

"The peasants who have coca plants on their properties or on public lands nearby," Luis said, "have no need for the refined powder that the people of more advanced civilizations demand. Do as they do, and chew the leaf."

"No, thanks." Bob sniffed the broken leaf, and a faintly bitter scent assailed his nostrils.

Luis chuckled. "It will make your mouth numb, so you will think your dentist has given you an injection. Chew a little more, and your throat also will be numb. In a very short time, perhaps a half-minute, certainly no more, you will feel as though you are floating. All your problems will disappear, and you will be happier than ever before in your life."

"You've chewed coca leaves, I take it."

"Every Doradan has done so at one time or another," Luis said. "It is not physiologically habit-forming, although doctors say that people become psychologically addicted to it."

Bob looked around. "Is anything else grown on this property?"

"No other crop would be as valuable. This farm has more than nine hundred acres, and two crops of the coca plant are grown each year."

"What becomes of it?"

"It is processed into cocaine at a small plant on the premises, a very simple process. Some is sold for medical purposes under licenses granted by the United States, Great Britain, France, and the Low Countries."

"What of the rest?" the Legat asked.

The Captain-General of Doradan police looked somewhat ill at ease. "All is sent off to different countries in Europe. None to the U.S.A. or Canada."

"The demand is there, and prices on the black market are going through the ceiling. So what makes you think we and the Canadians aren't getting shares of this stuff?"

Luis's eyes widened. "Your laws prohibiting the importation are very strict."

"Hey, friend, you're a professional. Unless you sleep through your classes at Quantico you know better than that. I'll bet you a dinner that ninety percent of the cocaine grown in this field crosses the U.S. border. And is consumed there."

"The problem is that we have no law in Dorado to prevent the growing of the coca plant."

"It's one thing for a handful of peasants to grow a few plants of the garbage and kill themselves at an early age," Bob said. "But this farm is different. This is large-scale cultivation for export purposes. And I'm sure there's no export tax on cocaine, either, which means that Dorado doesn't benefit. You'd be doing your country and mine a big favor, Luis, if you brought in a few of your men armed with machetes and cut down every last one of these weeds."

"That is impossible," Luis said. "This farm is the property of Colonel-General Belamon. The commander of the Doradan army. And the brother of Presidente Belamon."

8

Samson Grant had a Saturday-night date with a girl he had met recently, but deliberately planned to dine with his mother, who had been complaining that she saw him infrequently. She was cooking a crown roast of pork, his favorite, and spent the entire late afternoon in the kitchen. Samson played six innings of baseball with a semi-professional team that was delighted to use his services when he was available, and as soon as he returned home he took a shower.

He was dressing when the telephone rang, and he was not surprised to hear from the weekend duty officer at the Field Office. "You had a call just now from a woman named Claudia," the Supervisor said. "I wasn't sure whether it's personal or professional, so I thought I'd better get hold of you."

"Strictly business."

"Well, she wants to see you right away. She claims this is urgent."

"Then it is," Samson said. "Is Mr. Daniels or Mr. Butler around?"

"No, they've both gone home."

"Then I'll have to stop in at the office. I'll be there in ten minutes."

Mrs. Grant came into the room as he was buckling his gun belt. "You aren't going to work! Not now!"

Samson shrugged. "I'm sorry, Mama."

"How long—"

"Turn the roast down to low, Mama, and let's hope for the best."

As soon as Samson reached the office he called the SAC at home, interrupting him as he was fertilizing a flower patch. "I hate to bother you, Mr. Daniels," he said, "but this is an emergency. One of my best informants wants to see me right away. If she produces she expects to be paid off at once, so I'd like authorization to take some cash with me."

"How much do you want?"

"A couple of hundred, sir. I'll pay her according to the value of what she has to offer, of course. Fifty to a hundred if it's little stuff. If it should be really big the two hundred can be a down payment."

"Put the Supervisor on the line," the SAC said, "and I'll okay two hundred. Since you're in a hurry you can fill in the financial requisition form later."

A short time later, after parking his Bureau car down the block, Samson wandered into the waterfront saloon. No customers were on hand as yet for the biggest night of the week, but Claudia was ready for them in a slinky, low-cut dress that matched her scarlet lipstick.

She greeted the agent with a broad smile of welcome and drew him a beer. "In some ways you can be quick."

He perched on a bar stool. "What's new?"

"I told you I'd come through for you, and I have. Now you can do the same for me. Henry is spaced out tonight, but for real, and what he doesn't find out won't ever hurt him."

Samson had no intention of sparring with her. "What have you learned?"

"I just picked this up. A freighter called the *Margot S.* is loading at the Paul Thoman dock in South Winthrop. Taking on mostly Ford Granadas and a couple of bigger cars."

He handed her $100. "There will be more if this tip is accurate. Let me use your phone."

Pouting slightly, she pointed to a corner behind the bar.

Samson called the Field Office, asking the duty officer to send two agents to meet him as soon as possible in South Winthrop.

Saturday-evening traffic was in the mess that developed every spring and that lasted until late autumn. Cars from New York and New Jersey were heading north, cars from Massachusetts and Rhode Island were moving south, and the locals were spreading out in all directions as they went to drive-in restaurants and movies, miniature golf courses, beaches and picnic grounds.

Samson disliked using his siren, but he had no choice, so he plugged his flashing light into the car's cigar-lighter socket and pressed his siren button. The noise was deafening and the glare of the revolving light on the dashboard hurt his eyes, but traffic cleared out of his way with alacrity, and by stepping hard on the gas he soon reached the South Winthrop industrial quarter. He turned in the general direction of the dock area, with which he was unfamiliar, and a weathered sign, PAUL THOMAN AND SON, guided him to his destination.

A two-story concrete building blocked his view of Long Island Sound as he parked his car between the building and a domed oil reservoir. The agents who were joining him hadn't yet arrived, but he couldn't wait for them and broke into a run. If the Ford Granadas being shipped were part of the loot stolen from All-American Car Rentals their original Vehicle Identification Numbers had been left intact, in all probability, and after a quick verification through NCIC he would be in a position to capture a large haul.

He turned the corner of the building, then stopped short. No freighter was tied up at the wharf, and aside from several small pleasure craft the harbor was empty.

A light was burning inside an office at one end of the warehouse, so Samson hurried to it, showing his credentials to a man sitting behind an old-fashioned rolltop desk. "I was told a freighter called the *Margot S.* was loading automobiles here," he said.

The man peered at him over a sheaf of papers. "She sailed."

"How long ago?"

The man shrugged. "An hour or two."

"What's her destination?"

The man picked up a ship's manifest and studied it. "Kingston, Jamaica."

Samson was certain now that he was on the trail of something important: the destination listed had to be phony, as there was no market on the small island of Jamaica for an entire shipload of second-hand automobiles.

As he was absorbing the information the two Special Agents dispatched from the Field Office arrived.

"Go down to the Coast Guard station about a mile down the waterfront road," Samson told them, "and get a cutter that can follow that freighter out to sea. With any luck we can overhaul her before she passes the twelve-mile limit. I'm going to call the S-A-C and ask him to get us a search warrant from the District Court in a hurry. We'll save time if you'll bring the cutter around to the wharf here, and we can be on our way."

The agents hurried away.

Samson telephoned Dave Daniels at home and explained his problem.

"I'll try to find Judge Garrity right away," the SAC said, "but that might not be too easy on a Saturday night. Give me your number, and I'll get back to you."

Samson chain-smoked as he waited, pacing up and down for twenty minutes until the telephone in the little office rang. He snatched it from its cradle before the Paul Thoman employee could reach for it.

"All set," Dave Daniels told him. "Judge Garrity has signed the warrant, and has read it on the phone to the commandant of the Coast Guard station. I'll have someone bring it down to the docks, so it will be there by the time you return to port with the freighter in tow. Good hunting, Grant!"

Samson became feverish as he had to wait another five minutes before the white, 110-foot U.S. Coast Guard cutter pulled up at the wharf. In his impatience he leaped to the deck while she was still maneuvering toward her berth, and almost fell into the water.

The Captain and the two agents from the Field Office awaited him on the deck.

"Can you catch the *Margot S.?*" Samson demanded.

"The first problem is to locate her," the Captain said, leading the way to the bridge so he could take personal command of the search. "Long Island Sound is bigger than you think, and we don't even know whether she's heading for the open Atlantic by way of Montauk or whether she's sailing down by way of New York."

The cutter gathered speed as she sliced through the waters of the harbor, heading toward the Sound.

"I'd think she'd sail by way of Montauk," Samson said. "She may have farther to travel, but she avoids the congestion in New York Harbor."

"You're probably right," the Captain replied, "but let's find out before we commit ourselves."

Samson wondered how he intended to accomplish that feat, but asked no questions.

The Captain began to issue call numbers on his radio, and it soon developed that two smaller Coast Guard ships were already on patrol in the Sound.

"I saw a freighter sailing in the general direction of Montauk, sir," one skipper reported. "But I'm afraid I didn't pay any particular attention to her name."

"How long ago?" the Captain wanted to know.

"A half-hour to forty-five minutes," the skipper of the smaller vessel said. "I didn't log her position or her speed."

The Captain gave the order to sail toward the open Atlantic by way of Montauk Point. "Even if we do find the *Margot S.,*" he said, "this is going to be close. She'll be near international waters by the time we overhaul her."

Only now did it suddenly occur to Samson that he had forgotten to telephone either his mother or his Saturday-night date. But he couldn't ask for the use of Coast Guard facilities for personal calls. So the roast would be dried out, and his mother would spend all day Sunday feeling sorry for herself. As for his date, she'd believe he had forgotten tonight's engagement, and wouldn't speak to him again.

Samson knew nothing about the sea, so the frequent conversations the Captain held with the masters of other Coast Guard vessels meant nothing to him. Occasionally a young lieutenant, junior grade, jabbed a colored pin into a chart attached to a bulkhead, so it appeared that various positions were being plotted.

The cutter was moving so rapidly she churned up a thick wake behind her, and even though the night was warm the air at sea was chilly. Samson shivered and wished he'd brought along a sweater to wear beneath his lightweight jacket.

A half-moon vanished behind a thick bank of clouds, the stars disappeared, and the night grew darker. But the navigator relied on radar and a large panel of instruments, and the cutter did not slacken her pace. Samson looked at the many dials, was unable to read any of them, and felt like an ignoramus. The Captain and his officers were awed by the FBI, but the truth of the matter was that he knew even less about the Coast Guard's business than they knew of his.

The voyage seemed interminable, and Samson wanted a cigarette, but nobody else on the bridge was smoking, so he refrained, too.

Ultimately the Captain took pity on his guests. "Gentlemen," he said to the three agents, "I suggest you go down to the wardroom for some coffee. I'll let you know when something is about to happen."

An ensign conducted the FBI representatives to a small cabin, where they poured coffee for themselves from a hot plate and found seats around a rectangular table. At least Samson could smoke here, and he was glad he worked for the Bureau. A career as a Coast Guard officer would give him galloping claustrophobia.

"Does anybody know what flag the *Margot S.* is flying?" he asked the ensign.

"Yes, sir. Greek," the young officer said. "But that doesn't necessarily mean she has Greek ownership. She could be flying what's known as a flag of convenience, meaning she was registered in Greece. But her owners could be American—or any one of a hundred other nationalities."

Samson believed in being thorough. "If we can, let's check that out while we're hunting for her."

The ensign went away, returning a short time later with a slip of paper. "This may not be much help," he said. "The *Margot S.* is one of about nine freighters owned by a company called the Pier Twenty Corporation. They have New York offices in Wall Street, and others in London, Piraeus, and Singapore. But our registers don't give the nationality of the company's stockholders and directors."

"We'll get that information later," Samson said. "All in due time."

"Would you gentlemen like a sandwich? Or some soup? I know we have tunafish, and we always carry tomato soup because the Captain lives on it."

"Later for me, thanks," Samson said. "I won't have much appetite until we get our hands on that cargo."

The other agents said they felt as he did, so no one ate.

All at once the cutter's pitch seemed sharper, and her roll became more pronounced.

"We've reached the Atlantic now," the ensign said.

Samson looked out a porthole, saw some lights blinking in the distance, and guessed they were off Montauk Point. Unable to judge distances at sea with any degree of accuracy, he had no idea whether they were sailing a half-mile or a mile and a half from land. He didn't like being at the mercy of others, but there was nothing he could do about it.

"Maybe we ought to get back up to the bridge," he said.

The ensign was polite. "As you wish, sir."

When they climbed to the open deck Samson saw that the cutter's guns, fore and aft, had been unlimbered and were ready for action in the event they should be needed. It was good to know that any demands he might be required to make would be supported by artillery.

"Any luck yet?" he asked when they reached the bridge.

"Merchantmen are obliged to use predetermined shipping lanes," the Captain explained. "Four blips show up on our radar screen, which means there should be four merchantmen sailing within a twenty-five-mile radius. It won't take us long to overtake all of them, so we'll soon find out whether one is your freighter."

Samson felt himself becoming tense, as he always did before a caper.

For a long time no one spoke, and only the throbbing of the cutter's engines broke the silence on the bridge.

Then the Captain gave a quiet order, and a pair of powerful searchlight beams stabbed into the night.

"Ship off our port bow, sir," the lieutenant said.

The port searchlight was adjusted, and picked up a fishing

trawler rising and falling on the Atlantic swells as she plowed eastward.

The lights were extinguished, and the cutter sailed on.

The process was repeated a short time later, and a tanker, riding high in the water after unloading her cargo of oil, was revealed in the glare of a searchlight.

The wait was more difficult, and Samson had to curb a desire to fidget.

Ultimately the lieutenant broke the silence again. "Ship off starboard bow, sir."

In the gleam of a searchlight they could see a freighter of about seven thousand tons. Patches of rust showed above her waterline, and white paint was peeling from her superstructure. She had an open hold aft, but her cargo was concealed beneath tarpaulins.

"She's flying a Greek flag," the lieutenant said.

The Captain studied the name on her bow through his glasses. "She's the *Margot S.*," he said.

Samson tried to speak calmly. "I assume you'll request her to stand to," he said, "and then put a shot across her bow if she doesn't obey."

The Captain's laugh was rueful. "To tell you the absolute truth, Mr. Grant, I'm not going to do anything. We've sailed well past the twelve-mile limit. In fact, we have about four miles of international waters separating us from United States jurisdiction."

Samson's disappointment was so intense he couldn't speak. Directly ahead was a cargo that well might consist of stolen automobiles, and by seizing it he well might be able to trace the ring to its source. But nothing whatever could be done.

The Captain would be subjected to a court-martial trial if he halted the freighter on the high seas. And Samson knew he himself would be severely disciplined, too, if he actively disobeyed the law. Criminals were free to do as they pleased, but both the FBI and the Coast Guard were required to observe the letter of the law they were sworn to uphold and protect.

The situation was so frustrating that Samson wanted to pound the nearest bulkhead with his fists. The freighter was within easy reach of the cutter, property worth a fortune could be recovered, and there was a chance that a major ITSMV ring could be smashed. But they had to watch the *Margot S.* sail away, untouched and untouchable.

Samson turned away and went below to the wardroom. All that could be done now would be to warn the harbormasters of United States and foreign ports to look for the ship and notify local law-enforcement authorities if she put into port. The Bureau's own Field Offices would be alerted. Interpol, the international police association, would be notified, too, and member nations also would be ready to pounce. But the *Margot S.* could be disguised by painting her another color and giving her a new name long before she reached port. Harbormasters and local police in many countries could be bribed.

The prize had slipped away, and Samson had to admit the fact. There would be no dramatic breakthrough in the case. Instead the Bureau would plod on, accumulating evidence bit by bit, utilizing its many investigative techniques with a patience learned through bitter experience.

He glanced at his watch and sighed. By the time he returned home the roast would be dried up and his mother would be asleep. As for the girl with whom he had made tonight's aborted date, he felt certain she would never again agree to spend an evening with a Special Agent.

Sid Benjamin and Linda Bartlett attended a performance of a new comedy trying out in Winthrop before going on to Broadway. The play was a hit, they enjoyed it, and both were in a festive mood when they left the Palace Theatre. Sid halted and let the crowds swirl past them.

"I feel like splurging tonight," he said. "We could drive down to the Silver Windmill, but we needn't really go that far. There are a half-dozen places right here in town that serve good meals. All within walking distance."

Linda replied by taking his arm and guiding him to the lot where his car was parked.

"It'll be the Silver Windmill, then?"

She shook her head. "I'll show you where to go. Start driving, and turn left at the corner, then right at the next corner."

He humored her by obeying her instructions.

Again she gave him directions.

Sid found himself heading toward a hamburger drive-in. "What's the gag?"

"I'm not joking," she said. "The play put me in the mood for a hamburger with onions, French fries, and a chocolate malted. And to hell with the calories."

He shrugged as he found a place to park. "We can't even get a beer here," he said.

"Right. No alcohol tonight."

Something in her tone caused him to look at her.

"Wait until we give the order." She began to chat about the play.

It was evident to him that she had something on her mind.

Linda waited until they were busy eating to unburden herself. "Sid," she said, "I've never thanked you properly for the night that I behaved so badly."

"You didn't, so forget it."

"But I did. I won't forget it, and I can't. At first I was too ashamed to mention anything to you, and the longer I've waited the more difficult it's become. But this is the night I let it all hang out."

"Look," he said. "You were under terrible tensions after the Ruiz girl was killed, and you reacted. Every agent goes through something like that. Sooner or later."

"I very much doubt that most agents are guilty of depraved conduct. But there I was, practically begging you to take me to bed. If you aren't using your chili sauce, pass me the packet."

He ate in silence for a few minutes, wanting to ease her guilts without dwelling unnecessarily on the subject. "You had a few drinks, that's all."

"Precisely the reason I'm not drinking anything stronger than a malted tonight." Linda raised her cardboard container to him in a toast, twisting in her seat to face him. "Until that night you never missed a chance to make a pass at me. Since then you haven't made one. Either verbal or physical."

Sid's discomfort became acute.

"How come?" she persisted.

"I don't want to draw diagrams, but the basic nature of our relationship changed."

"At first I thought you were so disgusted you didn't want any more to do with me."

"That's the most stupid remark I've ever heard an intelligent woman make!"

"Well, you've kept asking me to go out with you, so my estimate was wrong. I admit it."

"Hooray for that much," Sid said.

"In the interests of presenting complete evidence, I want it noted for the court record that I've accepted every single one of your invitations. Does that tell you something?"

He sidestepped the question. "I'm an investigator, not an interpreter."

Linda finished her meal, then wiped her hands on a paper napkin. "Sid, you've made it clear for quite a long time that you wanted me. Do you still feel that way?"

He grinned at her. "I'm prepared to put on an exhibition that will shock the family in the station wagon next to us. The parents and that whole mess of little kids."

She averted her gaze, then forced herself to look at him again. "Well, I've realized that I go for you, too."

Sid tried to speak.

Linda gave him no opportunity. "In full sobriety," she said, "I'm inviting you back to my apartment with me. Now."

He responded by putting the car in gear and leaving the drive-in lot so abruptly that there was no opportunity to throw their empty plates and malted containers into a trash barrel.

Carolyn and Dave Daniels attended a small dinner party, and the SAC excused himself frequently to call his office. Not until they returned home shortly before midnight, however, did he learn that Samson Grant's attempt to intercept the freighter had failed.

He offered his wife no explanation, as he never discussed current cases with her, so she wasn't bothered. She could see, however, that he was upset. "Shall I get us a nightcap, Dave?"

"You go ahead if you like. None for me."

"Coffee?"

"At this hour? I'd be awake all night."

"A glass of iced tea, then."

"Carolyn," he said, "there is no need for you to humor me."

She went to the bar and mixed herself a mild bourbon and water. "I'll take this upstairs with me."

"Let's stay down here for a little while," he said, and filled a pipe.

Carolyn knew he wanted to unburden himself.

"Working for the Bureau," he said, "has many satisfactions and advantages."

No reply was necessary.

"As a man moves up in the hierarchy, though, things become tougher. A street agent can fall on his face, and he makes up for it on the next round. A desk man in Washington shuffles papers the wrong way, but he recoups."

Paying no attention to the desires he had expressed, she mixed him a drink, too, and placed it beside him.

Dave sipped it, not even remembering he had said he didn't want it. "At my level," he said, "there's no margin for error."

"I don't believe that."

"Everyone at the top expects me to produce results. That's the name of the game. When a case has been opened, get it closed. When there's a problem, solve it."

"I've heard you say a thousand times in speeches that Special Agents aren't supermen. Are you trying to tell me that's what you're expected to be?"

Dave was untouched by her humor. "Yes. Because I'm an S-A-C. One of fifty-nine supposed supermen who provide the cement that holds the organization together. One of fifty-nine miracle makers."

"If you were to ask me, which you aren't," Carolyn said, "I'd feel compelled to tell you that you're spouting rubbish."

"The Bureau has a reputation to maintain," Dave said. "It shows up every year in the *Crime Reports.* We solve our cases. Bank robbers and espionage agents and kidnappers and saboteurs and all the other crooks who menace our society are caught and brought to justice. It's the momentum the Bureau builds up that makes us successful. Criminals freeze when we move into a case because they're convinced we'll nab them. So they make mistakes —and defeat themselves. That's why no S-A-C can afford to tolerate failures!"

"I see your point, dear, but I think you're exaggerating."

"At the present time," he said, "I have an ITSMV case that's dragging on. And tied in with it, perhaps, is a murder case that we aren't solving, either. I've had Joe Butler in charge of both because I wanted him to have something important to occupy his mind until the disposition of his son's case. Now I'm afraid I'll have to take charge myself, and that will just about kill Joe."

At last Carolyn understood what was disturbing him, and it wasn't the alleged infallibility of the Bureau. "Is your Ay-sack letting you down?"

"Not really. At least, I can't put my finger on anything specific that he's doing wrong. But he isn't getting results!"

She realized it would be wrong to remind him that he always became restless when a case resisted solution. It was a symptom he had displayed for a quarter of a century and, now that she thought of it, was one of the qualities that had led him through a series of promotions to his present level.

"Joe is worried half to death by this situation his son is in," Dave said, "even though he doesn't talk much about it. It's nasty, and there's no way Joe can help him avoid a hefty prison sentence. Not that he would. What worries me is that if I take him off this big case it'll break him, and he'll resign a year before he's eligible for retirement."

"You can't allow that to happen, Dave!"

"I don't intend to, if it can be avoided. He'd have hell's own time finding a good enough job to support a family. At his age there aren't that many available. I'd nudge him along on this case, if I could, but I'm afraid it has me stymied, too. So I'm afraid I'll have to give him a little longer, and meanwhile I'll see if there isn't some way I can break the logjam."

The Field Office was emptying, with most of the Saturday-night staff clearing their desks, but Ray Merrill continued to sit in his cubicle, making a supreme effort to organize the facts of the ITSMV ring case in his mind. Samson Grant's inability to halt the freighter and inspect its cargo tonight struck him hard, and he regarded it as a personal failure. He should have known the best way for the ring to dispose of a large number of automobiles would be to send them out of the country. He should have established a running surveillance of all the docks in the Winthrop district, and should have requested other Field Offices with jurisdiction over seaports and coastal areas to do the same.

Ray thought he was slipping, and was disgusted with himself.

The case was typical of the process of disintegration that was taking place in every aspect of his life. He felt low because Linda Bartlett was avoiding him, and he suspected she preferred Benjamin to him, but he couldn't blame her for that. Inasmuch as he hadn't really become deeply involved with her, it was wrong to use her attitude as an excuse to drink too much.

No, that wasn't the reason. He hoisted a few too many before dinner most nights because he had nothing else to occupy his time. He had to recognize the fact that he had become acclimated to marriage, and needed a wife. He'd do well to make the effort to know the nurse better, other than in bed. Or the woman from the insurance company; there were worse fates than inheriting a ready-made family.

First, however, he had to regain his self-respect. And that meant increasing the pace of the investigation in the ITSMV case. And solving the murder of Carlotta Ruiz.

Ray felt certain the freighter wasn't sailing to Jamaica with a cargo of Ford Granadas. But it was significant she might be heading toward the Caribbean, so, as an initial step, he would request the police of every nation, every major island in the West Indies, to keep watch for the *Margot S.* Some countries were reluctant to turn on the heat, but did respond to Bureau pressure, and it was essential that those cars be checked to determine whether they had been stolen.

The surveillance of the Poole woman was producing no results, and he didn't think it would, at least for the moment. But she might prove useful as a stalking horse who would rejoin Reyes when he returned to the country. Reyes was the key to the case, and the problem continued to be that of finding a way to pin the man down.

Every Immigration office had been alerted, and the Bureau would be notified when Reyes reentered the United States. In theory, anyway. In practice many of the tiny offices on the long border with Mexico were understaffed, loaded with paperwork, and it well could take one of them days to realize Reyes had passed through a particular checkpoint. By that time it would be difficult to pick up his trail again.

Perhaps the time had come to call the Drug Enforcment Agency into the case to help speed a solution. Ray's pride in the Bureau, his knowledge that the FBI rarely required outside assistance, made him reluctant even to consider the possibility. But that was foolish. The Bureau and the DEA were arms of the same government, and sought the same goals. His attitude, like that of his superiors, was a hangover from Mr. Hoover's era, but times had changed, so it was stupid not to take advantage of any special expertise the DEA could offer.

The last of the stenographers had departed, so Ray went out to a typewriter in the bullpen and pecked out a memorandum to the ASAC requesting that the Drug Enforcement Administration be called into the case. The Bureau, as the originating agency, would remain in charge. Unless something extraordinary and unexpected developed.

Experience told Ray that the case was ripe for development, but such action rarely was self-generating. Something was needed to pry it loose. The screws should be tightened on informants under the Bureau's control, and more liberal rewards should be offered to those who were paid. Something had to be done to kick the case off dead center.

At last Ray was ready to leave the office. Habit almost led him to Pete's for a nightcap or two, but the time had come for him to use willpower, and he drove straight to his apartment. He had beer in his refrigerator, as well as a bottle or two of bourbon in a kitchen cabinet, so he could drink himself into a stupor if that was what he wanted. Which it wasn't. He knew he wouldn't touch the hard stuff when by himself at home, and at most he might drink a can of beer.

Barring an emergency he had all day tomorrow to kill, and wouldn't return to the office until Monday morning. Instead of frittering away the day, maybe watching a ball game on TV, reading until he lost interest in a book, and then drifting down to Pete's because he disliked being alone, he'd organize the day.

He had been lethargic and sorry for himself long enough, Ray decided, and he was damned if he was over the hill at forty. He loved the Bureau, he had no desire to work anywhere else, and he fully intended to break this ITSMV case. That, in turn, would spur the SAC to send him off to school at Quantico, and in another year or two he'd have his next promotion.

He felt as though he had been ill, and was just beginning to recover.

Stella Butler was staying sober and, for once, hadn't touched a drop of booze. Instead she devoted her full attention to the young attorney who sat opposite her and Joe in their living room.

"I realize a Saturday evening is an odd time for a conference," the lawyer said, "but I didn't want to wait until the beginning of the week."

"We have nothing better to do," Joe said, and sounded listless.

It occurred to Stella that he had aged in recent weeks. She wanted to comfort him, just as she wanted solace for herself, but didn't know what to say or do.

"You've seen Joey again, Mr. Potter?"

Alan Potter nodded. "Late this afternoon, for two hours. My third visit to him this week."

Husband and wife leaned forward on the sofa.

The attorney shrugged. "He's the most uncooperative boy I've encountered in the five years I've been in practice."

Stella's sigh shook her whole body.

"I'm tempted," Potter said, "to report to the court that I'm getting nowhere with him, and that I'm reluctant to accept a public fee for my services. All that holds me back, so far, is that someone must represent him."

"It might as well be you," Joe said. "No offense intended. What has he told you?"

"Very little, Mr. Butler. I gather he had no hand in stealing the car used in the various bank robberies, but he sat behind the wheel during all three. The best I can say for him, and it isn't much, is that he didn't actually go into any of the banks and participate in the actual holdups."

"Does that mean he'll get a lighter sentence?" Stella asked, finding it difficult to swallow.

"Somewhat lighter, perhaps," Potter said. "Mr. Butler would know the answer to that one better than I would."

"It depends on his attitude," Joe said. "If he shows the court some sign of repentance. If he indicates, even obliquely, why he took part in these insane crimes, he could throw himself on the mercy of the court. His age, plus his clean record, might have an effect."

"Unfortunately," the attorney said, "he appears to have no intention of doing any of the things you suggest. All I can get out of him is that he did what he did, he'll plead guilty, and he'll take the consequences."

"We know," Joe said.

"The reason I've come to you tonight, Mr. and Mrs. Butler, is because you know your son, and I don't. I'm hoping you can suggest some way I can get to him. Perhaps you're aware of a key that will open him up."

"We don't know him at all anymore," Stella said. "When I visit him he's very sweet and pleasant, but he doesn't say anything that has any meaning. And when his father goes—"

"I've stopped going," Joe said. "I get so aggravated I want to slug him. He behaves like a thousand other punks I've seen, kids who automatically label anybody from the FBI as the enemy. I don't understand Joey, and maybe I never did. I don't know what makes him tick. If he won't cooperate with you he'll just have to pay the consequences when the court throws the book at him."

Stella wilted and looked away.

"The prosecutor has hinted," Potter said, "that Judge Garrity wouldn't mind having a talk with you in his chambers before the case comes to trial, Mr. Butler."

"I'll be glad to have a chat with him on any other subject. But I couldn't say any more to him about Joey than I've said to you right now. What's more, I won't compromise my position as a representative of the Bureau. I may have lost my son, but I still have my honor!"

Dinner with Lisa Talbot's family in their North Plymouth home proved to be less of an ordeal than Johnny Hedley had imagined. It was true that her father, who owned the local grain and hardware store, seemed to have the ability to look through him, dissecting someone who had the audacity to have become interested in his daughter. But Mrs. Talbot was a warm person who spoke a great deal without saying much, and who wanted to make certain everyone at the table ate second helpings of her chicken and liver dumplings. Lisa's two younger brothers were easy conquests: Johnny allowed them to handle his .38 after he emptied the chambers, and the boys were thrilled by the presence of a bona fide Special Agent under the family roof.

After dinner, while Lisa helped her mother clear the table and wash the dishes, Mr. Talbot took Johnny on an inspection tour of his fifteen-acre property, with his sons tagging along. The boys tried to persuade Johnny to shoot at an air rifle target they had set up in the backyard, but he had to explain that an agent was required to account for every round of ammunition he fired.

Eventually Mr. and Mrs. Talbot went off with their sons to a championship high school basketball game, and Johnny was alone in the house with Lisa. She suggested they adjourn to a swing on the side porch.

"From here," she said, "we can see everybody who walks past the house, but the forsythia is so thick they can't see us. And there you have the evening's excitement."

"I like it," Johnny said.

Lisa glanced at him, uncertain whether he was being sarcastic. "We have a couple of other choices. There's dancing at the Grange Hall, but the music is so awful I haven't gone since I was a sophomore in high school. We can go, if you like, but just remember I warned you."

"I don't feel much like dancing," he said.

"The other choice," she told him, "is a wild bingo game at the American Legion. As you can tell, the social life in North Plymouth is just overwhelming on a Saturday night."

"It was quiet in my neighborhood when I was growing up, too."

Lisa was still defensive. "I guess I just feel funny, asking you here for the weekend. Mom has always embarrassed me by making a fuss over anybody who has ever taken me out—"

"It's her way of being hospitable."

"And the boys were impossible, swarming all over you."

"You're wrong," Johnny said. "You work for the Bureau, so you see everybody at the office as being kind of ordinary. But your brothers think being an agent is the most wonderful, glamorous job in the world. That's the way I felt at their age, and I still feel it, or I wouldn't be doing what I am. Maybe they'll want to be agents when they grow up. Their attitude, multiplied all over the country, is what gives the FBI its stature."

"You want to know something, Johnny Hedley?" Lisa put the swing in motion. "You're a hopelessly old-fashioned square."

"I guess I am." He was plunged into the depths.

"So am I. Every single morning, on my way to work, I get a kick out of knowing I actually work for the Bureau. I don't do much of anything I wouldn't be doing at the Department of Commerce of the Bureau of the Budget. But I have enough small town in me to feel pleased and proud."

"I come from a big city," Johnny said, "and I chose being a Special Agent over a half-dozen other careers. The only time I regret it is when Mr. Merrill chews me out." He smiled, then sobered. "There's still a mystique that makes the Bureau what it is. In the past year or two a lot of people have blasted at us for mistakes, and I'm sure we deserve it, but we still stand in a class by ourselves. And that's good."

"Why?"

"Because we need public respect to help us do our job. You've been around the Bureau long enough—longer than I have, actually—to know we need the cooperation of every decent citizen. It's the only way crime will ever be eradicated."

"I could hear 'The Star-Spangled Banner' playing in the background while you made that little speech," Lisa said. "But I'm not laughing at you. Truly I'm not. I've seen agents coming into the office with hangovers, and I've had my share of being barked at without cause. But I think this country would be in worse shape without the Bureau."

"All I want is to work there for the next thirty years. The hours are crazy, the risks you take are enormous, and the pay isn't all that great. So I sometimes wonder why I ever got in." Johnny hesitated for a long time, and began to perspire. "I can't understand, either, why any girl in her right mind ever marries an agent."

"Do you advise against it?"

"Well, transfers aren't as frequent as they were, but an agent still moves around from one town to another a lot. I've seen fellows calling home night after night, telling their wives they're going to be late. Weekends get messed up. You can't talk about your work at home. And a lot of outsiders shy away from you."

"I've seen that, even on my level," Lisa said. "A couple of girls I know avoid me, and at least one fellow stopped dating me when he learned I work for the Bureau. But I don't care. I know in my own mind what's right."

He decided to proceed with subtlety. "Have you ever wondered what kind of a life you'd lead if you were married to an agent?"

She laughed.

He realized he hadn't been all that subtle.

Lisa spoke with deliberation. "Just lately," she said, "I've started to think about it."

He looked at her, and saw that she was returning his gaze.

They slid toward each other, and the swing moved more rapidly.

The headquarters of Alan Collins, the district head of the Drug Enforcement Agency, were located directly below the FBI Field Office in the Winthrop Federal Building, so he climbed a single flight of stairs for a Monday-morning meeting with Joe Butler. He listened to a description of the ITSMV ring case, was told the details of the Carlotta Ruiz murder, and then Ray Merrill was called in.

Collins, a short, slender man with prematurely white hair, grinned at the Supervisor. "You couldn't get along without me, I see. We get called in whenever the FBI needs to be bailed out."

Joe knew he was being needled, of course, and realized there was fire behind the smoke. All federal law-enforcement agencies were jealous of the Bureau's greater prestige, glory, and annual operations budget. "We know you people downstairs haven't had enough work lately to be earning your salaries, Al, so we've taken pity on you."

"What I like best about you guys is your generosity," Collins said.

The ASAC was in no mood for barbed pleasantries. "What's your reaction to these cases, Mr. Collins?"

"I can't deal in specifics," the DEA head said, "but they mesh with our general picture. There's always been a drug slopover from New York into Fairfield County. And heroin has been a constant problem in Winthrop, Hartford, New Haven, and the other major cities of Connecticut. Just in this past year, however, the cocaine situation has become worse."

"In what way?" Joe Butler wanted to know.

"The supply has quintupled," Collins said. "It's easier to take than heroin, and its use is more difficult to detect, short of a blood test. There's no physical dependency on it, although the addict does form a mental and emotional need for it that amounts to the same thing. Anyway, the demand has become overwhelming. There are drug fads, just as there are so many other kinds of fads. Dexedrine was the 'in' drug for a time. Then came LSD. Today cocaine is number one."

"In Connecticut?" the ASAC asked.

"Everywhere. But no matter how great the demand, the supply keeps up with it. We've had trouble tracing it because the sources aren't the same as they are for heroin and other opium products. We've had to find and develop an entire new set of informants. And that, as you know, takes time."

"Does the cocaine sold in this state come from Dorado?" Ray cut to the heart of the problem.

"I wish I knew," Collins said. "Either there or South America, obviously, but our tracers have been pretty feeble. This case of yours hints that Dorado might be the source, and that members of the ring are smuggling it into the country in stolen Monarchs and Buicks. But that's still a surmise."

"The key to the whole operation," Joe Butler said, "appears to be Hernando Reyes Gomez. But so far, I'm sorry to say, we haven't been able to touch him."

"Until I came in here and read your confidential file," the DEA head said, "I never heard of the man. Which indicates that he's been able to maintain a very low profile."

"We were hoping you could give us some data on him," Ray said.

"So far," Collins replied, "we've drawn a blank on the cocaine sources. Occasionally one of our operatives will pick up a small quantity on the street. From some minor peddler who can't lead us back to the big boys. We hate being humiliated."

"So do we," Joe Butler said.

"We've arrested only a few of the small fry," Collins said, "and without exception they've been Latin Americans. Which isn't surprising, considering the source of cocaine. A new crowd has taken control, and not even the top heroin people know them."

"Have you tried developing informants in the Andean countries and Dorado?" Joe Butler asked.

The DEA head was scornful. "Naturally. But a few of them have disappeared, and the others are too frightened now to work with us. We have yet to find one witness we can rely on."

"If Reyes is running this operation," Ray Merrill said, "he's doing a first-class job. I've got to say that much for him."

"Just off the top of my head," Collins said, "it seems to me that your best bet—and perhaps our best bet—is this young car thief you're holding in the federal lockup. Ramon Garcia."

"You're welcome to take a crack at him," the ASAC said with a bitter laugh. "We've pounded and cajoled him. We've threatened him and offered him a minimum sentence. Nothing has budged him, nothing has persuaded him to talk."

"In fact," Ray added, "we aren't even certain he knows anything to talk about."

Collins looked wistful and rubbed the knuckles of one hand with the palm of the other. "When I've seen what drugs have done to more youngsters than I care to remember, I sometimes wish the rights of certain federal prisoners could be forgotten for a few hours."

Every law-enforcement official felt as he did, and there was no need to reply.

"I'll send you a summary of what we've discussed in a two-oh-four, Mr. Collins," the ASAC said, referring to the form used by the Bureau in its communications with other government agencies. "Just to make this whole sorry business official."

"Keep in touch, gentlemen." There was a hint of mockery in Collins's tone as he shook hands.

The dignity of Joe Butler's position made it difficult for him to respond in kind.

But Ray felt hampered by no such restrictions. "The same to you, Al. And when we develop an informant who is hot, you can borrow him from us." He escorted the DEA official to the door, turned back, and dropped into a chair. "If we develop one. Which may be never, the way this case is marking time."

"If we don't get the breaks we'll have to make them," Joe said. obviously irritated. "And don't ask me how, because I have no idea. If we live long enough this case will work itself out, but the frustrations are shortening our lives. We've come up against a stone wall, and there seems to be no way around, through, or over it!"

9

The white cruise ship dropped anchor in the Ciudad Dorado harbor shortly before dawn, but there were few signs of life on board, and several hours would pass before the passengers arose, ate breakfast, and went ashore in tenders for a morning of free-port shopping and an afternoon visit to the Mayan temple in the mountains.

The battered little freighter made a detour around the larger vessel, and because of her size was able to tie up at a wharf. Day was breaking when an Inspector of Doradan Customs went on board, and in the cabin of the master, over cups of coffee laced with rum, he was handed a manifest informing him that ten Ford Granada sedans and one Cadillac Seville sedan would be landed.

All eleven vehicles were driven ashore by the time the sun rose, with the modest duty paid in cash by a stranger, claiming to be Venezuelan, whose calling card indicated he was the representative of the Simon Bolivar Trading and Import Company, Limited. He mentioned in passing that the remaining automobiles on board the *Margot S.* would be delivered to colleagues in other ports, a fact which the master of the ship corroborated.

All eleven cars promptly left the dock area under their own power.

Before the Inspector of Customs went ashore, refreshed by his coffee, he was handed an envelope by the master, and counted its contents with care. Retiring to his office, he was met by a lieutenant of Doradan police, who held out a hand.

The Inspector gave him one-quarter of the sum in the envelope. The lieutenant was supposed to receive one-half, under the terms of their agreement, but inasmuch as he was ignorant of the total he was in no position to complain.

At 9:30 A.M. the *Margot S.* cast off her lines and sailed out of the harbor.

The Inspector delayed the filing of his report on the motorcars that had entered the country because he felt a strong desire to visit a young lady who lived on the opposite side of Ciudad Dorado and tell her the news of his latest windfall.

The police lieutenant could not write his own report, as he was required to copy the statement prepared by the Customs Division.

The Inspector returned to his office at 11:20 A.M., and his brief report was written by 11:35.

The police lieutenant copied it by 11:45, making certain that a carbon was sent by special messenger, in accordance with recent instructions, to central headquarters. There it passed through several hands, and at 12:05 P.M. was given to the secretary to the Captain-General of Doradan police, who immediately notified her superior. Luis Alvaro de Silvera went into action, summoning the Inspector of Customs and the police lieutenant for questioning, making a series of calls on one of the few telephone lines in the city that operated without delays, and, finally, paying a personal visit to the waterfront.

At 1:14 he returned to his office and immediately called the Legal Attaché at the United States Embassy.

At 1:30 Luis Alvaro de Silvera and Bob Roberts met at their usual corner table in Ciudad Dorado's oldest and most distinguished sidewalk café.

"The facts are simple," Luis said. "Ten Granadas were landed by the *Margot S.* very early this morning. I wasn't notified. The ship sailed away, and will drop off the rest of her cargo at other ports. The cars were driven off."

The Legat won a battle to curb his temper. "Can any of the cars be recovered?"

The Captain-General of Doradan police shrugged. "By this time most of them have crossed the borders. They're being taken for sale in Nicaragua. Guatemala. Belize. Panama. Wherever. By now they have new licenses, and police outposts on the roads are few. Who will halt and search them? And how will the peasants we hire as police officers know where to find—much less read—the Vehicle Identification Numbers?"

"So we've been outsmarted again," Bob said.

"The two officials who broke my orders have been suspended, and an inquiry will be held."

Doradan inquiries invariably dragged on for months. "Luis, what do you know about the Simon Bolivar Trading and Import Company?"

"No company of that name is registered with our Ministry of Commerce and Industry, and none of our neighboring countries has heard of it, either."

"A fake," the Legat said. "Invented for the purpose of creating a front for the importation of motorcars. The only reason a phony company would be used is obvious. The cars had to be stolen."

"I am forced to accept that interpretation myself," the Doradan said.

Bob's tonic tasted flat. "Unfortunately, we can't prove it. The evidence has disappeared. We have the impossible task of tracing a fleet of cars that have either left or are leaving Dorado. Cars that ultimately will be bought by honest people who pay real money for them. Cars that will wind up anywhere from Buenos Aires to Mexico City. Cars we can no longer trace. Cars that the police of many countries lack the expertise to trace."

"We had our chance," Luis said.

"I don't suppose you put anyone on the trail of Hernando Reyes Gomez this morning?"

"His movements are being watched, as I promised you they would be. If he had left his house this morning I would have been notified."

The Legat nodded, his gloom increasing. "He's too sharp to have played any direct part in today's operation, and I'm sure Juan Garcia stayed under wraps this morning, too. The worst of this situation is that we're virtually certain Reyes is responsible for the entire caper, but we haven't scraped up enough evidence to haul him into court. In the States. Here. Anywhere."

"Soon I will have an ulcer, like so many of our colleagues around the world."

"I'll take copies of the ship's manifest, import Customs papers, and that calling card, just for the record. Not that they'll be of much use."

Luis reached into his crocodile leather portfolio. "I have had them prepared for you. In matters of little consequence the police of Dorado are very efficient."

Bob glanced through the documents before putting them into his pocket, and all at once something struck him. "Well. I see the Granadas weren't the only cars that came ashore this morning. There was also a Cadillac Seville."

"Indeed."

"You didn't mention it on the phone."

"It must have slipped my mind."

"I assume that it vanished, too, and has left the country?"

The Captain-General of Doradan police spoke with great reluctance. "No. As it happens, this fine car is still in Ciudad Dorado. It has been taken to a villa on the outskirts of the city."

"So we get a break after all," the Legat said. "Send someone out to get the Vehicle Identification Number and the secret number. You know where to look, so you may even want to attend to the job yourself."

"I regret that this is impossible."

Bob stared at him. "What the hell does that mean?"

"The Cadillac Seville has been delivered—as a gift of the nonexistent Simon Bolivar Company—to Colonel-General Belamon. I would lose my position and perhaps my personal liberty if I made the unfortunate discovery that he is the new owner of a car that was stolen."

Joe Butler thought seriously of requesting a short leave of absence when his son's trial was placed on the Federal District Court docket for the first week of the following month. Uncertain whether he had the courage to attend, he wondered whether he ought to go elsewhere for those days. Stella wouldn't leave, of course, and he couldn't allow her to face the ordeal without him, so he abandoned the plan.

Eleven days before the trial was scheduled, Joe received a telephone call from the Winthrop police lieutenant who acted as warden of the federal lockup. Mr. Butler," he said, "I wonder if you can drop over here this morning."

"I think so. What's up, Lieutenant?"

"I'd rather not discuss it on the phone. Come straight to my office without announcing yourself at the sergeant's desk."

The request was strange, but other matters intervened, and it was almost noon before Joe had the opportunity to leave his desk. He walked to the lockup, and went directly to the lieutenant's private office.

"I'll tell you what I know," the officer said, "and you can form your own judgment. Right after breakfast this morning one of our patrolmen who works as a prison guard came to me. He said that Joseph Butler, Junior, wants to see his father on a very urgent matter. But not to bother if anybody else learned about it."

Joe was startled. "He's said nothing to me since his arrest. Do you know what this is all about?"

The lieutenant shook his head. "You're welcome to the use of this office, and I'll have the same patrolman escort him up here. They can use the back elevator, which is private."

"Thanks," Joe said, and braced himself for an unexpected confrontation.

The lieutenant left, and too late Joe remembered he hadn't surrendered his .38. Not that it mattered; he couldn't imagine his son trying to take the weapon from him.

It was very quiet in the office, and Joe reached into his pocket for a cigar, but changed his mind.

At last the rear door opened, and Joey walked in alone, the door closing behind him.

The boy was scrawny and pale, and Joe felt a wave of love for him.

Joey glared at him. "I'm no stoolie," he said.

The comment made no sense. "It never crossed my mind that you were." An investigator's sixth sense told Joe to take no initiative and to let the boy's purpose emerge naturally.

"I don't want you to think I'm trying to get into your good graces, because I'm not," Joey said, and lighted a cigarette with a shaking hand. "I don't care what you think about me, and I want to make that very clear."

"I understand it perfectly," Joe said. "Why don't we sit down?"

To his surprise Joey nodded, and took a chair.

His father took another, with the light behind him, so the sun shone into the boy's face. Even under these circumstances a professional interrogator didn't forget techniques.

"I've had a lot of time to think these past couple of months," Joey said. "And I feel badly about one thing. Just one. You and Mom put a lot of time and effort and money into bringing me up."

And love, Joe thought, but didn't express his thought aloud.

"So I've been bugged by the thought that I'd like to repay you. Pretty corny, huh?"

Joe carefully clipped off the end of a cigar. "I think that's decent of you," he said, trying to sound casual.

"There was no way I could do it, and it'll be harder after I get to the penitentiary. In fact, from what I've heard around here, I could get myself killed after I'm sent up. Convicts hate stoolies even more than they hate cops."

Joe lighted his cigar, his face a mask.

"There's a fellow in the cell next to mine," Joey said. "Ramon Garcia."

Joe nodded.

"He says you questioned him one day."

"I believe I did."

"He hates your guts. He doesn't really know you, but he hates everybody in the FBI."

"I understand." Joe's antennae were stretching.

"So he thinks I'm pretty terrific, doing what I did."

"Of course."

Joey lighted a fresh cigarette from his stub. "Ramon and I have come to know each other pretty well. We play chess together."

"I hope you beat him," Joe said.

"For a while I did, but he's smart, and he catches on fast. We've gotten chummy, so he's been talking to me. About all kinds of things." Joey paused and looked out of the window. "I don't want anything from you. You got that straight? Absolutely nothing!" He didn't realize he was shouting.

"You have my word that I won't lift a finger to help you," Joe said, "and you know I've never broken my word to you."

"Okay, then." Again Joey paused. "Ramon talks all the time about his brother. The greatest, toughest, smartest man in the world. A tin saint. Ramon is keeping his mouth shut because he knows his brother will look after him when he gets out of prison. And his brother's boss. Somebody named Reyes. He's very rich, and Ramon is sure he'll be rich, too, after he serves his term."

Joe merely nodded, afraid he would break the spell if he spoke.

"They've got the greatest racket in the world, and they make the FBI look like monkeys. Ramon gets a big jolt out of that. I did, too, until I got to thinking I could repay you. Not that it changes the way I feel about you."

"Of course not."

"They've got the greatest racket in the world." Joey's eyes were enormous in his thin face, and he looked like a small boy again. "They steal cars on a big scale. I don't know much about that part. It's what Ramon did for them, and he doesn't talk about it."

Again Joe nodded.

"They ship the cars off to different places in Latin America. Ramon isn't sure just where, but he says that isn't important." The boy lowered his voice. "Sometimes they sell the cars for cash. But not always. Sometimes they trade them for cocaine. When he told me about that part, I made up my mind I had to let you know."

Joe silently thanked God for his son's hatred of drugs. At least he had instilled that much in the kid.

"They bring it back into the country in cars, too. Then Ramon's brother and this Reyes show up, and the drugs are handed over to them. They don't take any risks at all, you see."

"I see," Joe said.

"They've got people here who buy from them, and then off they go again. You can't touch them, and neither can anybody else. This Reyes is worth a mint, and Ramon says his brother is getting rich, too. That's why he isn't worried."

"I can imagine," Joe murmured.

"They're due to show up pretty soon on one of their regular trips, and then Ramon will have all the spending money he needs."

Apparently the boy had no idea how much he was revealing, and Joe steeled himself to forget that the informant was his son. The ITSMV ring case was breaking wide open, complete with ramifications beyond any that the Bureau had contemplated, and duty still came first.

"I suppose," he said, "your friend Ramon is still pretty upset by the death of his girl."

"That didn't bother him much. She was turning into a C-head."

In spite of his professionalism Joe was bothered by his son's familiarity with prison slang. A few months ago he wouldn't have known that a C-head was a cocaine addict. "Ramon knows she was murdered."

"Yeah." Joey's face worked, and he struggled for composure.

"She knew too much," Joe said, stating a Bureau conjecture as a fact. "And with Ramon in prison, his bosses were afraid she'd talk out of turn."

"That's what he thinks, although he doesn't seem to be sure. He's mentioned her only a couple of times."

Joe's vague nod seemed disinterested.

His son jumped to his feet. "Now we're even! You don't owe me anything, and I don't owe you anything!" He raced to the door, threw it open, and ran out, leaving the startled guard stationed outside to follow him to the elevator.

Joe chewed on his cigar, trying to regain his equilibrium. Then he reached for the lieutenant's telephone and called Stella. "I want you to meet me for a late lunch," he said. "Meet me at Pete's in an hour and a half. There are details I can't discuss with you, but it looks as though we have a son who is rejoining the human race."

He returned without delay to the Field Office, where he conferred at length with the SAC, to whom he repeated the whole conversation.

"This," Dave Daniels said, "is the break we've needed."

"Right. Now we know where we're going. Joey's revelations aren't worth anything in court, of course, because everything he said is only hearsay evidence, but at least we can bear down."

"I'll request the Legat in Ciudad Dorado to keep a close watch on Reyes and Garcia, and to let us know instantly when they leave the country. Meantime we'll tighten our own surveillance on the Poole woman."

"I'll alert the Drug Enforcement people," Joe said, "so they can be ready to roll, too."

"With any luck," Dave said, "we should be able to catch Reyes with his hand in the cookie jar. And, Joe, I'm pleased and relieved for you. I can imagine how much better you must be feeling about your son."

"It's good to know he isn't totally lost. I'm meeting my wife to tell her there's at least a chance he'll be headed in the right direction by the time he gets out of prison."

"The courts have been known to deal leniently with other informants," Dave said, his voice gentle, "so I'm sure they'd take this act of your son's into consideration before he's sentenced."

"He's no less guilty," Joe said, "and I still think it would be wrong for me to ask the prosecutor to show him leniency. Joey wasn't plea bargaining when he opened up to me, and I couldn't live with myself if I gave up my principles."

Four days later, shortly before noon, Legat Bob Roberts telephoned the Winthrop Field Office. "Our friends," he said, "have just taken Pan Am flight four-sixteen to Miami."

The Miami Field Office was alerted, and a high-level decision was made at Bureau headquarters in Washington to permit Reyes and Garcia to proceed with their business.

The pair went to a Miami Beach hotel, where they booked a suite for overnight use, and the FBI immediately obtained a court order to tap their telephones.

Reyes made a call to Louise Elizabeth Poole, in which he asked if the "usual" reservations had been made. She replied they had been confirmed for the following day, and that she would be waiting for him. He also requested that she notify "Frank" of his impending arrival, and she said she would.

The Winthrop Field Office obtained a court order making it

possible for a tap to be placed on the woman's telephone, but by the time the arrangements were completed it appeared she had already been in touch with the man called Frank. She did not use her telephone again. Meanwhile the agents maintaining the surveillance were ordered to be ready to follow her, and three pairs were given the assignment. They would leapfrog behind her when she drove off so that no one car would follow directly behind her continuously. When she looked in her rear-view mirror, she would be less likely to realize she was being tailed.

At 9:30 the following morning Reyes and Garcia left the Miami Beach hotel and drove by taxi to the Miami airport. The driver of the taxi was a Special Agent, and others followed in another taxi. As soon as the agent in charge of the operation learned that the pair were flying to New York on Eastern Airlines Flight 911, seats were obtained directly behind those reserved for them, and two agents made the flight.

The New York Field Office picked up the surveillance when the flight terminated.

Louise Elizabeth Poole left her house at 2:00 P.M., carrying two pieces of luggage. She drove only a short distance to the far side of Winthrop, where she checked into a room at the Sound View Motel, built the previous year.

A court order was obtained that enabled the Bureau to tap the woman's telephone there and to install equipment that would enable agents to listen to conversations taking place in the room. Assuming that Reyes and Garcia would check into the same place, another court order made it possible to install devices in their quarters and to tap their telephones, too.

A check made by agents of the Winthrop Field Office revealed that one of the proprietors of the Sound View Motel had a questionable background, so the taps were installed without the knowledge of the management.

Linda Bartlett was ordered to move into the motel, and managed to obtain a room adjacent to that of the Poole woman. Listening device monitors were set up, and teams of agents were assigned to duty around the clock.

Reyes and Garcia rented a car at Kennedy Airport and drove to Connecticut, arriving at the Sound View Motel at 4:40 P.M. They were given rooms across the corridor from the room of

Louise Elizabeth Poole. Sid Benjamin was ordered to move into the place, and was able to obtain a room on the second floor, directly above that occupied by Reyes.

At 5:00 P.M. the three suspects left the motel in the rented car, and Sid Benjamin took advantage of their absence to install listening devices in the rooms.

The trio drove to the main lot of All-American Car Rentals in Winthrop, where they turned in the automobile. The irony of their having legitimately rented a car from All-American was not lost on the agents.

Two unidentified men were awaiting the trio at the car rental lot, and turned over a Continental Mark IV two-door sedan to them. The three suspects then drove back to the motel, with Reyes at the wheel.

Reyes went to the motel bar, where he spent the next hour and a half, drinking mild highballs and talking with no one. Garcia and the Poole woman retired to the latter's room, where they had sex relations. Subsequently they rejoined Reyes, and all three went into the dining room, where they ordered a large meal.

Meanwhile agents had checked the Continental Mark IV, and learned it was a stolen vehicle.

Dave Daniels, after conferring with Joe Butler and Ray Merrill, decided to make no immediate move to retrieve the car. "We're after bigger game than a single stolen motor vehicle charge," the SAC said.

After dinner Garcia went to the bar, where he ordered one stinger after another, drank until he became intoxicated, and then went off to bed. Meanwhile Reyes and the Poole woman had retired to the former's room, where they had sex relations.

The entire staff of the Winthrop Field Office was on duty.

In midevening the early edition of the following morning's Winthrop *Herald* was delivered. In its classified section Johnny Hedley found an ad offering a Continental Mark IV sedan for sale. The ad bore the name of Hernando Reyes Gomez and listed a telephone number.

An emergency check with the telephone company revealed that there was no such phone number.

Dave Daniels immediately consulted with Joe Butler and Ray

Merrill. "There's no doubt in my mind," he said. "This ad is a signal."

"It bears out our interpretation of the ad that kicked off this case," Ray said. "That had to have been a signal, too. If you'll remember, Ramon Garcia and the Ruiz girl allegedly knew nothing about any car being for sale."

"If our information about drugs is correct," Joe Butler said, "this should mean there will be a pickup or delivery tomorrow. We're moving down to the wire in a hurry now."

"Bartlett has searched the Poole woman's luggage, and has found no drugs or other incriminating material. Benjamin has gone through the luggage of the men, too, while they were at dinner, and has come up with blanks. Neither Reyes nor Garcia is even carrying a handgun."

"I still think we should make a thorough search of the stolen Continental," Ray said.

"I'm tempted," the SAC said, "but we're taking too big a risk. We don't know the extent to which the management of the motel may be involved in the ring's operations. The car is parked right outside the window of the manager on duty, and we were almost caught when we took the VIN earlier tonight. If we really search that car we well might be seen, and Reyes could become so alarmed he'd call off his whole operation."

"I agree," Joe Butler said. "We've had the two men who delivered the Continental followed, and they've holed up in a New Haven rooming house. We'll continue to keep tabs on them, but we won't arrest them until Reyes himself makes some overt move."

New staff assignments were made, and with so many agents involved in one capacity or another, it was necessary to give Johnny Hedley a key job. He was ordered to take up a post at dawn, disguised as a gas station attendant, in the service station located directly across the street from the motel parking lot. There, armed with a two-way radio, he would notify a pair of agents parked around the corner the moment that Reyes or one of his associates appeared and approached the Mark IV.

Three other Bureau cars would be cruising in the immediate vicinity, and all four would tail the Continental, leapfrogging to avoid calling undue attention to themselves.

Sid Benjamin was relieved at the motel, and was assigned to accompany Samson Grant in the lead surveillance car. The SAC regarded them as the most aggressively active members of the staff, so they would have the primary responsibility for moving in at the appropriate time.

At Joe Butler's request he was given charge of the operation. Accompanied by Ray Merrill, he would direct the surveillance and would determine when arrests were to be made. This assignment was in line with a Bureau policy: when dealing with dangerous persons it was customary for a SAC or an ASAC to be present personally in the field and to assume the ultimate responsibility. This prevented younger agents from taking premature action that might unnecessarily risk lives.

An all-night vigil was maintained at the motel, and at dawn the agents moved to their action stations.

Linda, who had slept for a few hours on top of one of the motel room beds while others maintained the vigil at the listening posts, awakened when the personnel was changed. She had fully expected to participate in the climactic operation, and was upset when the new arrivals brought her no instructions.

Either she had been forgotten or was being left out deliberately, and she had no intention of accepting the snub. For the sake of security she went to a pay telephone booth in the lobby, noting as she passed the manager's duty office that a light was burning there. A few moments later she had the SAC on the line.

"Mr. Daniels," she said, "the relief team couldn't remember my new assignment."

"I was hoping to spare you the fireworks, Miss Bartlett."

She thought of Carlotta Ruiz slumped on a couch, her throat cut and a knife protruding from her back. "I've worked on this case from the beginning, sir," she said, her voice strident, "and I intend to be in on the kill. If I must, I'll work alone."

The SAC didn't want a woman agent subjected to risks when it could be avoided, but understood how she felt. "Team up with Hedley," he said, "and join the surveillance unit."

Linda swallowed her indignation. She and the new first-office agent were relegated to the bottom of the list. "Yes, sir," she said, and rang off.

One of the men told her where to find Johnny, and she walked across the street to the gas station, where she found him concealing his two-way radio behind one of the pumps.

"You and I are elected to bring up the rear of the procession. Where is your car?"

He pointed it out to her adjacent to the street.

"Give me the keys, and as soon as you do your thing, join me. I'll be waiting for you with the engine running. This is one caper I don't intend to miss!"

Moments later Samson Grant's car pulled to a stop around the corner, and Sid Benjamin handed his partner a container of the black coffee they had purchased at an all-night diner.

"I've heard," Samson said, "that you get higher scores at target practice than anybody else in the office."

"Could be." Sid sipped his coffee.

"Then I'll drive, and you ride shotgun."

The gesture was generous. Samson, as the senior of the pair, could have given himself either assignment, and was deliberately allowing his partner to achieve the greater credit in the event of a crunch. "That's decent of you," Sid said, and meant it.

Samson shrugged. "I don't drive toy cars at amusement parks, but I'm pretty good on highways." He snapped on his radio, and they settled down to wait.

Three other pairs of agents reached the scene soon thereafter, as did two other cars manned by representatives of the Drug Enforcement Agency. Joe Butler, parked a block away with Ray Merrill, smiled grimly. "Nobody can accuse us of being understaffed for this job," he said.

Ray made himself more comfortable behind the wheel and nodded. "I'm afraid we're being relegated to the role of playing traffic cops." That was what happened when an agent grew older, and he disliked the whole system.

Joe could sympathize with him, but was satisfied to be in the rear trench. At this stage of the operation. If a real crisis developed, Bureau tradition would require him to lead the troops into action, and then he and Ray would have their fill of excitement.

This situation had developed because of what Joey had told him, and he couldn't help feeling proud of his son's contribution. Even though the kid couldn't have helped if he weren't in jail. This was no time to think of Joey and the miserable future that awaited him. All that mattered right now was a ticklish job. Joe realized the assessment he and Dave Daniels had made could be in error and that Reyes and his associates might not be playing a direct role in whatever might develop as a result of the want-ad placed in the *Herald.* The Bureau could be made to appear foolish, and Reyes could get off with no punishment worse than a few months' imprisonment for driving a stolen car. With a smart lawyer helping him he might even claim he didn't know the Continental had been stolen. He had squeezed out of trouble in the Galveston ITSMV ring case, and what he had done once he could do again.

Soon after daybreak a light spring rain fell, making the roads slippery. The drizzle lasted no more than a half-hour, but a fog enveloped the Long Island Sound coastline.

At 7:10 A.M. Hernando Reyes Gomez and Juan Garcia went into the motel dining room for breakfast. A Special Agent disguised as a waiter went to the men's room, and from there reported on his two-way radio that the pair had shown up. He also said that a waiter had taken fruit juice and coffee to the room of Louise Elizabeth Poole.

The entire task force was ready for immediate action.

At 7:35 A.M. Reyes and Garcia appeared in the parking lot.

Johnny Hedley instantly notified the network.

There was a delay, however, while the two men waited for the Poole woman, who showed up ten minutes later in a pink two-piece suit, her makeup suitable for a formal gala.

"They're getting in the car," Johnny said. "They're starting. They're turning left as they come out of the parking lot." In order not to appear conspicuous he strolled to his own car, where Linda had already turned on the engine.

Samson Grant and Sid Benjamin donned hats with snap brims and fell in behind the Mark IV. This was the most delicate phase of the operation. Louise Elizabeth Poole was acquainted with both and knew them as FBI agents; if she recognized them she could give away the entire surveillance operation. But she was seated in the front seat between Reyes, who was driving, and Garcia, who seemed to be lecturing her.

She did not glance in the direction of the car that followed, and was in no position to look in either the left or right rear-view mirror. For safety's sake, however, the two agents continued to wear their hats.

One by one the other cars joined in the procession. Johnny and Linda thought they were bringing up the rear, but the ASAC and Supervisor Merrill took up that position.

Rush-hour traffic was heavy. Factory workers were driving to work at the industrial plants that lined the waterfront, office employees were heading to their downtown jobs, and the wet streets further slowed the long line of cars.

The agents rode bumper to bumper, giving no other vehicles an opportunity to cut in. A green light turned red at Lower Winthrop Boulevard, cutting off the last four cars in the procession. But Joe Butler did not hesitate. "Plow right on through," he ordered on his two-way radio.

A traffic policeman blew his whistle furiously, but stopped when Ray Merrill slowed sufficiently for the ASAC to show the officer his Bureau credentials.

At the corner of South Main Street and Lower Winthrop Boulevard the second car in the procession slipped past Samson Grant, who deftly squeezed as far to the right as he could to aid in the maneuver. It was unnecessary for the ASAC to give orders: the agents were timing these moves themselves.

When Reyes approached the ramp of the Turnpike the next Bureau car moved up into the lead position.

Only the Drug Enforcement Agency representatives held their places in the line. Never having practiced leapfrogging with the Bureau's agents they took no chances of snarling the maneuver now. Their inability to participate kept Johnny Hedley and Linda Bartlett behind them, with the ASAC and Ray Merrill still in the anchor spot.

"From here," Linda said as they gathered speed and moved onto the Turnpike, "we can't even see what's happening."

"What do you suppose they'll do to us," Johnny asked, glancing at the ASAC in his rear-view mirror, "if we move up?"

Linda's laugh was reckless. "They can't fire us until after the caper ends, I know that much."

Johnny responded by shooting out of line, passing the two DEA cars, and drawing back into position behind the other Bureau cars.

"Now," Linda said, "we can take our turn leapfrogging. This is more like it!"

Joe Butler thought of rebuking them, but refrained. He didn't want to use the radio unnecessarily, and he hated to chastise subordinates who were guilty only of an eagerness to miss nothing important.

"Number two to number one," he said instead, reporting to Dave Daniels, who was sweating out the caper in his office. "Caravan is heading east on I-Ninety-five. So far we're under control."

The speed limit was fifty-five miles per hour, but Reyes soon was driving at sixty-five, forcing the others to do the same. Every half-mile the Bureau cars leapfrogged, and soon Johnny was riding directly behind the Mark IV.

Linda saw the consternation mixed with surprise on Sid's face when he recognized her, and she smiled. It was sweet of him to be concerned for her safety, but he seemed to be forgetting she was an agent, too, and had every right to participate.

"Do you suppose they're armed up there?" Johnny asked.

"According to the final instructions we were issued this morning," Linda said, "we were told to assume they have firearms. They may have been carrying them on their persons, or they may have hidden them in the car. Either way, we're instructed to take no chances."

"Any idea where they're driving?"

"No, but we'll find out soon enough."

In the car directly behind them Sid Benjamin was furious. "I'm going to rip into Linda for this!" he said. "There are enough of us taking part in this operation that she doesn't have to stick her neck out!"

"Women agents demand the same rights as men," Samson said, swallowing a laugh because he realized his partner's interest in Linda was serious.

As they approached New Haven it became necessary for the Mark IV to halt at a toll station, and the agents had to do the same. Because of the delay between cars, however, Joe Butler resorted to a somewhat different technique, ordering two of the agents' vehicles to utilize the far right-hand lane, ordinarily used by state troopers, and to flash credentials' signs at the attendants as they passed. This maneuver made it possible for both cars to fall in directly behind the Mark IV again.

The others struggled to catch up.

As soon as they moved past New Haven, heading eastward, Reyes increased his speed to seventy miles per hour.

Samson Grant leapfrogged into the lead behind him.

"If a trooper gets into the act," Joe Butler said, "this could become complicated. And awkward." He called the nearest State Police barracks on his radio, identifying himself in code. "Let me talk to the lieutenant in command," he said.

The trooper on dispatcher duty switched him.

"Sergeant Whitman," a deep voice said. "The lieutenant hasn't come in yet."

Again the ASAC identified himself. "There's a Mark Four heading east on the Turnpike at a high speed," he said, "and there's quite an escort keeping him company. We'll appreciate it if you'll notify all of your patrol cars on the road not to interfere."

"Yes, sir. Do you want any help?"

"Not at the moment, thanks. Your cars are too easy to identify, and we don't want the Mark Four to know he's under surveillance. But we'll keep in touch."

Another toll booth loomed ahead, and the technique employed at the last was used again.

This time Johnny Hedley was the first through the far right lane and fell in behind the Continental.

Reyes began to push, quickly achieving a speed of seventy-five, then going to eighty.

"Full alert!" Joe Butler said. "He must be wise to us now, so we'll have to take him. Who has the lead?"

"Hedley and Bartlett," Linda replied.

Joe made a muffled exclamation that sounded like a curse.

Reyes increased his speed to eighty-five miles per hour, roaring down the left-hand lane and forcing other cars to swerve out of his path.

Linda plugged in the flashing light, and Johnny touched his siren button.

Reyes responded by increasing his speed to ninety, and was still accelerating. The blonde beside him sank lower in her seat, and Garcia turned to look at the car behind them.

Linda drew her .38 from her shoulder bag. "Hold steady, Johnny!" she shouted over the scream of the siren. "I'll have to wing him."

"Take him!" Joe Butler order over the radio. "This speed is dangerous."

Sid Benjamin saw Linda rolling down her window. "Move up, Grant," he said. "Reyes is our pigeon. We can't let Linda play games with him!"

Samson Grant laughed exuberantly, pushed his gas pedal to the floorboard, and squeezing between Johnny Hedley and the fence in the center of the road, achieved a speed of 107 miles per hour.

Samson's siren wailed.

"I'm not using the flasher," Sid said. "I don't want the light distracting my aim."

Juan Garcia leaned out his window and fired at the pursuing car. The shot went wild.

Bureau policy placed strict restraints on the use of firearms, but the fact that Garcia had shot at two agents gave Sid the green light. He rolled down his window.

Samson continued to drive at a speed faster than that of the Mark IV, and as he roared past the larger vehicle Sid squeezed the trigger of his .38.

The Mark IV swerved, almost overturning, and Reyes fought hard to bring it under control.

By this time Samson was in front of him.

"I got his rear left tire," Sid said, and sounded calm.

"Neat," Samson said, and his admiration was genuine.

The danger was not yet ended. The Mark IV rocketed from one side of the road to the other, almost plowing into a trailer truck as it lost speed and forcing a small car to drive onto the shoulder.

A sweat-drenched Johnny Hedley remained close behind the wildly swerving Continental, gradually reducing his own speed. He had scored high honors in the driving course at the Academy, but in this situation anything could happen.

The other FBI cars crowded still closer.

"Take them alive, if you can," Joe Butler ordered. "Don't fire again unless you must. But—if they don't surrender—shoot to kill!"

Every Special Agent understood. Bureau representatives used firearms only when necessary, and then utilized them in earnest.

The Mark IV smashed through a section of fence on the right shoulder as it finally came to a halt, twisting back halfway in the direction from which it had come.

Samson and Sid leaped out of their car together, pistols in their hands as they ran toward the Continental. "Come out one at a time!" Sid called. "With your hands up!"

Linda and Johnny approached on foot from the other side of the Mark IV, with several other agents directly behind them.

Meanwhile two State Police cars arrived on the scene, and halted all traffic behind the caravan.

The left-hand door of the Mark IV opened, and an ashen-faced Hernando Reyes Gomez emerged, slowly raising his hands high over his head.

Juan Garcia opened the right-hand door and started to leave the car.

"Drop that gun!" Samson ordered. "Or I'll shoot!"

Garcia's .357 Magnum fell to the ground.

"Both of you," Samson directed, "face the car, with your hands on the roof."

Reyes and Garcia hastened to obey, and immediately were searched for concealed weapons.

Louise Elizabeth Poole slid out of the car, saw what was happening to her companions, and began to scream. Suddenly she found herself looking into the muzzle of a .38.

"Save the hysterics until later, dear," Linda told her. "Get your hands on the roof. I'm frisking you."

Joe Butler was already making his report to the Field Office as Ray Merrill brought their car to a halt a few feet from the Mark IV.

"This is a good morning's work," Dave Daniels told him. "We've just picked up the pair who delivered the Continental to Reyes yesterday, and we bagged three others with them."

The Drug Enforcement agents were combing the Mark IV, two of them searching the interior while the other pair examined the contents of the trunk.

There was no fight left in either Reyes or Garcia as handcuffs were snapped onto their wrists.

But Louise Elizabeth Poole had no intention of remaining silent. "I've done nothing wrong! You can't prove that I have."

"Just put your hands behind your back, like a good girl," Linda said, handcuffing her. "We'll have lots of time for a chat later."

One of the Drug Enforcement agents beckoned, and two of the FBI men began to take photographs as Joe Butler and Ray Merrill walked to the Mark IV.

A section of the rear seat had just been ripped out, and nestling in the stuffing was a glassine bag filled with a white powder.

Joe and Ray watched as the bag was removed, and the drug agent cautiously smelled the contents. "Cocaine," he said. "This haul is worth a fortune."

Joe turned to the leader of the ring. "You've been quite a busy fellow, Reyes, what with stealing cars and peddling drugs. What do you have to say?"

Hernando Reyes Gomez drew himself up to his full height and managed a faint, contemptuous smile. "I know my rights. I have no comment to make on any subject except in the presence of my attorney."

"Give us his name, and he'll be waiting for us by the time we get back to Winthrop. What about you, Garcia?"

Juan Garcia glowered at the ASAC, then cursed in Spanish.

Samson Grant stepped forward and addressed him in the same tongue. "Aren't you in enough trouble, Chico? Don't make things worse for yourself."

Joe turned to the Poole woman. "What about you?"

"I know nothing about stolen cars or drugs or anything else," she said. "These gentlemen happen to be my social friends, and I know nothing about their business affairs."

"Drive them to Winthrop in separate cars," Joe said, "and allow them no contact with anyone until they've been questioned."

Ray halted one of the agents shepherding Garcia. "Be particularly careful that this one has no contact of any kind in the lockup with his brother. Keeping them totally separated can be useful." He offered no explanation.

"Gentlemen and Miss Bartlett," the ASAC said, "congratulations to all of you. Grant and Benjamin, you'll get commendations for your part in all this. I've never seen better driving or more accurate shooting. Hedley, you did well, so I won't censure you for joining in the leapfrogging."

Johnny grinned, and his older colleagues knew how he felt. He had conducted himself creditably in his first full-fledged caper, and never again would he be regarded as a neophyte. The greening of Special Agent Hedley was ended.

He could hardly wait to give Lisa Talbot a blow-by-blow account of what he had done, and he was tempted to take her aside as soon as he returned to the office. But he would try to wait until tonight, when he intended to present her with an engagement ring. The occasion would be more fitting as a way of assuring his future wife that he had chosen the right vocation.

Joe Butler looked at Linda. "As for you, Miss Bartlett," he said, "you gave me a few anxious minutes. I froze when I realized you intended to take on Reyes and Garcia yourself. I applaud your initiative and courage. As much as I deplore your judgment."

"Amen to that," Sid said, and put an arm around the girl's shoulders.

Linda's smile was guileless, and when she spoke she was ostensibly replying to Sid, but her words were actually directed at the ASAC, too. "I just want to remind you," she said, "that I'm a Special Agent. Not an auxiliary."

"Ouch. I guess I deserved that." Sid laughed and, ignoring the presence of others, hugged her.

Ray Merrill averted his gaze and walked rapidly to his car, his feeling of satisfaction evaporating. He had convinced himself that Linda meant nothing to him, and he was making progress in his campaign to become better acquainted with the nurse. The reason Benjamin's intimate gesture bothered him, he knew, was that it reminded him he was too old for women of Linda's generation.

The time had come for him to adjust to realities. He had played a major role in what promised to be the breakup of a large

ITSMV ring, and the case had an unexpected bonus in its drug tie-in. Not too bad for a middle-aged man. All the same, he envied the youngsters who still felt energetic after a full day's work as street agents. He couldn't yet afford to worry about himself, of course. There was a lot of mopping up still to be done.

Joe Butler joined him in the car, and sighed as he settled in his seat. "You want to know something, Ray? I ought to be doing nip-ups, the way this case is developing, but I'm too tired. I wish I had your stamina."

10

The arrest of Hernando Reyes Gomez had an electrifying effect on the minor members of the ITSMV ring who had been taken into custody, particularly when they realized the evidence against him was sufficiently substantial to guarantee that he would be sentenced to a long term in prison. Several of them began to talk, hoping the prosecution would deal leniently with them, and as a consequence four other members of the gang also were arrested.

"For all practical purposes," SAC David Daniels wrote in a summary airtel to the Bureau, "the Reyes ring is smashed." Later he repeated the remark in a press conference.

There was still work to be done on the case, however, and a number of agents from the Winthrop Field Office spent hours interviewing members of the gang who were willing to reveal what they knew of the operations. Gradually a pattern emerged.

Reyes had never become directly involved himself, and always acting through subordinates, had paid small sums to young hoodlums who had stolen automobiles for him. These cars had moved through an underground assembly-line system, with one in four being sold to unsuspecting, legitimate buyers in the United States. The sums earned from this part of the enterprise had paid all of Reyes's bills.

Three out of four cars had been shipped to Latin America, and their sales had represented a clear profit, which Reyes had kept. Over the years he had expanded his scheme to include the importation of cocaine from Dorado, usually brought into the

United States in stolen motor vehicles. The Drug Enforcement Agency was still at work on this aspect of the case, and was attempting to track down the major buyers who had purchased the cocaine. Alan Collins of the DEA told Dave Daniels and Joe Butler he felt confident that his agents, aided by informants who were beginning to come forward, ultimately would round up everyone who had been involved in the smuggling, purchase, and resale of the cocaine. A few small fry might escape the dragnet, but they were not important.

Reyes refused to cooperate in any way with the FBI or the prosecutor, adopting the strategy that the less the authorities knew about him, the fewer the charges that would be preferred against him. The U.S. Attorney and his assistants were confident, however, that they had enough evidence against him to send him to the penitentiary for many years.

The government of Dorado offered limited cooperation, and the federal authorities did not press for more data than was volunteered. Reyes's connection with the brother of the President of Dorado was delicate, and there was no need to bring it into the open in order to obtain a conviction. Legat Bob Roberts revealed in a confidential memorandum from Ciudad Dorado that the embarrassed President Belamon had ordered the uprooting and destruction of the coca plants being grown on his brother's farm.

Reyes had one modest bank account in Winthrop, with another in New York, and when the FBI could uncover no others the belief developed that the bulk of his fortune was deposited in Swiss accounts. The Bureau sent a special emissary, accompanied by an official of the Treasury Department, to Switzerland in the hope of persuading banks there to release information regarding Reyes's finances.

Linda Bartlett was given the task of trying to persuade Louise Elizabeth Poole to tell what she knew about Reyes's business, but in several sessions she accomplished nothing, and the assignment was handed to Samson Grant.

"She's tough," Linda told him. "She knows we have no case against her that will stand up in court, and I haven't been able to budge her. Good luck."

Samson had the prisoner brought to one of the interview rooms in the federal lockup.

She was wearing a green jumpsuit with her customary low neckline, her makeup was impeccable, and her manner indicated weary disdain. "Don't you turkeys ever give up?" she demanded, lighting one of her long cigarettes and blowing a thin stream of smoke across the table.

"We're just hoping you'll be sensible," Samson said.

"I'm the most sensible person you've ever met. I can't tell you anything about Hernando or about Juan Garcia. They've been social friends, nothing more, and they never discussed business with me. If they were stealing and selling cars, that's news to me. If they were peddling drugs, I'm that surprised. The broad who has been questioning me went over that ground a hundred times, and you won't get anywhere, either. Why not admit you're beaten? My lawyer is going to have me out of here in another day or two."

"There are angles we haven't discussed with you," Samson said. "For example, we know you went to bed with both Reyes and Garcia the day before all of you were picked up."

A flicker of amusement appeared in Louise Poole's eyes. "What does that prove? If I want to sleep with good friends, that's my privilege."

"It so happens," Samson said, "that we could turn you over to the state. There are stringent vice laws in Connecticut."

"They'd apply to me," she retorted, "only if I accepted money for my favors. You'd have to prove I did."

He knew her point was valid, but he had to keep trying. "You live in a fancy house, and you drive a jazzy car."

"I'm lucky. I have expensive tastes, and I have the ability to indulge them. There are no laws against that, either."

"What's the source of your income?"

"I could tell you it isn't any of your business, sweetheart, but I'll let you in on a secret. I have sound investments. Made for me by the trust department of the Winthrop National Bank and the local office of one of the biggest brokerage firms in America. Check me out, and you'll find I'm telling you the truth."

"We already have," Samson said with a rueful smile, "and you are."

"I think it's dreadful," Louise Poole said, "that the FBI wastes time persecuting innocent people when there's so much crime in this country. And if I must, I'm prepared to tell a jury exactly how I feel."

Her physical appeal would make her an effective witness, which she well knew, and she also realized the evidence against her was circumstantial. "I'm sure the jury would be interested in your trips to meet Reyes in Ciudad Dorado. Not to mention your trips together to Miami Beach and Palm Springs."

"Oh, we never traveled together," she said. "There's no way you're going to bag me on a Mann Act violation. There's no law that prevents me from meeting a friend at a resort, you know. Check the hotel registers and you'll discover we never signed in anywhere as man and wife. We always had separate suites."

"I've got to hand it to you," Samson said. "You're pretty sharp."

"A girl has to look out for herself these days."

He knew she had won. Sometimes the Bureau had to admit defeat, and he consoled himself with the thought that the ring had been smashed and its leaders could not escape prison. It was even possible the Poole woman was as innocent as she claimed, thanks to the precautions she took, and he had to concede she was no menace to society.

"Lady," he said, "I give up. I'm going to recommend that we release you without delay and drop all charges against you."

Louise Elizabeth Poole rewarded him with a dazzling smile. "An FBI agent with brains. You're very sweet."

"You don't need me to tell you this. Stay out of trouble when you get out."

"I intend to be very careful of the people I associate with. Luckily, I have some dear friends in legitimate industry. And banking."

She was so brazen about her profession that he couldn't help laughing. "I'll bet you do."

Her smile was demure.

He stood, indicating the session was at an end.

As she rose, too, she looked him up and down with slow

deliberation, and the invitation in her eyes was impossible to misinterpret. "When somebody is nice to me," she said, "I like to be nice in return. You know where to reach me."

As Samson walked back to the Field Office he wondered why he seemed to attract the wrong women. Claudia. Louise Poole. Hookers, low class and high. Ultimately, damn it, he'd meet the right girl and marry her.

A girl who wouldn't mind—well, not too much—living with a man who couldn't call his hours his own, who had to work nights and weekends, on holidays and right around the clock when necessary.

It occurred to Samson that he had made his basic decision. He would tell the people who had offered him a job that he wasn't really interested. For better or worse he'd spend the rest of his active career in the Bureau. There was a need for him, and he knew he was doing a job. He was no token black, and he'd move up the ladder on merit. There were places other blacks could fill in the Bureau, and somebody had to serve as an example, so he had elected himself.

His inability to persuade the Poole woman to talk was of no consequence. Feeling in better spirits than he had in a long time, Samson walked with a light step.

Ray Merrill had put his head on a guillotine block and the blade was poised, ready to drop, but he could blame only himself. The SAC, ASAC, and case supervisor had held several long meetings to determine strategy, and he had volunteered for the assignment. Of his own free will.

Eleven men would go to prison for their roles in the ITSMV ring, and Hernando Reyes Gomez and Juan Garcia would pay a stiff additional penalty for importing and selling cocaine. But the murder of Carlotta Ruiz was as yet unsolved, and no progress had been made. Reyes insisted that his lawyer attend every interrogation, and had shrugged off questions. Garcia cursed, refusing to admit he had even known the girl.

So a new strategy had emerged, and Ray went to the federal lockup to carry it out. Ordinarily the burden would have fallen on Joe Butler, but his son's trial was impending, and he was in a sorry state, unable to concentrate. So Ray had offered to undertake the job, even though he knew a failure would be held against him by the pencil pushers in Washington who had never conducted an interrogation.

Ray sat in one of the interview rooms in the federal lockup, chewed on the stem of his pipe, and did not bother to raise his head when Juan Garcia was admitted to the room.

Garcia glared at him, took a chair, and finally broke the silence. "You creeps have been buggin' me ever since you brought me here. Why don't you leave me the hell alone?"

"If you wish," Ray said, "you're entitled to demand that your attorney be present during our talk."

"I ain't needed him all the other times, and I don't need him now!"

"What I don't understand about you," Ray said, "is your loyalty to Reyes. After all you've done for him, he isn't even paying your legal expenses."

"So I got enough bread to pay for my own lawyer. Don't make somethin' out o' nothin'."

"I really don't care about your friendship with Reyes. I was thinking about your brother."

"You leave him out o' this!"

Ray chewed on his pipestem.

"You're throwin' the book at me and Hernando. Okay. Ramon ain't got any connection with us, so leave him alone."

"You haven't spoken to him lately?" Ray's voice was mild.

Garcia's anger almost overcame him. "How the hell could I? I seen him in the cell block a couple of times, but we can't get near enough to say hello, even. And the security is so tight I can't get a message to him!"

Ray shrugged. "The boy is in a great deal of trouble, which I'm sure you'll appreciate more than he does. He was apprehended driving a stolen motor vehicle, and he assaulted an FBI agent without provocation. He has problems."

Juan Garcia grimaced.

Ray was encouraged, believing he was on the right track. If the man had any weakness, it was his affection for his younger brother. "But that's just the beginning. He had a girl. Carlotta Ruiz. She was murdered."

Garcia's face became blank, and he nodded vaguely.

"We believe he was responsible for killing her."

"You gotta be nuts! Ramon was right here, behind bars, when she was killed."

"According to our information, he grew tired of her, and arranged to have her murdered."

Garcia cursed at length in Spanish. "You creeps always screw up! You sure don't know Ramon. If he was tired of her, he would have walked out on her, like he done to fifty other chicks. None of them got killed!"

"I thought you'd be interested in knowing the situation he faces, that's all." Ray rose, putting his pipe in his pocket. "Think of what I said about loyalties, and maybe we can have another chat. One of these days when I'm not too busy."

He pressed a button, and a guard appeared to conduct Garcia back to his cell.

"Joe," Dave Daniels said, "I'm putting you on sick leave for the rest of the week."

"There's too much to be done around here," Joe Butler said. "We aren't finished with Reyes—"

"We'll manage. What with your son coming to trial next week you have enough on your mind. Go home and stay there. That's an order."

The ASAC muttered something unintelligible under his breath and shuffled out, his gait that of an old man.

Dave watched him, then glanced at his watch and reached for the telephone. "I'm not leaving for my outside appointment for another fifteen minutes, so there should be time to squeeze in whoever is next on the schedule."

In a few moments Linda Bartlett and Sid Benjamin entered the SAC's office, and were waved to chairs.

Sid, almost always brash and self-confident, looked thoroughly uncomfortable.

Linda presented a calm facade, but the way she fingered her leather belt betrayed her nervousness.

"You wanted to see me?" Dave asked, prompting them.

Sid took a deep breath. "We want to get married."

"We can't find the paragraph in the new edition of the *Manual* that refers to the marriage of two agents," Linda said, "and we aren't sure whether we need your permission."

"I won't pretend I'm surprised," Dave said, biting back a smile and maintaining the suspense. "Everybody in the office has seen this coming. Are you intending to resign, Miss Bartlett?"

"No, sir! Single or married, I'm a Special Agent!"

"How do you feel about that, Benjamin?"

"Well, Mr. Daniels," Sid said, regaining some measure of poise, "seeing that nothing would persuade me to quit my job, I can't blame Linda for wanting to stick around, too. Unless there's a regulation that won't let us get married."

"Suppose there were?" Dave asked.

"I'd resign," Linda said promptly.

"And if I had to," Sid added, "so would I. My job means a lot to me, but I've discovered Linda means more."

"That's as it should be," the SAC said, and finally smiled. "You're creating something of an administrative headache for the Bureau, you understand. Whenever one of you is transferred, the other will have to be given the same transfer."

A delighted Linda and Sid looked at each other.

"I'm sure you realize you'll have your problems," Dave said. "Family life can be rough when one partner works for the FBI."

"We know," Sid said. "But we'll work it out."

"I'm sure you will." The malleability of the younger generation was extraordinary, Dave thought.

Linda remembered her manners. "We're going to have a small wedding," she said as she stood, "but we hope you and Mrs. Daniels will come."

"You couldn't keep us away." Dave rose and walked around his desk. "Right now I'm going to kiss the bride, and this is a memorable occasion. I've spent more than twenty-five years in the Bureau, and this will be the first time I've ever kissed a Special Agent."

Ray Merrill let forty-eight hours pass before he returned to the lockup for another session with Juan Garcia, and one glance at the prisoner's gaunt face told him he had adopted the right tactics.

"You guys," Garcia said, "always try to turn friends against each other. It's an old trick, but I been thinkin' about it, and this time it ain't gonna work."

Ray's shrug was a model of indifference. "The reason I'm here is to tell you, before we notify your brother, that he's going to be charged with responsibility for the murder of Carlotta Ruiz."

"No!" Garcia shouted and jumped to his feet.

"We've accumulated evidence that satisfies us," Ray said, "and the U.S. Attorney is confident he can obtain a conviction. Your brother will spend the rest of his life in prison."

The last of Juan Garcia's aplomb was shattered. He held his hands to his face, then let them fall to his sides, and when he spoke his voice seethed with hatred. "You're real bastards. You got me caught in a vise, and you know it."

Ray stuffed his pipe with care.

"What happens if I talk?" Garcia asked in a strangled voice.

"That depends on what you say." Ray showed none of the tension he felt.

"Suppose I lay it on the line about the killing of that broad. What'll you do for my brother?"

"Ramon Garcia has no previous prison record," Ray said, "and under appropriate circumstances I wouldn't be surprised if the court would give him a minimum sentence. I make no promises, you understand, because I'm in no position to make them. But I wouldn't be surprised if he got out on parole after serving no more than eighteen months."

Garcia sat abruptly, and again hid his face behind his hands for a moment. Then he reached in a pocket of his shirt for a cigarette.

Ray lighted it for him.

Inhaling deeply, Garcia looked at him, then stared down at the table. "The Ruiz chick was killed on Reyes's orders," he said. "She knew too much about the way we did business. He kept his mouth shut with just about everybody, but he couldn't turn her on in bed, so he bragged to her. Tryin' to impress her. So she knew everythin'."

Ray nodded, but did not interrupt.

"You heard enough?" Garcia became savage.

"Who committed the actual murder?"

"The hit man was a punk. Name of Hector Gonzales. A Puerto Rican. He's hidin' out in Mexico City with bread Reyes gave him, and he's under orders to stay there until the case cools off. He's been stayin' in a dump we use for a lot of our people. The Hotel King Carlos."

Ray had only one more question. "Will you testify for the prosecution?"

Garcia pulled himself together, managing to regain some semblance of dignity. "First get my brother off with a light sentence," he said, "and then I'll talk my guts out about Reyes."

Ray returned to the office, where he reported at once to the SAC, who immediately called the Legat in Mexico City, then notified the Bureau in Washington.

While they awaited the results of the move they got in touch with the U.S. Attorney, who took the unusual step of paying a visit to the Field Office. After hearing the story of Ray's conversation with the elder Garcia, he agreed to request a minimum sentence for Ramon Garcia, provided the actual killer was apprehended.

At 6:00 P.M. Dave Daniels telephoned home and told Carolyn he would be delayed indefinitely. Guests were invited to dinner, but would understand, and he would return home as soon as he could.

At 8:00 P.M. a clerk went to a delicatessen around the corner for two ham and cheese on rye sandwiches, and a stenographer prepared two large containers of coffee on a hot plate.

At 9:20 P.M. the SAC's secretary, who had also remained at her desk, buzzed her employer. "Mexico City is on the line," she said.

A moment later the Legat in the Mexican capital was speaking to Dave. "We're under control here," he said. "The local police picked up Gonzales, and he's given them a verbal confession, which he'll sign later tonight. I've put in an extradition request, and I've been assured it will be honored without delay."

"Good," Dave said. "I'll ask Washington to put a couple of Marshals on an early flight, and they can pick up Gonzales as soon as you can clear him through the red tape."

"No later than tomorrow evening," the Legat said before he rang off.

Dave called the Bureau and made the necessary arrangements for the departure of two Marshals, who would bring the murderer of Carlotta Ruiz back to Winthrop from Mexico City. Then he closed the door of his office and took a bottle of bourbon from his desk.

"We're seeing daylight in the Reyes case at last," he said, and they toasted each other.

"It's strange," Ray said, "but I always feel let down after a big one."

"That's a natural reaction," the SAC told him. "Also, you're stale, Merrill. You need a change of scene."

"No, sir. I—"

"You're going off to the Academy the week after next," Dave said, cutting him off. "And I'm recommending you for an immediate promotion as soon as you finish school."

"Thank you," Ray said, but looked unhappy.

"Don't tell me I've figured you wrong, that you want to remain a Supervisor for the rest of your career."

"Not really, sir. But the farther I get from the street, the more I realize I'm turning into a doddering old desk man."

"Wait until you're my age before you complain," Dave said. "As an Ay-sack you'll have plenty of chances for street action. More than you'll want. Just remember that at this stage of your development the Bureau needs your brains more than it does your ability to leap over walls."

"I guess you're right, sir." Ray felt a sense of loss, which was absurd.

"Your problem," Dave said, "is one that every senior official in the Bureau has had to face. You're not a kid anymore, and the younger men could tear you apart in a free-for-all. But you have something they lack. The experience and expertise that solves cases. You gave this whole Reyes investigation drive and direction, and don't forget it. If it weren't for your contribution we'd still be floundering." Dave shook his hand and departed.

Ray wandered back to his own cubicle, feeling somewhat confused. The Winthrop Field Office was his only real home, but he'd be leaving in less than two weeks, and probably wouldn't return.

John Xavier Garrity had been a partner in a major Winthrop law firm before going to the United States House of Representatives, where he had been the district Congressman for a decade. Appointed to the federal bench as a judge of the District Court, he had spent the past nineteen years as a jurist, and was regarded as an institution. His habits were fixed, so his bailiff and law clerk were surprised, on Friday shortly after noon, when he retired to his chambers instead of going to the Winthrop Country Club for the usual round of golf that inaugurated his weekend.

A short time later SAC Dave Daniels of the FBI arrived, and Judge Garrity sent his clerk out for sandwiches. The two men conferred until midafternoon behind closed doors, and soon after Dave departed Judge Garrity summoned his secretary.

The trial of Joseph Butler, Junior, which was scheduled to begin on Monday, he said, would be postponed for twenty-four hours. He gave no reason for the delay.

Joe and Stella Butler were notified, and the postponement meant their torture would be extended for an additional day. They drank sparingly, afraid of the effect liquor would have on them, and on Saturday night they went to a restaurant for dinner, but could not eat. Unable to sleep, read, or watch television, they went to church on Sunday morning, and were startled when a prayer was offered for their son.

Friends crowded around them to wish them well, and Stella maintained her composure until she arrived home. Then she collapsed, and Joe put her to bed. He scrambled some eggs, which they ate sparingly, and that afternoon he pretended to watch a baseball game on television, but saw nothing.

That night he and Stella were so exhausted they slept.

Judge Garrity arrived unexpectedly early at his Federal Building courtroom on Monday morning, and went straight to his chambers, where he made a brief telephone call.

A short time later a Marshal appeared, with Joseph Butler, Junior, in tow.

"He isn't dangerous," Judge Garrity said, "so you can take off the cuffs. And wait outside."

Joey was astonished when the Judge shook his hand and waved him to a leather armchair.

"You're entitled to have your lawyer present," Judge Garrity said.

"No, sir. Thanks. They told me you wanted to see me, and that's okay with me."

"All right. I suppose you know I sentenced your two companions to prison on Friday."

"Yes, sir."

"The reason I'm trying you separately—and the reason I wanted a chat with you today—is because I'm curious. I'm told that you played a very important role in the breakup of an automobile and drug smuggling ring. And gave information that has now led to the apprehension of a murderer."

"That was supposed to be private!"

"Oh, I'm very discreet. I hear all sorts of secrets that I never tell anybody, so you can rely on me."

The youth nodded, unaware of the humor behind the Judge's words.

Leaning back in his swivel chair, Judge Garrity looked sleepy. "Could you tell me, just between us, why you passed along all that information?"

"I'm not sure," Joey said. "I've been trying to figure it out myself. But it wasn't because I wanted anything in return, that's for sure. I pulled a big goof, and I'll pay for it."

"I understand. That much was made very clear to me. I just wondered what motivated you, that's all."

"I guess sitting in prison has given me a different slant on the law," Joey said. "I'm not making like a reformed drunk or anything like that, but it ate into me that a bunch of crooks were making my father and his crowd look foolish. My father and I don't have much use for each other, but he's trying to do a job protecting the public, and the way these characters were laughing really bugged me."

There was a tap at the door, and the bailiff came in with a pitcher of milk, and then withdrew.

"Have some," Judge Garrity said, filling two glasses. "It's good for your stomach. Helps you relax."

Joey accepted a glass, but remained tense.

"It isn't easy being the son of an FBI agent," the Judge said. "Oh, it's great when you're very little and when you're first starting school. Everybody looks up to you, everybody envies you. But all that begins to change in a few years."

Joey stared at him.

"Pretty soon other kids are saying, 'Just because your old man is in the FBI doesn't make you anything special.' And before you know it, you start having fights. With fellows your own age, with older boys, with everybody. You have to keep proving yourself. Children can be merciless, and the hazing never stops."

Joey nodded, and was openly astonished.

Judge Garrity pretended not to notice. "Things change again when you get into your teens. Other boys sneer at you, taking it for granted that you're a goodie-goodie, and even the girls avoid you. Pretty soon it dawns on you that you've got to prove you're regular, even though your father is an FBI agent. You're one of the first to start smoking. You prove yourself by drinking beer, and you're one of the first to try the hard stuff. You probably experiment with pot—"

"Have you been talking to my parents?"

"I haven't seen either of them, young man, and I haven't spoken to them. Where was I? You become part of the crowd that plays practical jokes, like locking the door of the girls' room at school, or setting fire to wastebaskets."

Joey slumped in his chair, his glass of milk forgotten.

"By the time you get out of high school you're pretty tough. Because you've had to be. You can look after yourself, and you've been in plenty of scrapes. You're accepted now, but you still have to keep proving yourself. To Joe Butler, Junior, as well as to your peers. Besides, you've formed patterns that are harder and harder to break. So, before you quite realize what's happened to you, you've driven the getaway car in three bank robberies. Finish your milk."

Joey gulped the contents of his glass. "How do you know so much about it?" he demanded.

Judge Garrity smiled. "My boys, who are older than you, had to grow up as the sons of a man who sits on the federal bench. Your problems haven't been unique."

The U.S. Attorney and defense counsel Alan Potter arrived at the courtroom simultaneously, and after depositing stacks of documents on separate tables in front of the bench, they chatted amiably about the stock market's activities of the previous day. Several reporters drifted in, taking places in a row reserved for the press, and court officials began to filter in.

Just before the doors were opened to the general public Stella and Joe Butler came in, both of them drawn and weary, and took seats directly behind the defense table. Potter broke off his conversation and came to them.

"How does it look?" Joe asked.

The attorney shrugged. "There isn't much I can do. He refuses to make any defense. The facts are open and shut, so that's about the size of it."

Joe nodded and stroked his wife's hand.

Joey came in through a side door, wearing a suit, shirt, necktie, and shoes that his mother had delivered the previous day. A Marshal accompanied him to the defense table, and he embraced his mother without speaking.

Stella managed to maintain a grip on her emotions.

Joe and his son did not acknowledge each other's presence.

The main doors were opened, and twenty-five or thirty people came in, scattering as they found places. Several were friends and neighbors of the Butler family, and a few were buffs who attended trials for the sake of entertainment.

Dave Daniels slipped in and took a seat in the rear.

The bailiff rapped on the bench with a gavel. "His Honor, John X. Garrity."

Judge Garrity entered from his chambers, directly behind the bench, climbed to his padded leather chair, and arranged his robes as he sat.

Everyone in the courtroom had stood, and when he nodded they resumed their seats.

"The United States versus Joseph Butler, Junior," the bailiff said, and read the charges in a monotone.

Judge Garrity cleaned his glasses, sipped from a glass of water, and riffled through some papers.

Joey stared straight ahead, his face rigid.

Stella clenched her husband's hand.

It was difficult for Joe to breathe, and he inhaled deeply.

"How does the defendant plead?" Judge Garrity asked.

"Guilty, Your Honor," Attorney Potter said.

"Does he wish to take the stand?"

"No, Your Honor."

Judge Garrity looked at the U.S. Attorney. "Does the prosecution wish to question the defendant?"

"In view of his plea, Your Honor, the prosecution waives that right."

"Well, I want to question him," the Judge said. "Swear him in."

Joey moved reluctantly to the witness stand, where the bailiff produced a Bible and observed the usual ritual.

"Your name, age, and occupation," the Judge said.

"Joseph Butler, Junior. Nineteen years old. Unemployed."

"Weren't you a college student?"

"Yes, sir, but I dropped out this past semester."

"Do you want to say anything in your own defense?"

Joey looked at the closed double doors at the rear of the courtroom. "No, Your Honor."

"Were there any extenuating circumstances that you might want this court to take into consideration before passing sentence?"

"No, sir." Joey's voice was expressionless.

Stella stifled a sob.

"You may step down." Judge Garrity turned and looked at Joe. "Mr. Butler, will you be good enough to take the stand, please?"

Joe was surprised, but hastened to obey, and was sworn in.

"Your name, age, and present vocation, please."

"Joseph Butler. Forty-nine. Special Agent, Federal Bureau of Investigation."

"Your present position?"

"Assistant Special Agent in Charge of the Winthrop Field Office, Your Honor."

"How long have you been an FBI agent?"

"This is my twenty-fifth year."

"Did you have any connection with this case?" Judge Garrity spoke quietly.

"Yes, Your Honor. My agents made the arrests of the two men sentenced last week, and of the present defendant."

"Mr. Butler, you and I have dealt with one another for several years. We work for the same company, so to speak, and both of us are dedicated to the pursuit of justice. In view of your rather special interest in this case I anticipated that you might get in touch with me regarding it, but you haven't done so. Would you care to state your reasons?"

"The defendant has entered a plea of guilty, Your Honor. It's my conviction that the cause of justice would not be served if I asked that he be given special consideration because of his relationship to me." Joe's mouth felt dry, but his hands were sweating and a cold trickle of perspiration ran down his back. He couldn't imagine why he was being subjected to an ordeal he regarded as unnecessary.

"You may stand down, Mr. Butler," Judge Garrity said, and waited until Joe resumed his seat. "The defendant will stand before the bench."

Joey rose and moved to a place in front of the defense table.

"Joseph Butler, Junior," Judge Garrity said, "you are aware of the unlawful and antisocial acts you performed, and you are prepared to accept the full consequences. This court has no intention of adding to the travail of your parents by delivering a sermon to you at this time. There are aspects of your case, in no way relating to the fact that you happen to be son of a senior FBI agent, that prompt me to deal with you leniently. I don't wish to place them on the public record, but they will be included in this court's sealed verdict. Suffice it to say that this court believes you are prepared to do penance and live hereafter as a law-abiding, decent, and useful citizen." He paused to sip water.

Stella looked at her husband, hope mingling with her fear.

"You are placed on probation for a period of two years," Judge Garrity said, "in the personal custody of FBI Special Agent Joseph Butler, Senior."

Stella could no longer hold back her tears.

Joe choked.

Joey was stunned. Then the last of his defenses crumbled, and he began to weep, too.

"You will report to this court's Probation Officer every Friday, and I further charge you with responsibility for reporting to me in person once each month on your progress." Judge Garrity rapped on the bench with his gavel. "Court is adjourned for one hour."

Everyone stood as he went off to his chambers.

Stella made no attempt to curb her emotions as she kissed her son.

Then it was Joe's turn, and he could feel the bones in the thin body he hugged. "Well, boy," was all he could manage.

"Oh, Dad." Joey clung to him, and sobbed.

They became aware of flashbulbs popping, and were surrounded by reporters, who began to ask questions.

"I wouldn't know what to say," Joe told them.

Dave Daniels materialized beside them, and came to their rescue. "Give them a break, fellows," he said. "You have your story and your pictures." He waited until the reporters and photographers gave way, then shook hands quickly with Joe, kissed Stella, and departed.

Joe put a protective arm around his son's slender shoulders. "Joey," he said, "let's go home."

When the SAC arrived for work the following morning he found his assistant waiting for him. "What is this?" Dave asked. "You're on leave."

"We talked most of the night," Joe Butler said, "and I want to get a few basics settled with you. Then I can go home and sleep."

The secretary brought them coffee, and Dave closed the door.

"Stella and Joey understand that we aren't necessarily bound to this area," Joe said. "We can have his probation transferred. But we decided—and it was Joey's thinking, really—that we'll stick it out here. With people who know what he did, rather than with strangers who might pick up some rumors. Joey wants to rehabilitate himself in Winthrop, and my wife and I are behind him one hundred percent."

"I can see your point," Dave said. "But there's one drawback. In another two years you'll have been passed over for promotion. Younger men will start moving up to Inspector, and you'll end your career as an Ay-sack."

"As if that mattered," Joe said. "My son is rejoining the human race. He's going off to enroll in summer school at the University today, and he floored me by saying he might join the ROTC. It wouldn't surprise me, after he gets his degree, if he applies for Special Agent training!"

"I can see," Dave said, "where your promotion isn't all that important. Nothing would make me happier, Joe, than to keep you in your present slot—"

"Then that's settled. What I don't understand is why Judge Garrity let Joey off with probation. He hinted that he knew Joey was responsible for the tip that led to the bust of the Reyes gang. Did you happen to see his sealed verdict?"

"No. I had no reason to make the request."

"In my position I can't ask, but it's odd. I kept my word to Joey and didn't even tell the U.S. Attorney that he was our informant. So I can't imagine how Garrity could have known."

Dave shrugged.

"I guess it doesn't much matter."

"It doesn't. Go home and take the next couple of weeks on leave, Joe."

"I will. I want to get acquainted with my son. Thanks for all your support, Dave."

"Forget it. You'd have done the same for me."

"I'll have to call the Director today and tell him the news."

"I spoke to him yesterday. You and Stella will be hearing from him, and Joey will have a letter of his own."

Joe looked at the white flag bearing the Bureau insignia in gold. "Sometimes I wonder how an idiot like me had the brains to hook up for life with this outfit." He expected no reply, and left abruptly.

The SAC accepted another container of coffee from his secretary and settled down to the morning's routine. The night report consisted of trivia. The Resident Agencies were quiet. Nothing of consequences had come in from the Bureau either on the teletype or in the early mail. The day promised to be dull, and that suited his mood. The Winthrop Field Office had enjoyed more than its share of excitement lately, and deserved a respite.

Later he'd call Judge Garrity to thank him and report on the progress in the reunited Butler household. Joe had no idea how the Judge had learned the whole story of what Joey had done, but that wasn't surprising. Even the most experienced investigators sometimes failed to recognize evidence right under their noses.

Johnny Hedley stood on the threshold. "May I see you, Mr. Daniels? Urgent."

Dave sighed and waved him in.

"The new Supervisor hasn't come in yet this morning, so I took the message. The New London Resident Agency called to report the development of a new ITSMV ring case in the New London-Groton area." Johnny handed him a single sheet of paper on which he had written the salient facts.

"It looks," the SAC said, "as though your squad won't be doing much loafing. Tell the Supervisor I want to see him as soon as he arrives, and we'll get this case organized."

"Yes, sir!" Johnny's grin of pleasure and anticipation was as great as a child's at the approach of Christmas.

That, Dave Daniels thought, explained the essence of the FBI.